PROMISE ME

ASHLEE ROSE

Ashlee Rose
Copyright © 2020 Ashlee Rose

First Edition

The author has asserted their moral right under the Copyright, Designs and Patents Act, 1988, to be identified as the author of this work.

All rights reserved. No part of this publication may be reproduced, copied, stored in a retrieval system, or transmitted, in any form by or by any means, without the prior written consent of the copyright holder, nor be otherwise circulated in any form of binding or cover other than that in which it is published and without a similar condition being imposed on the subsequent purchaser.

This is a work of fiction. Names, characters, businesses, places, events and incidents are either the products of the authors imagination or used in a fictitious manner. Any resemblance to actual persons, living or dead, or actual events is purely coincidental.

Cover: Irish Ink
Formatting: Irish Ink
Editing: Lindsey Powell

Robyn,
This is for you, thank you for everything. You claimed Conor as your book boyfriend from the moment I typed the first word, he is officially yours x

OTHER BOOKS by ASHLEE ROSE

ENTWINED IN YOU SERIES:

SOMETHING NEW

SOMETHING TO LOSE

SOMETHING EVERLASTING

BEFORE HER

WITHOUT HER

STANDALONE:

UNWANTED

ALL AVAILABLE ON AMAZON KINDLE UNLIMITED ONLY SUITABLE FOR 18+ DUE TO NATURE OF THE BOOKS.

PROLOGUE

CONOR

I'm a dead man walking.

I promised him I wouldn't go near her, promised him that I would treat his sister like she was my little sister.

But that was a lie.

Because Darcey Sawyer was not my sister.

She was my best friends' sister.

She was forbidden fruit. Forbidden fruit that I have waited four years to touch, four years to have one little taste.

Tonight was that night.

Because Darcey fucking Sawyer was turning eighteen, and of course her rich as fuck parents were throwing her the biggest party known to man.

I am Conor 'King' Royce, and this king needed his queen.

-

ASHLEE ROSE

DARCEY

Four years ago Conor Elijah Royce came into my life, crashing in when I was least expecting it, and it hasn't been the same since.

He was my brother's best friend. They met in Buck Hall Private School and have been inseparable ever since their first meeting.

From the moment I laid my eyes on him, I was addicted.

His light green eyes with dark, almost black, rings around his iris' pulled me in.

I wanted to kiss his perfectly-pink, plump bow lips.

His chocolate hair was long on top and shaved round the sides, which had me wanting to run my hands through it.

He made my insides squirm with something I couldn't quite put my finger on.

He's hot, he's an alpha, he's vicious, and he's set his sights on me.

He had everybody fooled, thinking he was God's gift, especially my brother.

He was the 'King' of Buck Hall and everybody knew it.

He was everything I shouldn't want.

Forbidden fruit.

I hated him but wanted him, now more than ever.

PROMISE ME

Tonight is my eighteenth birthday party.

Tonight is the night that I will get my moment with Conor fucking Royce.

The king was about to take down this princess in his kingdom, and I was going to fall to my knees and bow in front of him.

PART One

CHAPTER 1

CONOR

I still remember the first day I saw her. I had just turned sixteen. It was a week or so after I had met her brother Chase at Buck Hall Private School. Every rich kid in Exeter went there if their parents could afford it.

My parents couldn't.

I managed to get in on a gifted scholarship. I didn't want to go, but meeting Chase made it bearable. I couldn't stand the stuck-up kids who looked down their noses at the transfer kid, like I didn't belong there.

The truth was I didn't, but I was going to make sure they never looked like that at me again.

Chase invited me over to his house one afternoon after school, and to be honest, I jumped at the chance.

You see, my home life isn't great. I have a dad who comes and goes as he pleases, and an addict for a mother who couldn't give two shits if I was dead or alive.

When my dad is home, he makes my life hell. I am his human punching bag. At six-foot-six, I am a lanky, scrawny kid who doesn't have a hope in hell of standing up against him.

But I made a promise to myself that one day I would.

-

After school, Chase and I walked towards the bus that took us to a stop just outside his house; the kid had it made. Me on the other hand, had to walk three miles just to get to school. I was gifted a uniform that I had to wash and look after myself. I had no hope in anyone doing it for me.

"Thanks for coming back with me," Chase said, nudging me with his shoulder. His blonde hair messy, like a curly mop, his grey eyes smiling at me

"No problem, dude," I replied, nudging him back, a small smirk gracing my face. "Nice just to get away from my shithole of a home." I sighed.

Chase leant across and wrapped his arm around my shoulders. "Don't worry, man, I've got you. I promise you." He smiled then dropped his hand and pulled out his phone.

"Is there anything I need to know or not know? Don't want to put my foot in it." I laughed, nerves kicking in.

"Not really, all I will say is, I have a younger sister, she is a no-go. Like never. Understood?" His eyes flitted up from his phone, his grey eyes narrowing on me.

"How young?" I asked, teasing.

"Conor..." He glared at me.

"I'm joking, man." I laughed a light chuckle. "Yeah, cool, I wouldn't go there, bro. I promise you," I said, holding my fist up for our infamous fist pump that we have done from day one.

"Then you have nothing to worry about." He smiled as the bus approached the stop outside his house. He stood up, grabbing his ruck-sack off the floor and swinging it onto his back. I stood up after him, shrugging my bag onto my back and taking a deep breath as we walked off the bus.

Once off, I stood, jaw hitting the floor at the size of his house as the gates started opening slowly, the sound of them dragging along the stony driveway. There were black iron gates at the entrance, and a gravelled path behind them that was long and winding towards the front of the house. The gravel path was lined with huge oak trees. You couldn't see much from the outside due to the thick green hedges that were neatly trimmed into rectangles, keeping what was hidden behind a mystery. The house was something else.

We walked down the gravelled path in silence. I felt his eyes burning into me, probably not sure on my facial expression. I literally couldn't get over this house. This is what dreams were made of. I was like a kid in a candy shop for the first time. When you're piss-poor and come from nothing, you want every single bit of it. I wanted it. All of it. I would be lying if I said I wasn't envious.

Jealous? No.

But envious, yes.

I was only human after all.

He walked slightly in front of me, jogging up the six steps that lead to the double front doors. The house was built in light, cream bricks and was even bigger up close. The double oak front doors both had gold lion knockers on. Tacky if you asked me, but that is just what pompous people do. Have to have something extravagant just for a knocker. I rolled my eyes at my thoughts.

All the windows were large, sash windows with white Georgian bars running down them, separating the panes into six squares. I walked into his house behind him, my eyes scanning the hallway. It was a bit out there, that was for sure. Every door handle was gold, the staircase had a solid gold bannister that swept all the way up.

Evenly placed up the stairs were those god-awful portraits of weird looking historic people. Honestly, they freaked me out. I stood, kicking the floor with the toe of my converse as nerves crippled me. I felt so out of place. I had never felt more like an outsider than I did right now.

I looked through to the lounge and there was a white, solid marble fire place with slightly burnt logs sitting inside it, and a large gold ornate mirror sat proudly above it. Just underneath were your typical family portraits, then two single ones of Chase and, I am assuming, his sister. It was hard to see from where I was standing.

The carpet in the lounge was a thick, luxurious cream. I wanted to take my shoes off and feel it between my toes. Carpet was a luxury from where I came from. Shit, any floor was a luxury. I had hard-wood, you know, the floor that you lay the carpet on top of.

My eyes scanned the high ceilings, the skirting at the top looked decorative, and the huge gold chandeliers hung from ceiling roses which finished this over-the-top room of perfectly.

"Mum," Chase called out. "We're home." He dropped his bag on the floor, and I copied.

I felt uneasy and uncomfortable. Completely out of my comfort zone.

I heard clicking of heels on the marble floor, my eyes looking for the source of noise when I saw his mum. Long, wavy honey-blonde hair and crystal-blue eyes. She didn't look old enough to be his mum. Her smile was so wide, I could see all of her teeth.

"Chase, darling," she cooed as she walked up to him, pulling him in for an embraced cuddle and kissing the top of his head before letting go and looking me up and down.

"You must be Conor." She smiled at me, pulling me into an embrace. "So nice to meet you," she said softly.

"You too, Mrs Sawyer," I said politely.

"It's Zara, please" she replied. "Follow me, I've made

fresh lemonade." She flicked her hair over her shoulder and walked down their extravagant hallway into an even bigger kitchen.

I swear, their kitchen is the size of my entire house. Fucking ridiculous.

The kitchen had off-white shaker kitchen units and a shiny black, flecked with gold, granite worktop. I knew his family were rich, but surely this was just showing off?

There was a huge island sat in the middle of the kitchen area, wine racks sitting underneath them, fully stocked of course. The window overlooking their field of a garden which was huge, the low sun beaming through and bouncing off the high-gloss worktop.

To the left was a square room that had floor to ceiling windows which, I suppose, was like an orangery but actually in their kitchen. There were a couple of sofas and a fuck-off huge television on the wall.

The dining room was part of the kitchen but sat to the left of the room, and it was all open-plan. The dining table was made out of the same granite as the worktops; it must have sat at least twelve people. The dining chairs were high-backed velvet, black chairs which, of course, you guessed it, had gold knockers on the back. Why the hell you would need them on the back of the chairs I would never know. I shook my head slightly as I followed Chase.

We were sat at the dining room table with fresh lemonade, cookies, crisps and hot dogs whilst our school books were scattered everywhere.

"Conor," I heard Zara call as she came and sat at the table, taking a cookie off the plate and biting into it, moaning softly as she appreciated the taste. "Tell me about your family, where do you live?"

"There's not much to tell." I shrugged. "My mum doesn't even know I exist, my dad is never home and I live in a shithole."

I watched the cookie fall from her perfectly manicured fingers and hit her floral bone-china plate. Her mouth formed in the perfect 'o.'

"Sorry for swearing." I beamed up at her. Chase's eyes were on mine, narrowing in on me with a shocked expression before moving his eyes to his mum.

"No, no it's fine," she said, letting out a small laugh, flapping her hand over towards me then picking her cookie back up. It most certainly wasn't fine. I swallowed hard, worried I had fucked it up already.

Zara stood up, pushing her chair out and filling a water bottle, placing it on the side and grabbing a banana. "Darcey," she called down the echoing hallway.

"We've got to go sweetie," she said as she packed the water and the banana in a small bag, then hung it on the kitchen door handle.

"Conor," she said as she walked over to me, placing her hands on my shoulders. "You are always welcome here, okay, whatever the time."

I smiled back at her. "Thank you, Zara, I really appreciate it."

And I meant it.

I was grateful for her kindness.

I turned my attention back to my school work when I heard her voice. The sweet sound sent shivers down my spine, my hairs on the back of my neck standing up, goose-bumps smothering my body.

"Ready, Mum? Hi, Chase," the voice said sweetly.

I looked over my shoulder, my green eyes on her. Her long honey-blonde hair, like her mum's, sat down under her ribs. Her blue eyes met mine as her cheeks flushed slightly. She was in a leotard, ballet tights and a small pair of silk shorts pulled over the top, her ballet pumps were wrapped round her neck. Her long, toned legs were never ending. I couldn't pull my eyes from her.

She fisted the bag on the door and pulled out the banana that her mum had packed for her as she started unpeeling it.

"Who's your friend, Chase?" she asked, taking a bite of her banana then walking towards her brother, kicking him with her converse in his shins.

"Conor." He groaned, bending down to rub his leg, his eyebrows pulling together as he narrowed his eyes on her.

"Hi, Conor, I'm Darcey." She smiled sweetly, bolts of electricity shooting through me before she turned and walked back down the hallway, but not before giving me a cheeky wink over her shoulder.

"Hi, Darcey," I mumbled, somehow losing the ability to speak to her. I didn't even know if she heard me, but I didn't care.

In that moment, I felt my heart flutter. How could she have affected me in that way? I didn't even know her.

She was beautiful.

But I couldn't go there.

I couldn't break my promise no matter how much I wanted too.

I let out a deep sigh as I pulled my eyes from the empty doorway before looking back down at my school books on the table.

"Fourteen," Chase growled, giving me a swift elbow to the ribs.

"Fuck you," I muttered under my breath, wincing as I flipped my middle finger up at him.

"I warned ya, bro." A snort of a laugh coming out as he shook his head at me.

CHAPTER 2

DARCEY

It had been two years since Conor Royce came crashing into our lives. He had basically moved in. My mum and dad felt sorry for him, so now he spends most of his time over ours, occasionally going home.

I hated him.

At first, I thought he was nice, cute and everything I wanted, but the more I got to know him, the more I realised he wasn't any of those things. He was vicious, calculated, manipulative, an absolute arsehole, but he was hot as sin.

I can't quite put my finger on what made him change, but he did. He made me despise school. Luckily, he was leaving this year, after he and Chase decided to sit a few extra exams to better their chances of getting into the army on this enrolment. I would finally get to leave him behind with the school, and hopefully he would be out of mine and my family's lives for good. You don't normally still hang around with your senior school friends once you finish school, you all go on to your own adventures, so I'm hoping Conor gets his grips out my brother and leaves.

I sighed when I threw my duvet back on my bed. I didn't want to go to school, the weekend, like always, had gone far too quickly, and it was made even worse knowing that I would be seeing Conor in about an hour.

I stretched up, then left my bed before getting in the shower. My muscles ached from my ballet mock-exam this weekend. I was so desperate to get into the Royal London Ballet School, so I needed to keep up the hard work.

I had to pass.

Then I could be out of Devon and into London. This was my dream, and I wasn't letting anyone ruin that for me.

I had a quick shower, then hopped out and pulled my uniform out of the wardrobe. It was a warm summer day, so at least we didn't have to wear our boxy, stuffy blazers. I did my buttons up to my collar on my white shirt and tightened my dark, green tie-knot neatly, so it sat in my collar.

I slipped my chequered green and black pleat skirt on, tucking my shirt in, then pulling my knee high black socks on before slipping my Doc Martens on. My feet would melt but they were so comfortable.

I pulled half of my hair up and tied it into a pony-tail, then left the rest tumbling down. I smudged some nude, pink lipstick on and flicked my lashes with a coating of mascara. I grabbed my black school ruck-sack on the way out of my bedroom, running down the stairs and straight into the kitchen, picking up a slice of toast with honey on before kissing my mum goodbye.

"Have a good day, darling," she shouted down the hallway as and I made my way out the front to wait for the bus.

Great. I groaned when I saw Conor standing with Chase. I knew he was going to be there, every fucking morning, but it was still a kick in the teeth when I actually saw him standing there.

I took another bite of my toast as I stood next to them, Chase smiling at me. Conor's eyes were drawing up and down my body, pulling his bottom lip in-between his teeth as if he was mentally undressing me.

"Why are you such a creep?" I sniped, frowning at him then looking him up and down in disgust.

"Darcey," Chase moaned at me, kicking the floor as he tightened his grip on his backpack before pushing his hand through his curly mop of blonde hair in frustration.

"A creep? Am I?" Conor asked moving closer to me, sniffing me then grabbing my last bite of toast out my hand and putting it in his mouth, smiling at me as he chewed it.

"What's wrong, were you not fed this morning, stray?" I shouted at him angrily, balling my hands into fists.

He rolled his eyes before laughing. "Alright, grunge." He snorted before he stood back next to Chase. It was only eight a.m. and my blood was already boiling.

I was grateful when the bus pulled up and I managed to get a seat midway down, on my own. I put my ear phones in and blasted *Blink 182* into my ears. I eyed Conor as he walked past me, behind my brother, winking at me as he did.

Ugh. He was such an arrogant prick.

I rolled my eyes before turning to face the window, watching the world go by. Fifteen minutes into the journey, I felt him near me. The hairs on the back of my neck standing, goose-bumps spreading over my body like wildfire as he sat down next to me.

"Hey, baby girl," he crooned, pulling my ear phone out of my ear. He made himself comfortable before looking over his shoulder at Chase who was too busy talking to some girl he was sitting with at the back of the bus.

"What do you want, Royce," I hissed at him.

"Oh, baby, do you really want to know?" His tongue darted out and licked his bottom lip as his hand rested on my thigh, squeezing it gently. My breathing hitched, my chest rising up and down a lot faster than I would have liked it to, showing him just how much he affects me.

"Leave me alone," I whispered, my voice quivering. I was trying to be strong, but my voice betrayed me. My eyes darted back and forth to his.

"I can't do that, angel," he whispered, his hand trailing near the edge of the hem under my skirt, running his finger and thumb across my bare skin before he whipped them away.

"As if I would really go near you though." He laughed. "Grunge."

He stood up, cockiness all over his face before he turned around, leaning down so his face was in front of mine, his hand grabbing my cheeks and squeezing, pulling me closer to him, our lips so close. My heart was jack hammering in my chest.

"But let it be known, I may not be able to have you yet, but I don't want anyone else having you. Got it?" He said through gritted teeth, dropping his hand from my face.

Tears started to sting my eyes, but I wouldn't let them fall. I wouldn't cry in front of him.

In that moment, a glint of kindness shot through his eyes as he saw my reaction, but it was soon replaced with anger again as he laughed at me then walked back up to Chase.

"What was all that about?" I heard Chase ask.

"Oh, nothing, just wanted to make sure she knew we

had a test today." I heard his lies spilling out of his mouth. How the hell was my brother friends with him?

He was the spawn of Satan himself.

I was grateful when we pulled up at school, jumping out of my seat and darting off before Conor and Chase caught up with me. I saw Robyn standing there waiting for me.

"Hey, girl," she said, her red hair tied into a bun. "You okay?"

"Wonderful," I grumbled, looking over my shoulder and frowning at Conor whose eyes were glued to me. I could feel them burning into my soul.

"Conor being a dick?"

"When is he not a dick?" I sighed.

"True." She shrugged as we walked towards our lockers. "Ready for the test?" she asked as she dropped her bag in front of her locker.

"I think so, I hate calculus. When am I ever going to use it outside of here, honestly? What ballet dancer do you know that does calculus?" I started laughing as I offloaded some of my books into my locker, as did Robyn.

"I know." She laughed with me, slamming her locker shut.

I let out a deep breath when I felt his presence near me.

Robyn's eyes were looking behind me. "Incoming," she muttered, dropping her eyes to the floor.

I turned around to see him smirking and walking towards me, Chase nowhere in sight.

Brilliant.

He stopped in front of me, dropping his text book on the floor, his stupid grin getting bigger as he pushed his dark, chocolate hair back over to the side.

"Pick it up, grunge," he demanded, his little army of girls behind him snickering.

Bitches.

"No," I said before turning my back on him when I felt a tug on my hair, pulling me back around and bringing my face close to his, him inhaling my scent.

"I said..." He tightened his grip, tilting my head back as his eyes burned into mine. "Pick. It. Up." He continued through gritted teeth, slowly, his breath on my face before letting go of my hair.

I dropped to the floor like a submissive, crouching down in front of him but trying to be mindful to keep my legs as close together to each other as I could, I didn't want to be giving the whole school a flash of my underwear. I grabbed his text book and stood slowly, one hand holding my skirt down before clutching the book to my chest, trying to take a moment to register what the actual fuck was going on.

How the hell had I become this girl that did every single thing he said?

The girls all had their phones out, standing behind

their king as they continued to giggle. I didn't give a shit if they were filming me, they were as pathetic as him.

I held it out to him, my eyes not leaving his, trying to show him that he didn't intimidate me. But he did, he was so intense.

He snatched the book from me, then shoved me into my locker, pressing his body up against mine, his scent intoxicating me. He stroked his finger down my face before running it along my jaw-line, then gliding his hand down my body, stopping at my hips. He pressed his knee in-between my legs, pushing them apart with his knee and standing even closer to me, his body pinning me to the metal locker.

"Next time, baby girl, don't make me ask twice." He smirked, his eyes on me the whole time.

Within minutes he was walking away, down the halls, and I couldn't stop watching him.

I finally let out the breath I had been holding, my heart hammering in my chest. My eyes moved from him as he disappeared into the distance, then I turned to face Robyn. Her mouth was lax and open from what just happened.

He owned this school, like the fucking king he was.

But he wasn't the king to me, no, not in my world. In my world he was no more than the joker who karma was going to catch up with sooner rather than later.

I hoped.

I walked into the exam hall, Robyn behind me as we searched the rows for our names. I gave her a small smile and mouthed, "good luck," as I took my seat, letting out a sigh of relief when I saw Chase sitting next to me.

"How you feeling?" I asked him.

"Yeah, okay, going to boss it." He laughed, turning around in his seat and raising his eyebrows at me. "How about you?"

"Yeah, not bad, think I've got it." I nodded slightly, nibbling the inside of my mouth.

"Course you've got it. You'll be fine, Darcey." He reached back and stroked my hand. "Promise," he muttered before turning around in his seat.

I took a couple of deep breaths and laid my pencil, pen and calculator out next to me, when my eyes were pulled up to see *him* walking towards me, tongue-in-cheek, his eyes hazy and narrowed. He held his hand up to high five Chase.

"Hello, baby girl," he said quietly, bending down and whispering in my ear in a chilling tone before sitting down on the table next me, inches away. I let out a moan of frustration before throwing him a dagger stare. He rubbed his finger in-between his lips slowly, while his eyes were on my bare legs.

I felt myself blush. I hated that my body reacted to him in a completely different way than I wanted it too. I pushed my thighs together, turning my boots inwards, trying to cover myself somehow.

"Don't shy away from me," he said curtly. "My eyes are allowed to roam your body." He smirked, pulling his bottom lip between his teeth.

"Only for this last year at school, then I'll be rid of you," I spat, shaking my head as I picked my pencil up and started tapping it on the wooden exam desk.

"Ha." He laughed a little louder than I would've liked. "I'm not going anywhere, grunge, mark my words. You will never get rid of me. I am here forever, baby," he said in a threatening manner.

The thought of having him in my life out of school was soul destroying. I needed rid of Conor Royce, once and for all.

"Okay, quiet down," Mr Spink bellowed across the hall. "You have three hours, your time starts now." His balding head shining from the hall lights. He pushed his glasses up his nose as he started his walk down the aisle. I instantly relaxed, knowing that Conor couldn't talk to me for three hours.

And it was bliss.

CHAPTER 3

DARCEY

I walked out the exam room to find Robyn standing against the wall, waiting for me.

"How did it go?" she asked as we started walking down the corridor.

"Yeah, not bad. It's done now, isn't it? Not much I can do." I let out a giggle. "You?"

"I think alright." She scrunched her nose up. "Like you say, not much we can do now."

"Exactly." I smiled, wrapping my arm round her and pulling her into me. "It'll be fine."

We went out for lunch as we had a free period before our last lesson, it felt good getting out and away from Conor for a while. We walked towards a little coffee shop, just outside the school gates, which was a usual hang out for us all.

I sat cradling my iced latte, waiting for Robyn to join

me at the table. She smiled as she walked over, dragging her chair out and sitting opposite me. I rolled my neck, running my hand round the back of it.

"You okay?" Robyn asked.

"I am, I just feel so tense. Think I've been more worried about the exam than I liked to admit." I nodded, twirling my cup round in my palms.

"Is it just the exam?" Robyn asked, tapping her fingers on the table.

"What do you mean?" I acted dumb, I knew what she meant.

"Conor," she replied bluntly, pressing her lips into a thin line, her eyes on mine.

"No. God no. I hate him. And I can't wait to tell him how much I hate him."

"Love, hate or just pure hate?" She smirked at me then took a sip of her tea.

"Oh, pure hate." I nodded confidently.

"Mmhmm," she muttered quietly, taking another sip of her tea. I just rolled my eyes.

I was so grateful when our last class was over, I felt exhausted and it was only Monday.

I stood at the bus stop after hugging Robyn goodbye and agreeing to meet up on Wednesday for a catch up.

I popped my ear phones in and tried to blend in, away from his highness. He came crashing down the narrow bus aisle with his arm wrapped round Marie, licking his lips as he walked past me. He literally made my skin crawl, but I was glad that he was pre-occupied because that meant that he would leave me alone and hopefully go back to his swamp, instead of coming to our house again.

I ran off the bus, then walked quickly with my head down, making my way towards my house. And as per, Conor, my brother, and now Marie, were also behind.

Great.

I didn't stop to speak to my mum, just ran straight upstairs, slamming my door behind me. I couldn't cope with him in my life like this, day in and day out. It was exhausting.

I kicked off my Doc Martens, throwing them across the room then loosened the knot in my tie, when there was a knock on the door. I huffed, swinging the door open to see Conor standing there.

My heart started racing.

I couldn't help but let my eyes trail up and down his body.

In the year that I first met him, he was scrawny; nothing more than a handsome face. But now, he was toning himself up, his muscles more defined.

He was hot.

So, so hot.

"Baby girl," he muttered under his breath, leaning against my bedroom door frame, his leg crossed over the other and twirling his finger round in the palm of his hand.

"Conor." I sighed, batting my eyes down to my socks.

"What's got you in a mood? Is it because I've bought Marie back?" he said, stepping into my room, making me edge back towards my bed.

"No," I said in barely a whisper.

"Then what is it?" he asked, his eyes narrowing in on me.

"You," I said as the back of my knees hit the bed, making me fall onto it.

He leant down, kneeling on the bed, pressing his knee in-between my legs, smirking down at me.

My breath caught, my insides burned.

You can still want someone you hate, right?

"Admit you want me," he said, winking at me, sliding his hand slowly up my thigh.

"I don't," I said as confident as my voice would allow.

"Then why is your body betraying you?" He licked his lips. "Your breathing has quickened, your lips are parted as if you're waiting for me to kiss you, and you're flushed," he continued, leaning his mouth to my ear. "Tell me, are you wet for me, angel?"

"Conor," I moaned quietly, wanting him to stop this, but also at the same time wanting him to carry on. I felt his weight shift as he knelt up, wrapping his long, thick fingers around the knot in my tie, pulling me up so our lips were nearly touching.

"Even though you're legally old enough for me to touch you, it won't happen. Not yet, anyway. Just don't forget you belong to me, baby girl."

He leant down, brushing his lips against mine, a spark coursed through me, shooting from my heart straight down into the unknown in-between my legs.

It took everything inside of me to not kiss him back.

He let go of my tie, pushing me back down onto the bed. He winked at me, wiping the corner of his mouth with his thumb pad, then re-adjusted his trousers.

"Bye, grunge." He sniggered as he walked out the room.

My heart stopped, my body ached with the need to have him, but my hate for him consumed all of those feelings in an instant.

Damn you, Conor fucking Royce.

-

CONOR

"Fuck." I hissed, balling my fist outside her bedroom door. I nearly lost the tiny bit of control I have over myself. I pushed my hair back over to the side in frustration, my eyes hazing over as I go to find Marie. I needed to fuck, just to help get Darcey out my system for a few minutes, until it's time for me to finally have her. And I will have her, but that means breaking my promise to Chase, and for Darcey, that is something I am willing to do.

I run down to the basement to see Chase and Marie watching some shit on tele.

"Where you been?" Chase asks, leaning back and looking me up and down.

"Had to take a leak." I shrug. "Get off my back." I laugh, running my hand through his messy mop of blonde hair.

"Whoa, alright." He laughed back, punching me in the top of the arm in retaliation.

"Marie," her name slips off my tongue. "Come with me a minute." My tongue darts out, licking my bottom lip before pulling it back with my top teeth. Like an obedient puppy dog she jumped up off of the bean-bag, bounding over to me.

"Be back soon, bro," I shouted over at Chase. He just put his thumb up as he turned the X-box on.

I grab her hand, dragging her out of the basement and up to the room that the Sawyer's gave me a year ago. I pull her into my room, closing the door with my foot before pushing my hungry mouth on hers, imagining the whole time that she was Darcey.

Marie pulls away, grabbing and pulling at my shirt, before her greedy hands are on my belt.

"Call me baby girl, like you do that grunge girl," she whispers in my ear.

The anger suddenly builds up inside me.

Baby girl is Darcey's name, no one else's. She is and will always be *my* baby girl.

Only her.

Only mine.

"No," I growl as I push my trousers down then throw Marie on the bed.

"Undress," I bark at her as I grab a condom out the drawer, tearing the packet and rolling it down on my cock.

As predicted, she does what I ask, of course she does. She would be silly to ignore me. I lean down onto the bed, grabbing her hips and flipping her over as I slam myself into her without any warning. I squeeze my eyes shut as I continue my harsh pounding, her horrible mewing noises escaping her mouth as her hands scrunch up my bedsheets.

"Oh, Conor," she moans.

The anger grows in me even more, so without thinking, I stretch my arm out, grabbing her tie then reaching forward, I push it into her mouth, gagging her.

"Quiet," I growled. I didn't have to look at her, and I definitely didn't want to hear her calling my name.

My eyes dart open when I hear my bedroom door open. Turning my head to look over my shoulder, I see Darcey standing there.

Fuck. My heart started pounding, I saw the hurt in her eyes in an instant.

"I fucking hate you Conor Royce," Darcey shouts, throwing the glass of lemonade she had in her hand to the floor, watching it shatter, just like her heart.

"Fuck you. I hope your dick falls off," she screams, her voice strained as she runs into her bedroom.

I pull away from Marie, pushing her away from me across the bed, completely sickened and disgusted by her, and by myself. My skin crawls, making a shiver run down my spine.

"Get out," I hiss at Marie, and she done just that. Grabbing her clothes and running out of my bedroom.

I have fucked up.

She is never going to forgive me for this.

CHAPTER 4

DARCEY

Two Years Later

It was the morning of my eighteenth birthday party. I didn't want a party, but of course, Chase did with his many friends, including Conor.

After that night I caught Conor balls-deep in Maria, or Marie, whatever her name was, he seemed to mellow a bit. Don't get me wrong, he was still vicious, depending on his mood, but I just made a point to stay out of his way.

There were a few occasions I would have to sit next to him and entertain him for a short period of time, but I wouldn't do it out of choice. No. I hated him more and more each day.

I was booked into the salon with Robyn and my mum today to have our hair styled. Is it wrong that I want to bail on my own party?

I sigh as I open my bedroom door, to see Conor

coming out his room, his stunning green eyes on mine.

"Grunge," he mutters, his eyes looking me up and down.

"Dick." I flip my finger at him.

"Oh, baby girl, don't be like that," he cooed before laughing and walking towards the stairs, me following behind him. It took everything in me not to run and push him down the stairs, watching the king fall, this princess smiling with satisfaction.

Why did he have to be so damn hot?

My body wanted him.

My heart, on the other hand, constantly reminded me to stay away from him.

He was bad news.

Trouble.

"Chase, my man," he boomed as he high-fived my brother.

I stood in the kitchen, watching their sickly bromance. As I stared at them, I looked at how much they had both changed in the last two years.

Chase's honey-blonde hair was now shoulder length and long enough for him to get it into a man bun. He also sported more stubble now-a-days.

Conor on the other hand, flew off the charts, rocketed in fact. The side and back of his head were shaved short, making it hard to see just how dark his hair was. He still had his long hair on top which he sported in a side parting, and I still dreamt of running my fingers through. I moved my eyes down to his smug, stupid, handsome face. I was never into too many piercings, but he made it look hot. One of his ears was pierced which he wore a small stretcher in. He had both conches pierced, his helix and his tragus. I had my helix and tragus done too, but not because he had his done. Me and Robyn went together, sort of a best friend bonding thing.

He turned on his heel facing me, his eyes looking me up and down as he walked closer to me, bending down and levelling his perfect plump lips in line with my ear.

"What you wearing tonight then, baby girl?" he whispered as Chase walked down to the basement and out of sight.

"Does it matter?" I asked, ignoring the deep flutter in my stomach.

"Of course it does," he said, licking his lips. "Because this is the night we are going to stop fighting each other. This is the night I am going to own you. Mind, body and soul." He winked at me.

"I don't think so." I scoffed, letting out a little laugh as I flicked my long, honey-blonde hair over my shoulder. Even though I wanted him to own me in every way, I wouldn't let it happen.

He was my nemesis.

My Achilles heel.

My distraction and weakness.

"Okay, babe. We will see." He smirked confidently, his eyes on my body, my eyes on his. I focused on his full-sleeved tattooed arms and neck. I couldn't quite believe he had done that to himself. His torso and back were covered too.

"Told ya, baby, you'll be mine." Standing there so bold and confident in himself, rubbing his hands together. He has big hands. He has started having his fingers and hands tattooed, I'm not sure if it is a rebellious thing or not. Or just a way of coping.

Shortly after Conor started Buck Hall, his mum was found dead after overdosing on heroine, then shortly after that happened his dad skipped town. He hasn't heard a word from him since.

He turned up the evening his mum died with my mum, he was black and blue after falling to the hands of his father. It wasn't the first time, I knew that his father laid a hand on him before, but after the night he was brought home by my mum, that was the last time his father touched him. I am aware that he tried, waiting outside the gates of school, but he never got near Conor. Chase wouldn't allow it, and neither would my parents.

Part of me felt sorry for him, but most of me doesn't. I know that sounds harsh, but you write your own paths in life, I am a firm believer of that. He didn't have to be a heartless prick to me because of his upbringing.

Karma comes back when you least expect it.

That's why I am working so hard on my ballet and to be a good person. I was hoping to find out next week if I have made it into The London Ballet college. I had back-to-back lessons next week with my uptight, stuffy ballet mistress but it would all be worth it. I knew I was good enough. I have been doing this since I was five, this was my life. I could do this in my sleep.

I was so deep in thought, I hadn't realised he was still standing there, his eyes burning into me. I pulled my eyes from him, losing the connection between us as he stepped back and away from me.

"Ready, darling?" my mum called out as she sashayed her hips down the hallway. She always looked so pristine. She was wearing tight, skinny high-waisted jeans and a loose crew neck tee. Her long golden hair was in waves.

"Yup," I said quietly, gripping my phone and bending to pick my Doc Martens up from the shoe closet. I sat on the chair that was situated in the entrance hall as I pulled them on, my mum tutting at me.

"What?" I quipped at her.

"Why are you wearing those?" she questioned me, her eyes firmly peeled to my battered boots.

"Erm, cos I want to." I challenged her, all the while Conor was smirking at me. My eyes flew to him, a furious look plastered over my face. "What are you smirking at?" I snapped at him.

"Darcey!" my mum shouted.

"What?" I sniped.

"What is wrong with you?" She shook her head in disgust.

"Him. That's what is wrong with me," I hissed at her as I finished doing my laces up. I looked down at my black leggings and *Chicago Bulls* basketball jersey. Maybe I should've made a bit of an effort?

I rolled my eyes. "Fuck it," I groaned as I stormed out the door.

I heard my mum apologise to Conor for my behaviour as she followed me. He was such a dick.

I slammed the car door on my mum's range rover, pushing my sunglasses onto my face, the spring air warm on my tanned skin.

As I went to put my ear phones in, I heard her voice. "I don't think so, young lady," she said, pulling them from my ears. "What has gotten into you?"

"Nothing, just Conor." I shook my head.

"The boy lost his parents, we are the only family he has."

"Yay." I rolled my eyes at her. "He isn't as innocent as you think he is."

"What is that supposed to mean?" she quizzed me as she pushed the button to start the engine.

"Just forget it, Mum. Can we go? Robyn is waiting," I said, my tone clipped.

"Fine." She shook her head at me before pulling away from the house.

I was relieved when we pulled up outside Robyn's house, I messaged her just as we pulled outside her gates, so we wouldn't have to drive in and then wait to drive back out again.

"Hey, boo, hey Zara," Robyn called out as she hopped in the back of the car. "Whoa, I can feel some tension in here," she said blasé. "What's happened?"

"Nothing," I snapped.

"Darcey is being mean to Conor," my mum piped up, looking at Robyn in the rear view mirror and raising her perfectly shaped brows.

"Mmhmm, but he does deserve it though." She shrugged, a smirk on her face.

"Not you as well? The poor boy has been through enough. What is wrong with you two? Do you both have a crush on him?"

"No!" we both shouted in unison.

"Christ no," I said after, shaking my head.

"Then what's the issue?"

"He is a dick, Mum, alright? That's all you need to know. He might be golden-boy to you and Chase, but he is a prick to me."

"Language." She scowled, tutting and shaking her head at me.

"Well, stop asking me then." I rolled my eyes and

looked out the window. The conversation was over.

We pulled up at the salon and I have never been so relieved. My mum kept going on about how wonderful Conor was, and how me and Robyn should stop being so cruel to him. Halfway through her conversation I put my earphones in and drowned the noise out. I felt bad on Robyn, but she would understand, she knew how he was.

I sat down in the chair with my usual stylist Kera as she pulled my hair out of its messy ponytail then ran her fingers through it.

"What we doing today?" she asked, smiling at me in the mirror.

"I don't know, maybe an up-do of some sort? Or something off the neck?" I let out a little laugh.

"I'll work my magic, leave it with me." She winked at me. "Drink?"

"Please, I'll have a champagne seeing as I'm eighteen," I said a little louder, so my mum heard.

Her eyes wandered over. "One glass," she warned as she closed her eyes, enjoying her hair wash and scalp massage.

Within minutes she was back with a bubbly glass of champagne, Robyn accepting hers as well. I closed my eyes and let Kera's expert hands style my hair. I already wanted tonight over. I've got ballet all weekend, so I won't be having a heavy night, whereas Chase and Conor will no doubt get so drunk they won't even know their names.

ASHLEE ROSE

As long as he stays away from me, it'll be fine.

CHAPTER 5

After a couple of hours in the salon we arrived home. We all walked up the six steps leading to the oak front doors. I pushed through them, anxiety sweeping over me instantly when I saw the caterers and party planners making my eighteenth look like something you see on 'My Sweet Sixteen.'

As much as I was grateful for my parents throwing a party, this wasn't what I wanted. I would rather have had a quiet night in with my family and Robyn, sitting with a nice takeaway, a few wines and a girly film.

This was not my idea of fun.

Yet, Chase had talked my mum and dad into it for his "social status." He was a cool kid; the cool kids needed the biggest parties. I wasn't a cool kid. I was the unpopular nerd who got bullied by her brothers' best friend. How sad was that? All of a sudden, I was having a pity party for one. I kicked my boots off and left them in the middle of the hallway as I started walking upstairs, Robyn walking up behind me.

I let out a sigh of relief when I got to my bedroom without having to see the devil himself. I opened my door, letting Robyn through first, watching as she dropped her bags and flopped down on my bed.

"I don't know about you, but I feel knackered."

"Same, hun," I muttered as I sat next to her.

I pulled my phone out before connecting it to my Bluetooth speaker and turning *Blink 182 – "Always"* up, but not too much that we couldn't speak. The house was big enough to not have my mum banging on my door to turn it down.

"Have you decided what you're wearing?" I asked Robyn who was twiddling with a loose curl from her messy bun up-do.

"Hmm, think so. I chose a bandeau midi-dress. In my favourite colour obvs, red." She let out a small smile, nudging me. "How about you?"

"Black skater dress." I nodded kicking my feet together. "I feel like getting drunk, but I can't because of ballet tomorrow, and the last thing I want to do is fuck up. Especially with Ms. Camilla, she would have my arse for showing up hungover."

"Darce, it's your eighteenth, have a bloody drink. You're sensible, you know when to stop."

"Hmm, I suppose a couple wouldn't hurt." I shrugged before standing up and stretching my arms up.

PROMISE ME

"Better start getting dressed."

I groaned as I walked towards my walk-in wardrobe. I peeled my leggings and jersey off and discarded them to the floor. I pulled my underwear drawer out, trying to find something discreet that wouldn't show under the dress I chose to wear. After rummaging, I found a seamless black thong and black-laced bra. I slipped them on and looked at myself in the mirror. My breasts were a good handful in size, so not too big. My legs long and toned, my stomach flat and defined; I had ballet to thank for my abs.

I was five-foot-seven, quite tall for a girl but not too tall. I wrapped myself in a black, silk dressing gown before walking out to my bedroom and sitting down at my dressing table. Robyn wasn't in the room, which made me think she was getting a drink for us. Suddenly, I felt like drinking wasn't a good idea. I can keep my distant from Conor when I've not had a drink because my brain kicks in, tells me that it isn't a good idea to not go near him, but drunk Darcey around Conor is a recipe for disaster.

Maybe I should just have the one? Robyn comes bounding into the room with two bottles of champagne.

"It's your party," she shouts, excitement apparent in her voice. She placed one of the chilled bottles on my dressing table in front of me.

"Where did you get these from?" I ask, laughing before popping the cork and letting out a little shriek as the bubbles spill over the bottle.

"Erm, from the bar set up downstairs. They were just sitting in a massive chiller, so I thought, why not?" She laughed with me before taking a swig of her bottle.

"So, boo, I was thinking that maybe I would just stick to the one drink," I said before taking a small sip of the champagne.

"Nah." She shook her head ferociously from side to side. "Nope. It's your birthday. You *need* the drink, especially when you see how hot Conor looks. Mate," she said, fanning herself with her hand. "Honestly, Darce, you're going to lose your shit." She winked at me as she started undressing and pulling her dress out of its bag.

"Oh, man, okay, maybe I do need the drink," I said sheepishly before taking a big mouthful, trying to calm my growing nerves.

"Mmhmm, you do." She nodded as she slipped her red dress up her body, smiling at her reflection in the mirror as she started applying her make up.

After applying my foundation, I worked on a dark, smoky-eye look. I finished my eyes off with eyeliner then flicked my long lashes with mascara. I added some bronzer to my visible cheekbones, then finishing my look off with bright, red matte lipstick.

I rubbed my lips together before getting rid of any stray lipstick that had smudged. I tightened the hair toggle on the bottom of my fish-tail-plait that Kera did for me, pulling it round and over my shoulder so it's sitting under my ribs.

I stood from the table, satisfied in how I looked, then dropped my robe, grabbing my skater-dress and slipping it over my little curves. The neck-line dipped a little lower than my parents would like, but it was my birthday and I was eighteen. I'm technically an adult.

"Babe, do me up," I asked Robyn, who had now started on my champagne. I stood in front of her as she clasped the zip and yanked it up.

"There we go." She smiled as she re-adjusted her dress as she stood.

I sprayed my perfume then stepped into my faithful Doc Martens.

"Mate." Robyn giggled. "Your mum is going to lose her shit that you're wearing them again."

"I know." I laughed with her, then poked my tongue out, grabbing the champagne off of her and downing what was left in the bottle.

"Ready?" Robyn asked.

"Ready as I'll ever be." I let out a small sigh, nerves crashing through my body. "Do I look okay?"

"Babe, you look like fire. So hot. You're a rocket. Completely out of this world. Conor isn't going to be able to keep his eyes off of you," she said grabbing my hand and yanking me out of my bedroom and down towards the party.

I held on to her until we got downstairs, to see the

house was brimming. I hardly knew these people, me and Robyn kept ourselves to ourselves in school, where most girls had cliques. We weren't about that, we were happy with it just being us two. I barged my way through the crowds to get to the kitchen, seeing my mum's face straight away.

Shit, she was pissed.

"Darcey, why? Why the boots?" she asked annoyed, her brows knitted together, and she looked me up and down.

"Because I like them and they're me," I sniped at her. "Plus, it's my party and I'll wear the boots if I want too" shrugging my shoulders up at her.

"Christ." She rolled her eyes and shook her head, still muttering, before slipping into the crowd.

I looked behind to see Robyn trying not to laugh. We walked out into the marquee where the DJ was set up, and over the back was the bar which we made a bee-line straight for.

"Ladies," the guy behind the bar said in a husky, low voice.

"Hey, can we have four shots of tequila and four vodka and lemonades please?" I batted my eyelashes at him.

"Sure thing." He smiled back and winked at me as he tended to our drinks. I blushed.

"Thirsty?" Robyn asked.

"Like you wouldn't believe."

But the truth was, I wasn't just thirsty for a drink, I was thirsty for Conor Royce. I needed to keep my distance from him.

The bartender passed us our tequila shots first, then went back to make the vodkas.

"Ready? 3... 2... 1..." I shouted as we both knocked back the shots, then sucked on the lemon. I winced. Christ, it was awful.

"That was fucking disgusting," Robyn spat.

"I know, but we have another one each to do, so quick. Let's just do it and get it over with," I suggested, shoving the tequila into her hand.

"Ready?" I asked before knocking it back. That one actually didn't taste too bad.

The music was booming through our bodies, "Roses" by SAINt JHN blasted through the marquee.

"Ladies," the bartender crooned as he slid the four vodkas over to us.

"Thank you." I smiled, grabbing my two plastic glasses and walking towards the dance floor when I felt his eyes on me. My heart pounded in my chest at the thought of him. I looked round the marquee, but I couldn't see him. I knew when he was close; My skin covered in goose-bumps, the hairs on the back of my neck standing tall.

My body always reacted to him, whether I wanted it

to or not.

"What's wrong?" Robyn asked, sensing my mood instantly.

"I can feel him," I muttered. Just as the words left my lips, there he was, standing in the crowd. And fuck me, Robyn wasn't lying when she said what he looked like tonight. I tried everything to pull my disobedient eyes off him, but I couldn't.

I was hypnotized, being pulled towards him.

He was wearing a black, tight fitted shirt with a grandad collar, his neck tattoos showing over the top. He styled it with black, skinny jeans and Doc Martens.

I scoffed slightly. Why was he wearing Doc Martens? He has *never* worn shoes like me. He is all about his trainers.

His head was dipped slightly, his hands pressed together, pushing his index fingers into his bottom lip as his eyes found mine.

It took everything in me to continue to the dance floor, pushing his haunted green eyes out of my head. I necked back my two cups of vodka before dropping them to the floor. I slowly ran my hands up the sides of my body before pushing them above my head, letting the music take over as I felt the beat pulse through me.

My hips moved side to side to the fast tones of the song. I was putting on a show, just for him as I knew he would be watching me.

As the song slowed, my hands were back up in the air as my body snaked along. Once the beat dropped, I started nodding my head along with Robyn, forgetting about everything and anyone around us, so lost in the music, which is where I needed to be.

To erase Conor Royce from my mind.

Once the song slowed down, the DJ dropped "Mr Brightside" by The Killers, people crowded the dance floor. Me and Robyn started jumping up and down on the spot, our hands above our heads which were being tossed from side to side as we screamed the lyrics to each other.

"Another drink?" I shouted to Robyn who was still jumping up and down to the song.

"Yes! Keep them coming." She smiled. "I fucking love this song." I laughed at her as I walked unsteadily over to the bar. The shots and the downed Vodka were starting to affect me, but I wasn't stopping now.

The poison felt too good running through my veins.

I stood at the bar, kicking one of my boots with my other foot, waiting to be served.

"Same again?" the bartender asked, his eyes soft and warm.

I smiled a silly grin at him, twiddling with the ends of my hair. "Please."

"No problem." He smirked before walking away to start the drinks and I let out a little sigh. I just wish it was me, Robyn and Chase here tonight. They are all I care about. All of this; it's not me. I know girls would die for a lifestyle like this, but not me. I am content in my own little bubble.

The bartender passed me the tequila shots, the lemon sitting in the clear liquid. I nodded slightly as I accepted them, knocking one back straight away, wincing. Fuck, they really were bad, but I couldn't stop, grabbing the other one and throwing it back, letting it burn my throat before I puckered my lips, shaking my head to rid myself of the taste.

I looked over the crowd to see if I could get Robyn's attention to come and help me with the drinks, but she was too deep in the music. I turned back around as he slid the four vodkas along to me.

"Thanks," I muttered. I hadn't thought this through. Damn.

I reached forward for the other two tequila shots when I felt the hairs on the back of my neck stand.

Before I could look for him, his hands were on my hips, his lips next to my ear.

"Baby girl," he whispered.

My eyes closed, and I rolled my head back against his chest. One of his large, tattooed hands ran up round my neck as he gripped the base of it.

As much as I hated his pet name for me, it did things to me that I couldn't even explain.

"Do you think that's a good idea?" he asked, nibbling

on my ear lobe. A small moan came from my mouth.

It was just the drink... Just the drink, I muttered over and over in my head.

"I think you've had enough, don't you?" he mumbled, moving his lips from my ear and brushing his hot mouth across the back of my neck. His grip round my waist tightened. His scent intoxicated me.

I was addicted in that instant.

But the hate I felt for this man was imprinted in me; that would never leave.

I snapped my eyes open, throwing my hand up to his and pulling him away, removing the contact and breaking the hypnotic state he had me under.

"I'm fine." I stepped away, side-eyeing him, grabbing the shot glasses and knocking them back in front of him. His eyes darkened as they hooded over. He just glared at me.

As much as my throat was burning, I needed to prove a point to him. I grabbed my vodka and drank it as quickly as I could before reaching over and grabbing the other three plastic glasses for me and Robyn. I'm sure she wouldn't miss the tequila.

"You need to slow down," he warned, his fist closed and resting on the bar, his eyes narrowing on the bartender.

"I don't think I do. I am eighteen and if I want to get absolutely shit faced, then I will." I shrugged as I went to walk away but he wrapped his muscular arm round my waist and pulled me back against him.

"Darcey," he said in a chilling tone, emphasizing my name. His hand that was round my waist slowly made its way to the neckline on my dress, his finger running down my cleavage.

My breath caught at the contact.

"Do you like that, baby girl?" he crooned in my ear, his lips pressing against my neck as he kissed me. My skin lit in that instant, the rest of the room blurring out around me, my head relaxing against his hard chest.

"I take your silence as a yes," he said before letting me go. "I'll see you later." He winked as he pushed past me and walked into the crowd.

"Fuck," I whispered quietly to myself.

I walked back over to Robyn in a haze, gripping onto the plastic cups a little harder than I should have done.

"Finally! Did you get lost on the way to bar?" she said, a little laugh coming out.

"Something like that," I mumbled, handing her the two drinks.

"Where's your other one?" she asked, looking at both of hers before she eyed mine.

"Oh, I drank it at the bar, needed my hands." I shrugged before taking a big mouthful, my mouth suddenly dry.

I needed to stay away from Conor if I knew what was

good for me.

    Last thing I needed was to fall into his hands tonight.

CHAPTER 6

CONOR

"Fuck," I groaned to myself, my jeans constricting my hard on. She looked stunning with her blue eyes surrounded by her dark eye makeup. Her red fucking lips... All I could think about was the ring that would be left round my cock from them.

She was wearing a tight, short, black dress that hugged her toned figure as if it was made for her. Her short skirt sitting just under her arse.

When she is mine, she won't be going out in something like that. Those sorts of outfits will be for my eyes only.

And then her fucking boots, that I secretly love, just topped her look off.

Making her look as hot as sin.

That one little moment with her was too much.

I have waited so long to have something from her,

something to give me the go ahead, knowing that she wants me as much as I want her.

And that was what she just did.

The delectable moan that left her beautiful lips was what I needed. Her scent was too much. Do you know the amount of strength it took for me to walk away from her? Especially with the way she is drinking, she doesn't know what it's like to be drunk.

All the boys in the room are staring at her, especially the fucking bartender.

This is her first night with alcohol, and she is being reckless.

I snorted a laugh at my thoughts. I was the same when I was eighteen. Fuck, I was the same when I was a lot younger than her. But now, at twenty, I've slowed down a lot on the alcohol front. Especially when me and Chase enrolled in the army. We both promised each other that if one of us didn't get in, the other would drop their application but luckily, we both did. We were to leave on the thirtieth of September.

I loved the thought of being in the army, but fuck am I going to miss Darcey when I am gone. I took a picture from the family photo album of her from last year's school summer fete, and once I'm gone I am keeping it on me, at all times. Having a little piece of heaven with me.

I walked over to Chase, Tyler and Ryan who were standing round a bunch of girls, all looking too desperate for my liking. None of them compared to Darcey. They were all batting their shitty false eyelashes at us all. Pathetic.

I took my whiskey off of Chase, holding it up to him.

"Cheers, fella," I said before knocking it back, the satisfying burn travelling down my throat.

"How drunk do you think Darce is going to get tonight?" Chase asked me, humour lacing his voice.

"Knowing grunge, probably not overly," slut number one piped up giggling. My mouth twitched at them using the vicious name I call her, and my temper rose.

"She's probably drinking water, *pretending* she is drunk," slut number two jibed before running her finger up my bicep.

"Fuck off," I snapped at her, stepping closer to Chase.

"Enough," Chase sniped at the desperate wannabes. "Have you seen her?' he asked me, his voice now full of concern.

"Yeah, she's pretty steamed already, to be fair. I did tell her to go steady, but when does she listen to me?" I shrugged.

"Never, mate." He rolled his eyes. "Come, let's go check on her." He placed his, now empty, cup on the table behind one of the girls before stalking into the crowd as I followed behind him. The girls went to follow but I shot them a glare, and they knew better than to ignore me.

PROMISE ME

My eyes were already seeking her out.

"Mate, she was on the dance floor earlier," I said in his ear loudly over the banging music. We split up, so I checked one side of the floor, Chase the other. I started to panic when I couldn't see her.

Robyn was talking to a guy which made me tense as they were *always* together. There was no one else here who she really spoke to. She was a loner, basically invisible to everyone at school.

But to me she wasn't.

She was all I saw.

I walked up to Robyn, grabbing her arm and pulling her back towards me. Her drink spilled out of her cup and onto her red dress. She threw me a look, her brows furrowed. She was fucked off.

"Where's Darce?" I asked, ignoring her icy glare. "Why should I tell you?" she slurred then giggled.

"Robyn, come on. Please." I gave her my best smile and my puppy dog eyes.

"I dunno, she went somewhere with the bartender, that's all I know. I promise," she muttered, now sensing the urgency and following me as I ran towards Chase.

We stood in the middle of the dance floor. "No luck mate, but Robyn seems to think she has disappeared with one of the bartenders," I shouted over the music. I didn't even know what shit the DJ was playing, it all merged into one.

"Yeah, she did, about twenty minutes ago," Robyn confirmed, her eyes wandering up Chase's body.

"Let's go check outside," Chase suggested before patting me on the chest as we made our way through the hustle and bustle of the crowd. The thing with this stupid house was that there was nooks and crannies everywhere. The garden was on acres and acres, but hopefully she wasn't too far.

Chase and Robyn ran in one direction, me in the other.

I ran out the oak doors, running down the steps that led down to the driveway. She wasn't there. I walked through the random smokers, just to make sure she wasn't hiding within them. I was the last person she was going to want to see, but at the moment in time I didn't give a shit what she wanted.

I could feel my temper rising.

I always had eyes on her.

I picked up my pace and started running towards the back of the house and into the garden. I continued to run along the side of the marquee and towards the pool house. My eyes were constantly darting, I just couldn't see her, I couldn't feel her.

I normally feel her presence.

She stood out anywhere to me.

She could be standing amongst thousands and thousands of people and my eyes would still find her.

I got to the pool house, grabbing the handle and trying to open it but it was jammed, or locked. I was banging on the glass and screaming for her.

"Darcey!" I banged again on the door. "Fuck," I growled as I walked back from the door then walked back up to it, kicking it with everything I had as it came off its hinges.

"Darcey," I shouted again.

"Con..." I heard her voice.

"Shut up before I shut you up. You want this, baby, I know you do. You wouldn't have been giving me the go ahead all night if you didn't, you little cock tease," I heard a man's voice say. The hairs on the back of my neck stood, my blood boiled and pumped through my veins.

I ran down the spiral stairs, searching the room as I did, when I saw her in the corner, pushed up against a wall behind the sun loungers, the bartender grabbing her and kissing her neck as his hands pushed up her thighs, making her dress rise.

Her eyes were on mine, silently pleading with me.

I jumped over the bannister of the staircase. I just wanted to get to her as quickly as I could.

I sprinted over to where she was, grabbing the bartender round the back of the neck, turning him towards me and punching him, hearing a crack as my fist contacted his face, tossing him to the floor when I saw Chase staring, Robyn's hands at her mouth.

"What the fuck?" Chase hissed as he ran over and kicked the bartender in the ribs. "What the fuck were you doing to my sister?" he shouted through gritted teeth, spit flying out of his mouth.

"She's a cock tease. She had been giving me the come-on all night. Nothing but a slut," the guy said as he went to stand, blood spilling out of his mouth when Chase kicked him again, giving him an almighty blow to the ribs before picking him up by the scruff of his neck and dragging him towards the doors.

"Stay with her," he barked his orders. I had never, ever seen Chase so wound up. But this was his baby sister.

I turned back to her, her black eyes smudged and her mascara running down her cheeks. Her red lipstick spread across her beautiful face.

"Baby girl," I said, breathless. I ran my thumb across her cheek. "Look at me," I demanded, and her scared, blue eyes flicked up to mine. "Did he hurt you or touch you?"

I couldn't believe the words were even coming out of my mouth. She shook her head, tears still streaming down her face.

"Are you sure?" I wasn't convinced. "Baby, please tell me what happened," I said, trying to hide the harshness of my angry voice.

"No." Her voice sounded small. "But he tried. He kept grabbing my legs and trying to force them open," she choked out. "Kept calling me a cock tease, then kissing me on my lips and neck." She started to shake. "He would have kept going if you hadn't shown up," she cried out before falling into me.

I wrapped my arms around her, holding her tight and kissing the top of her head. "Baby girl, nothing would have happened. I am always going to show up for you. When will you realise that you're mine? Always," I muttered. "Come, let's get you upstairs," I said softly as I ushered her out the pool house, Robyn behind us.

I needed to get her upstairs and in her room without any attention. This is where being a nobody comes in handy for her.

My baby girl.

This is not the night I had envisaged for us on her birthday.

CHAPTER 7

DARCEY

I felt numb as I sat on the edge of my bed, Robyn wrapping her arm around me.

"Boo, I'm so sorry. I shouldn't have let you go off with him," she said, guilt lacing her timid voice, her eyes burning into me.

I turned my head to look at her. "Don't you dare." I shook my head. "This wasn't your fault. I wanted to go, I needed to get Conor out of my head." I sniffed. "It's my fault," I said quietly, my voice shaking.

I nibbled on the inside of my mouth to try and stop my tears. Robyn had helped me get undressed and take my make-up off. She kissed the side of my head.

"I'm just popping to the loo, I'll be back in five. Will you be okay?" she asked, her face showing her concern.

"I'll be fine." I nodded, blowing my nose in my tissue. She smiled at me as she walked into the bathroom, closing the door. Conor and Chase had told my parents what happened, so they were currently trying to clear the house out while waiting for the police, not that they were going to do anything. I wasn't underage, he technically didn't do anything wrong, as such.

I threw my head back, focussing on the ceiling. What a fucked up night.

I was distracted when I heard a knock on my door and saw Conor standing there, still looking as handsome as anything in his clothes.

"Can I come in?" he asked quietly.

"You never normally ask." I rolled my eyes in humour before laughing. "Of course you can."

I shuffled up my bed slightly, wrapping my blanket round me to cover me up, now very conscious that I was only in a silk vest top and matching shorts. Conor had never seen me in so little. His eyes stayed on mine, not wandering down my body.

"Here," he said, handing me a hot cup of tea. "Thought it would help," he mumbled, fidgeting on the spot and then pushing his hands into his pockets, rocking back and forth on his feet.

"You can sit down." I smiled at him, my eyes looking at the spot next to me. "Thank you for this," I said, bringing the hot cup of tea up to my lips and taking a sip. I watched as he sat down warily next to me. We sat quietly for a moment or two, his eyes still on me.

"Well, I have never met this Conor before." I giggled, placing my cup on my side table.

"I'm not a complete monster," he said defensively.

"I never said you were." I raised my eyebrow at him. I felt sad that he thought that.

"I know you didn't, but I just want you to know, I am human. I do feel. I do have empathy." He sighed, pulling his eyes away from mine as he looked at his red, swollen knuckles.

"Maybe you should get some ice for that."

"I'll be fine. I just want to make sure you are," he said, his green eyes back on mine, and I swear I could see so deeply into his soul.

"I'll be okay," I assured him, then reached for his hand and gripped it tightly. "I will never be able to thank you enough for tonight. If it wasn't for you..." my voice trailed off before I started crying.

"Hey, come on, don't think like that. I was there. I would have always been there, Darce. I promise you," he said, pulling his hand from mine and wrapping his arm round my shoulders, pulling me towards him. I didn't say anything else, I just sat there, listening to his steady heartbeat when I felt his mouth on the top of my head. My heart fluttered.

I turned my head up to face him, his hand reaching to my chin and tilting it up slightly.

We were inches apart.

PROMISE ME

His mouth started moving down towards mine, our lips millimetres apart when we heard Robyn cough.

I bolted back towards the headboard, Conor shot up off the bed and walked towards the door.

"Okay, anyway..." he said, his eyes on Robyn, Robyn's eyes flitting back and forth from me and him. Her eyebrows furrowed, hands on her hips.

"I'm gonna hit the hay, Darce, I'm glad you're okay. Try and get some rest," he said before nodding and walking out the room.

I let out the breath I had been holding before falling back on my bed. "Shit," I muttered.

"Would you have kissed him if I wasn't here?" she asked, still standing in the middle of the bedroom floor, hands still firmly on her hips.

I took a moment to think about her question. I wanted to blurt out yes, but I knew I couldn't, I shouldn't.

"I don't know," I lied, my eyes narrowing in on her.

"You're a liar," she said, shaking her head before kneeling next to me. "You're allowed to be attracted to him, heck, the guy is a God." She grabbed her red hair from the back of her neck, holding it up and fanning her face with her spare hand.

"He is hot." I sighed. "And yeah, I probably would've kissed him if you weren't here." I let out a little laugh. "It's Conor fucking Royce, who wouldn't want to kiss him?" I shrugged at her.

"Exactly. I think you should go to his room," she encouraged as she slipped under the covers.

"What?" I asked her, shock on my face.

"Don't act dumb. You heard me. Go to his room, see what happens," she said before yawning and getting herself comfortable.

I contemplated it for a moment. I knew nothing would happen, he would probably push me away, but part of me was desperate to find out.

"Fine," I agreed. "But don't throw this back in my face when I start moaning about him."

"Yeah, yeah." She nodded, too engrossed in the tele. "Go," she bossed me.

"Okay, okay," I said, holding my hands up.

I threw my blanket off of me and stood, putting my slippers on. I walked over to my dressing table, pulled my fishtail plait out, then ran my fingers through my long, now wavy, hair.

I flicked my lashes with a light layer of mascara and rubbed some lip balm into my lips. I walked back over to the bed, grabbing my blanket, wrapping it back round myself.

I took a deep breath as I got to my bedroom door.

"Wish me luck," I said to Robyn who was quite happy taking over my bed.

"Good luck," she called out from her tele coma as I walked out the door.

I couldn't believe I was doing this, he probably wasn't even in bed.

I walked the few steps to his room from mine, knocking quietly on his bedroom door. I heard him on the other side of the door. I watched the handle with bated breath, waiting for him to open it.

"Darcey," he whispered, surprise on his face.

My eyes trawled down his body, his black shirt was undone and open fully, his tattoos spilling out. He still had his jeans on and he looked delectable. His toned stomach was so defined. It wasn't hard to make out underneath all his tattoos. My eyes studied the woman tattoo he had over most of his torso. I cocked my head then realised I had to speak.

"I... err..." I stammered. "I just wanted to say thanks, again."

Such a cop out.

"Did you?" A trace of a smile appeared on his lips, knowing he had caught me out.

"Mmhmm." I nodded, crossing my arms across my chest, suddenly embarrassed.

"Okay then, well... you're welcome," he said, still smiling as he took a step back before he started pushing the door shut.

"Wait," I called out.

"Yes?" he said in a snarky manner.

"Can I come in?" My eyes were wide as I stared into

his, my heart thumping so hard in my chest.

"You may." His gorgeous smile grew bigger, revealing his perfect white teeth. It wasn't fair, he shouldn't be allowed to be this hot. He stepped back, pulling his bedroom door open wider for me to squeeze past him.

I walked in sheepishly, feeling uneasy all of a sudden. He walked over to his bed, sitting himself down.

"Come over, I don't bite." A small smirk graced his face, his eyes hazy.

I walked over to him, closing the gap between us and sitting on the end of his bed. "Sorry for just turning up."

"That's okay," he muttered, his eyes on mine. "I wasn't doing much anyway, just listening to some music." His eyes flitted to his phone.

"What were you listening to?" I asked, tucking my legs under me, trying to peer over at his phone. He grabbed it then pulled it close to his chest. "Oh, I don't know..." he teased.

"Come on," I said, laughing then batting my eyelashes at him. "For me... Please?" I tried to beg, edging towards him, my arm darting out under my blanket quickly, my hand trying to grab his phone.

He pushed his phone above his head as my hand just touched it, and losing my balance, I fell onto him. His body tensed, his breathing quickened.

I didn't move, my eyes locked on him.

My heart was drumming in my chest.

I pushed my hands off his chest as I sat up, tucking my hair behind my ear and pulling my eyes from him, looking at his bed duvet.

"Sorry," I whispered.

"For what?" His voice was low and soft.

"For what just happened."

"Nothing happened." He slowly moved his arm down, holding his phone out for me to look at. My heart did a happy dance when I saw the song by Second Hand Serenade, "Fall For You."

"I love that song," I said quietly, playing with the label on my blanket.

"I know you do." He smiled at me. "I love it too."

I couldn't deny the pull between us, I always had a thing for him, but the hate always masked my true feelings, but things seem to have shifted between us. And I'm sure he felt it too.

He moved from the bed, walking towards his ensuite.

"Just going to get changed," he said quietly, throwing his phone on the bed. "Won't be a sec." He smiled as he disappeared.

Once the door was shut, I let out my held breath then fell down onto his bed consuming his scent. I laid with my eyes pinned to the ceiling.

What the hell was I doing here?

What was I expecting to happen, really?

He was the most popular guy in school, the fucking king. Would he really want to be spending his evening with me? The loner, the nerd, the grunge.

My subconscious was making me doubt myself, making me feel small and unsure if this was the right idea. I decided to get up and go back to my room. I groaned as I pulled myself up, wrapping my blanket around my frame and standing up when I heard his ensuite door open. *Too late.*

"Where you going?" he asked, rubbing his hand through his thick, brown hair.

He looked phenomenal.

He had a large grey vest on, the neck-line crew cut and sitting just above his pecs, hanging down over his cotton black shorts. My eyes marvelled at his tattoos, I loved every single one of them. He was like a piece of art, he was beautiful.

"I... erm... I was going to head back to my room," I confessed, kicking my slippers together.

"Why?" His eyes narrowed on me, quizzing me, but also looking a little stunned.

"I just... I don't know. I just didn't think you would want to spend your evening with me..." My voice trailed off as I bored my eyes into his light, green eyes. They were intoxicating.

"And why wouldn't I want to spend the night with you, Darcey?" he asked, stalking over to me.

His eyes drew up and down my body, the heat burning through to my soul. He pulled his bottom lip between his teeth. He stood in front of me, looking down at me as I now looked at my feet.

He made me feel intimidated.

I saw his hand move to my face, his fingers softly grabbing my chin and bringing my face up to look at him, my eyes studying his face.

"Because..." I said in barely a whisper, the air being knocked out of my lungs from his stare.

"Because?" he repeated, his eyes penetrated into mine then moved down to my mouth as he nibbled on his bottom lip. "You know nothing."

I went to respond but was stopped as his lips crashed onto mine.

My heart exploded into a thousand pieces inside my chest.

His hand was still on my chin, as if he was trying to keep me in place. My hands clung to my blanket, covering me. His lips were soft but harsh on mine, and he slipped his expert tongue into my mouth, massaging tentatively.

His mouth was rough, but in a good way. It was like he couldn't help himself, like he couldn't restrain himself with me.

I felt myself relax into him as our tongues continued to stroke one another in our slow, long anticipated kiss.

He was making sure I remembered this moment.

His hand moved from my chin to cup my face as he slowed his tongue before pecking me on the lips then pulling away, his eyes closed, his breathing harsh. Panic shot through me.

Did he regret it?

I let go of the blanket, moving my fingers to trail along my lips, tracing the feel of them as I looked at his face, his eyes dark and brooding.

We stood like that for a moment, I was frozen to the spot.

I couldn't believe the first boy to put their lips on mine was Conor Royce.

His big hands moved round my waist, pulling me into him, then they skimmed up my body as he pushed my blanket off of my shoulders and let it fall to the floor.

"Don't ever put yourself down, do you understand me?" he said in a firm tone.

I couldn't speak, just nodded. I had lost my voice. The feel of his hands on me set fireworks off deep inside me, my skin alight. His arms wrapped around me as he picked me up effortlessly, one of his arms under my legs, the other round my back as he walked me over to his bed before placing me down and pushing me over to the other side. He climbed in next to me, then draped his arm across me and pulled me into him.

His face nuzzled between my neck and face, his breath warm and minty. My lips were still tingling from his.

"You need to sleep, it's been an eventful night. Rest and I'll drive you to ballet tomorrow," he muttered as my insides melted.

I had forgotten about ballet, I needed to get my head back into it. I couldn't afford to fuck it up. Not now.

I snuggled into his duvet and breathed in his scent. It was a mix of soap, mint and cologne.

It was like my drug, my fix.

"Night, baby girl," I heard him mumble as my eyes gave in.

CHAPTER 8

DARCEY

I woke the next morning a little disorientated, blinking my eyes a few times before rubbing them and rolling over to see Conor next to me, asleep on top of the covers. I laid there for a moment, just looking at how perfect he was.

I saw him in a different light last night. Don't get me wrong, I'm sure Conor will be back to his normal self this morning, but for now, I wanted to revel in last night. He was sweet and attentive. Then my eyes widen when I remember the kiss. My fingers move to my lips, burning from the inside as my skin flushed.

I slipped out of bed quickly, walking round to the other side and grabbing my blanket off the floor before walking towards the door, opening it slowly, careful not to wake him. I crossed the threshold, turning my head over my shoulder, staring for just a moment back at him before closing the door behind me.

Once on the other side, I stood with my back to his door, my head resting back.

Holy shit, I kissed Conor.

A stupid smile spreads across my face as I walk towards my bedroom to see Robyn. I rush through the door, closing it behind me then run for my bed as I jump on her.

"Robyn, wake up," I said excitedly as I pushed down on the mattress, making her move.

"Darce," she groaned. "Piss off." She pulled the covers over her head, trying to hide. I rolled my eyes.

"Fine, I guess you don't want to know about my kiss with Conor then. I'll just go get ready," I said, teasing her as I made my way to the shower, smirking to myself, knowing that would get her attention.

"I'm up, I'm up, tell me." She came scrambling towards the ensuite. I laughed at her.

"Don't tell me you said it just to get me out of bed." Her voice was harsh as she scowled at me.

"Maybe..." I pushed my tongue into my cheek.

"I swear to God, Darcey Monroe Sawyer, if you have just bullshitted me to get me out of bed for no goddamn reason, I am going to lose my shit." Her hands were on her hip, her foot tapping.

I tried to hold in my laugh, but I couldn't. "I'm sorry. No, honestly," I blurted out through my giggle. "Oh God,"

I moaned, holding my belly where it was hurting from my laughter.

"Right, okay, I'm okay," I convinced myself, taking a deep breath. "Phew, okay, cool." I nodded as I turned the shower on.

"What do you mean *cool*? Did you or did you not kiss him?" she asked with a slight attitude. Oh man, she was not a morning person.

"Fine." I rolled my eyes with exaggeration. "If you really must know..." I trailed off, placing my hand under the shower to check the temperature.

"I haven't got all bloody morning, Darce. Stop being a tease," she huffed out, throwing her hands in the air.

"Okay..." I took a deep breath, I couldn't help rattling her cage. "Yes. We did kiss," I screeched as I ran on the spot excitedly. Robyn's mouth dropped open as she started jumping up and down on the spot before lunging herself towards me, hugging me as we continued jumping up and down. I let her go, her taking a seat on the toilet.

"Oh my God, you kissed Conor 'king' Royce, motherfucking Royce!" she screamed. "Was it hot? Oh, tell me, tell me."

"It was yeah, but he was soft, gentle..." My mind wandered away, back to that moment.

"And?" she jibed.

"And the most perfect first kiss." I sighed, holding my hand to my chest

"Swoon," she said in a slow, emphasized manner, stringing it out. "Did you talk about what happened?" she asked cautiously.

I shook my head. "There was no need to, and to be honest, I didn't want to speak about it. I just want to push it to the back of my mind. I want to just forget about it for the moment," I said quietly.

"How was it this morning?" she said, moving from the subject.

"He was asleep, I snuck out," I admitted, blushing.

"Why did you sneak out?" she asked confused, her leg crossing the other as her brows furrowed at me.

"Because, I remembered the kiss and panicked." I sighed. "Anyway, he said he is going to take me to ballet this morning. I'm not going to hold my breath, I'm sure the normal Conor will be back, I don't think he is actually *that* kind." I shrugged.

"Mmm, true, but you never know, he may have turned a new leaf?" she said, hopeful.

"Well, we can only hope and wait and see, aye babe," I said quietly. "Now, I need to shower, are you sitting in here or you going back to bed?"

"Back to bed, boo," she said, standing up and stretching her arms above her head. "Ciao," she shouted as she walked out the room.

I peeled my pyjamas off as I stepped under the, now steaming, shower. I didn't need to wash my hair, it was only going to get messy and sweaty after ballet.

I stepped out, wrapping myself in my towel and walking into my closet, grabbing my black leotard and pink tights. I slipped them on, pulling a pair of black leggings off my shelf before shimmying into them over the top of my opaque tights. I grabbed my ballet pumps and my pointe shoes, hanging them round my neck then bent down and grabbed my black holdall, checking that my towel and water bottle were in there.

I looked over at Robyn who had gone back to sleep, giving her a small smile before making my way downstairs. I dumped my bag on the kitchen side as I filled my water bottle up then put it back in my bag, along with my pumps. I wrapped my pointe shoes round themselves, covering them in the silk satin ties before placing them delicately in my bag.

It had just gone nine and I had to be at my class in half an hour. I flicked the kettle on and made myself a cup of tea, smiling at my mum as she waltzed into the kitchen and straight over to me.

"Darcey," she said, exasperated as she cuddled me. "We sorted it all last night, but the police want a statement," she said as she grabbed a cup for herself. "I wanted to leave you to rest last night darling."

"Mum, I don't want to press charges. Nothing happened. Conor showed up at the right time."

"Darcey Monroe, you will be pressing charges. What

if Conor hadn't shown up?" She shakes her head at me.

"Then I would be pressing charges, wouldn't I? But he did. Mum, I just want to forget about it. Please. I am fine, I promise. I was a bit shaken but I'm okay now." I smiled weakly at her as I finished making our teas. She shook her head, letting out a small sigh.

"We will be leaving in ten, okay?" she said, taking the cup from me and taking a mouthful.

"Actually," I said, dragging my converse along the floor. "Conor said he would take me."

"Oh, did he? In what car?" She raised an eyebrow, a small smile gracing her face as she took another sip of her tea.

"I'm assuming yours?" I muttered, taking a sip of my own tea.

"Oh right." She nodded her head up then dropped it slightly.

"Well, he may not want to take me anymore. He said it last night when he came to check I was okay." I needed to be careful of what I said around her.

"Okay, well, either way we need to leave in five, so if he isn't here in––"

"I'm here." He beamed, walking across to the junk drawer in the kitchen and grabbing Mum's keys. "Okay for me to take Darcey to her lesson, Zara?"

"Mmhmm." She nodded as she walked down the hallway. "Drive safely, Conor," she shouted as she walked away and into the lounge.

I looked over at him, a handsome smile creeping on his face.

"Ready, baby girl?" he crooned.

I nodded shyly, walking towards my bag that I dumped on the side and picked it up. I grabbed a banana on my way out, putting it in my bag as I started walking down the hallway. I looked over my shoulder to make sure he was following me; his eyes were on my butt before he dragged them up to meet mine.

I blushed a crimson red, flipping my head back around and opening the door.

I skipped down the steps and waited at the driver's side of my mum's range rover, watching him walking towards me. He was wearing a long white tee that was tightly cuffed at his muscly biceps, black skinny, ripped jeans and black trainers. He looked fucking amazing as per usual. I rubbed my lips together, trying to distract myself from him.

He unlocked the car, I opened the door and slipped in, dumping my bag at my feet.

"You okay?" he asked as he strapped himself in.

"Yeah, I'm not bad." I smiled at him, turning to face him. "You?"

"I'm perfect, thank you."

Wasn't that the truth.

I turned the radio on, James Bay "Us" was playing. I

reached across and turned it up slightly, the silence in the car was deafening. I couldn't work out if there was tension between us or not? Maybe it was me and my mind? Did he feel awkward after our kiss?

I had all this swimming round in my mind. This was not what I needed before my two hour lesson with my ballet mistress. I had to clear my head, but how could I clear it of Conor Royce? I was annoyed with myself for letting myself get distracted by him.

I turned to face the window, looking out at the trees along the road, sighing. I felt his eyes on me, but I refused to turn around to face him. I couldn't look at him.

When we pulled up at the ballet studio, I ran out the car before he had put the handbrake on. Pulling my bag over my shoulder, I push through the black, heavy, double doors.

"Darcey," Madame Camilla called out, a welcoming smile on her face.

"Morning, Madame," I greeted her, dumping my bag on the chair before sitting on the floor and undoing my converse, pulling my leggings down then slipping my pumps on for warm up.

My eyes drifted to the door when I saw Conor walk through them. My ballet mistress' eyes shot to him. I gave him a small nod in the direction of the chair seated at the side, instantly feeling nervous. I didn't realise he was going to be watching me, I thought he would have gone home.

Fuck.

Okay, Darce, it's fine. You have this.

Madame Camilla walked towards me. "Is he going to be a distraction, Darcey?" she asked, side-eyeing Conor.

I shook my head. "No, ma'am."

"Good, onto the barre," she ordered as she walked gracefully over, standing at the top, waiting for me. I stood next to it, the wall of mirrors sitting behind Conor.

"Okay, let's start with a demi," she called out. I gripped the barre with my left hand, keeping my back straight and my eyes on her the whole time as I bent my knees down, smoothly coming back up into second position.

"Good, give me another," she said, her eyes watching my every move.

I closed my eyes for a moment, I could feel the intensity of his stare as I moved.

"Grand plié," she bellowed as I carried out her command gracefully. I then moved into the barre before moving away.

"Straight to fifth," she said as I moved my left leg in front of my right, turning my left foot out as I rested my right foot on a point, then moved back into demi again, swooping my arm as I smoothly moved into the grande plié, moving front to back.

"Soutane to the other side, Darcey, and straight to

fifth please, then take the warm up from the top."

I did as she said before balancing in sous sous, turning, opening my arms and finishing, my feet turned and flat on the floor, my arm up in the air, my wrist curved slightly over my head. I stepped away from the barre and moved to the middle of the studio, ignoring the pull I was feeling to look at him. I kept my eyes on the floor and on Madame Camilla.

"Darcey, pointes please." She shook her head at me. I sighed before walking over and kicking off my pumps before sitting and slipping my pointes on and lacing them up round my ankle. I had a drink of water before walking back in front of Madame Camilla.

"You still think black swan is a good idea?" I asked, a little apprehensive.

"Black swan is always a good idea, it is a classic." She smiled at me. "Position, please," she commanded as the music started.

I stretched my arms up before going up on pointe. I flicked my eyes to Conor, his eyes hazy, his lips parted as he watched me. I pirouetted as I started my routine, doing everything in my power not to look at him.

"Stop," Madame Camilla bellowed.

"Darcey, you're stiff. Start again," she snapped.

I walked back to my start position, taking a deep breath as she re-started the music, going back into pointe, and this time I kept focussing on him. I needed to be able to get through this with him here.

I glided gracefully across the floor before going into an arabesque then gracefully striding into my leap, landing balletic and gliding into a pirouette, turning three times as I fluently moved into my leap, my head held high. I felt good, I felt this was the best I had performed this dance when all of a sudden, I felt a snap in my lower leg.

A blood curdling scream came from me as I collapsed to the floor in a heap, the tears falling. The pain was excruciating.

My surroundings blurred out around me, a small ringing in my ears as I heard Madame Camilla and Conor calling out to me, but their voices were muffled and far away. I turned my face to look round, my eyes brimming with tears when I saw Conor's face close to mine. He kissed my forehead as he demanded for Camilla to call an ambulance.

"Baby, you're going to be okay," he mumbled, wrapping himself round my body as I lay on the studio floor before blacking out.

CHAPTER 9

CONOR

I stayed lying behind her, my arms wrapped tightly around her. Her tears stained her beautiful face.

"It's okay, baby girl, I'm here," I mumbled in her ear. I wasn't sure if she could hear me, but I wanted her to know she wasn't alone. Her eyelids flickered before she slowly started blinking.

"Darce," I breathed out. "Baby, can you hear me?"

She nodded as the silent tears began to fall again.

Her ballet teacher was now on the phone to Zara after phoning the ambulance. Camilla, I think her name was, crouched down next to me, checking Darcey's legs. My eyes snapped over to her, I didn't like the fact that she was touching her but knew it was necessary.

"What do you think it is?" I asked her, my voice small as I kept my grip on Darcey.

"Well, I can't see a visible break, which is good, in a

way." Her eyebrows knitted together. "But it's got to be bad for her to have screamed like that and then black out for a moment." She crawled up to Darcey's head.

"Darling, the ambulance is on the way, okay? Can you tell me where it hurts," she cooed, running her hand through Darcey's honey-blonde hair. I watched as Darcey's hand moved to her calf as she wailed out in pain again.

"Okay, sweetie." She smiled down at her before her eyes flicked up at me. She didn't need to say anything for me to know that it was bad.

Her head turned towards the door as the ambulance crew arrived and she scarpered to her feet. I pulled her closer into me as Camilla filled them in before they were knelt down next to her.

"Sir, I'm going to need you to move," the fresh faced paramedic said, her face breaking into a small smile.

"No chance," I growled back. "I'm staying with her."

"You can stay with her, but I need to check her over, so I need you to move back, just slightly." Her hand was on mine, reassuring me in that moment to move. And I did, ever so slightly. My eyes narrowed on her as she rolled Darcey over on her back, talking to her calmly. Darcey's eyes were darting from the paramedic to me, so I reached over and took her hand, squeezing it, giving her the reassurance I wasn't going anywhere.

My eyes flicked up to see Zara, Chase, and her father,

Tanner, running towards us. Chase's eyes were on me as he saw her hand in mine. My eyes bored into him. He can think what he wants. I don't give two fucks at this moment in time.

"Darcey!" Zara screamed out through scared tears. My eyes moved from Chase to hers, she looked petrified. Darcey's eyes shot to her mum's as her tears began again. My heart was breaking.

Camilla stood from the ground, wrapping her arm around Zara's petite frame and taking her to the corner, Tanner behind them as Camilla explained what happened.

Chase just stood, looming over me.

A male paramedic crouched down next to me, placing a mask over her nose and mouth carefully then lying her head back down. He ran his fingers down her arm, pressing two fingers onto the underneath of her wrist, checking her pulse then noting it down. He stood slowly and grabbed the stretcher from the doors of the studio. The male paramedic knelt next to his colleague, pushing the stretcher next to Darcey's body before walking back round next to me.

"Ready?" the female paramedic asked.

"Ready," he said as he rolled her onto the stretcher that his colleague pushed towards us.

I still had her hand.

I wasn't letting go.

They lifted her carefully and started walking her towards the ambulance, Zara, Tanner and Chase running out behind us.

They laid her on the bed in the back of the ambulance, pulling two straps over her. I climbed into the back and sat on the chair next to her as the male driver climbed into the front of the ambulance, the female paramedic going over her vitals.

I watched as Zara, Chase and Camilla scrambled into the Range Rover, Tanner getting into his Jaguar. Chase's eyes burned into mine intensely from his seat as the female paramedic slammed the doors shut on them, breaking the contact. I let out a relieved sigh.

I was a dead man walking.

"Conor," her little voice said under the mask.

"Baby." My hand darted to hers, grabbing it and squeezing it. "I'm here."

"I'm scared," she admitted, a tear running down the side of her face before melting into her hair.

"Don't be scared, it'll be okay. I promise." My voice was trying to calm her and reassure. I had no idea how bad it was, but from the look on Camilla's face, it wasn't good.

"Darcey," the lady said softly, standing over her. "How's the pain?" she asked as she put a canular into her hand and connected a drip.

"Bad." She sobbed.

"It's okay, I'm going to give you some pain relief." She clicked the drip into place,

Darcey's head nodding slightly as the drip started flowing into her veins.

"It'll be okay," I soothed her, stroking my other hand across the top of her head, pushing her hair away from her face. Her gorgeous blue eyes didn't leave mine.

CHAPTER 10

DARCEY

As I was wheeled through to accident & emergency, my eyes sought out Conor. My heart swelled when I saw him with my holdall over his chest and shoulders, walking behind the paramedics. I couldn't believe he stayed with me the whole time.

The pain had eased after the drugs they had administered in the back of the ambulance. I had no clue where my parents and Chase were, I didn't know if they were in front of the ambulance or behind us.

As I was pushed through double doors, the female paramedic stopped, turning to Conor.

"You need to stay here. Follow the signs for the waiting room." I heard a small growl leave his throat.

I held my hand out, reaching for him, panic rising in my chest. He just stood there, his arms by his sides, his eyes on me as I was wheeled away, the double doors closing.

I was X-rayed, then scanned and wheeled into a ward whilst waiting for my results. I looked around the bare, empty walls feeling alone. I didn't even have my phone. I looked at the cannular in my hand and broke down. I didn't even know what I had done, all I knew was that, from my ankle up to my knee, there was a throbbing pain. I couldn't move it all that well, and currently had it elevated.

My eyes focused on the door when I saw the handle going. I wiped my tears off my face as I saw my family walk through the door, along with Conor and Camilla. My mum raced over to me, kissing my face and head before hugging me, the whole time my eyes were on him, his on mine. The chemistry crackled between us.

The doctor walked through, he was a young man. He had jet black hair pushed off of his face, and deep brown eyes.

"Darcey," he said softly, walking over and sitting on the edge of my bed. "Full house, aye?" He made a small joke, resulting in a little giggle from myself. My mum swooped my hand into hers, squeezing it tightly.

"Okay, so I have your X-rays and scans back." His smile disappeared from his face, and my heart sank to the bottom of my stomach.

"The good news is, there isn't a break. But from the scan results we can see you have torn your left Achilles tendon as well as having quite a big tear in your calf muscle. We are going to have to do surgery, just letting it heal on its own won't work, I'm afraid. We will be getting you prepped shortly, okay?" he said, patting the bed before standing.

"Mr and Mrs Sawyer, may I have a word?" he said before taking my mum and dad into the waiting room.

Once the door was closed, I couldn't hold back, the sobs left me. They were loud and pained.

I knew what this meant.

My dancing career was over.

I was never going to be going to college, I wouldn't be able to live my dream that I have had since I was five.

I put my head in my hands, hiding my face from the rest of the room, my heart shattering. I felt the weight shift on the bed. I wiped my eyes, dropping my hands and looking up. Camilla sat there, tears evident in her own green eyes.

"Darling, it'll be okay," she said, taking my hand and placing her other one over the top of it and patting.

"It won't. Come on, Camilla, you know injuries like this break ballet dancers, I'm not silly." I sighed, sniffing then pulling my hand from hers.

"But there is a small percentage that do come back to dancing. You've got to have faith, sweetie," she cooed.

I didn't answer. I just threw my head back into my pillow, focusing on the bright hospital lights in the ceiling.

I couldn't believe this was happening.

Why was this happening?

I didn't have the energy to fight with my thoughts.

"Baby girl," I heard his voice, crashing through me. I tilted my head up, his intense green eyes on mine. "You're a fighter, you will come back from this." He crept onto the bed and pulled me into him, kissing the top of my head.

In that moment, I felt calm, he pulled me from this nightmare, even if only for a minute.

My eyes flicked up when I saw my mum and dad walking back into the room, my mum had clearly been crying again. Conor hopped off the bed and stood next to Chase. Chase's eyes narrowed on Conor, and Conor threw an icy stare back at him.

My mum distracted me by placing a gown on the end of the bed. "The doctor is coming round to take you down in five, okay?"

I just nodded, I had no words.

She pulled the curtain round my bed as she started undressing me. I winced as she pulled my tights down my legs. I looked down at them, my left leg bruising by the minute. I pulled my bottom lip between my teeth to stop the tears coming out again.

"It'll be okay, sweetie, the doctor is going to fix you," my mum re-assured me, kissing me on the top of the head. "I promise."

-

My eyes fluttered open, looking round the clinical room. A nurse walked over, a warm smile on her face as she checked my observations.

"Hey, Darcey, how are you feeling?" she asked me.

"Okay," I muttered.

"I'll go get your parents," she said, placing the clipboard back at the end of my bed and walking out the room.

I reached over for the water on the side, taking a small sip and placing it back. My parents burst through the door.

"Oh, Darcey." My mum sobbed as she walked over to me, my dad with his arms wrapped round her. "Are you okay?"

"I'm fine, Mum." A small smile graced my face.

"I'm glad," she said, bending down and kissing me on my forehead. "We have spoken to the doctor, he has decided against casting it. He thinks you'll have a better chance of healing like this." She rubbed the back of my hand with her thumb.

"Princess, you look so much better. Your colour is back," my dad muttered. His mousy brown hair was thinning on top, his deep-set blue eyes still had a glisten to them.

"I think it's the drugs they've given me." I giggled. "I am so hungry, I haven't eaten this morning. Still got my banana in my bag." I groaned.

"Let me see if you're allowed to eat," my dad said, walking to find a nurse.

"So, Darcey Monroe, is there something you need to tell me." Her eyebrows raised, her eyes on mine. I darted my eyes from hers, fiddling with the light blanket that was over my legs.

"Like what?" I questioned her, knowing exactly what she was going on about.

"Conor," she said quietly.

"Nothing. I just think after what happened, and because he was the one that found me, I think he is just doing his duty to make sure I'm okay and distracted," I stammered the words then nibbled the inside of my lip.

"Hmm, okay," she said patting my leg, dropping the conversation just before my dad came back in.

"The doctor will be round in a moment, then the nurse will get you some food." He smiled fondly at me. Right on cue, the doctor walked in. I looked at his name tag as for the life of me I couldn't remember his name. Dr Cal Jones. I smiled sweetly at him as he made his way over to the bed.

"How you doing Darcey?" he asked softly, his dark brown eyes on mine. "Not bad" I mumbled.

"Okay, so the surgery went well, I decided not to put you in a cast as I personally think the healing time will be better in just a gator for the moment, then you can start doing some easy exercises and physio therapy which will help strengthen your calf muscle and Achilles tendon. At the moment I can't say whether you will be back dancing or not. Sometimes injuries like this heal absolutely perfectly, other times they don't. It comes down to the individual. But, I feel positive and I am hoping you make a speedy recovery, Darcey, I really do. Now, I will hand you over to nurse Cora who will be keeping an eye on you for the next couple of days while you are in here. Please, rest up," he said as he stood from the bed then turned to face my parents. "Mum, Dad, if you have any questions or concerns, please let nurse Cora know and she will come and find me."

He walked towards the door, facing me once more. "Take care, Darcey." He smiled at me before walking out and closing the door behind him.

I let out a deep sigh. Of course I was happy that the surgery went well, but I couldn't help feeling a little pessimistic that it would be my fate that I wouldn't be able to dance again.

"You'll be dancing again in no time," my mum said quietly as she came next to my bed.

"Zara, let's leave her be for a while, honey, Robyn is here," my dad muttered, wrapping his arms around my mum's waist and dragging her away, towards the door. My face lit up when he said Robyn's name.

"We will just be in the café," he said as his blue eyes twinkled at me, my mum's face crumpling by the minute as she was trying to hold off the tears in front of me. He managed to get her out of the room, giving me a wink as he pulled the door to.

I took this moment to just sit and reflect over the last couple of hours.

What an absolute rollercoaster.

I have gone from being excited about Conor and what could possibly happen and being psyched for my ballet exam, to now being laid up in bed after tearing my calf muscle and ruining my Achilles tendon, to potentially not having a dancing career anymore.

I sighed as I stared out ahead of me at the blank wall, the tears threatening to fall from my weepy eyes. I wanted to cry, a full on choked sob, I wanted to relieve the burning in my throat, but I just couldn't.

I rubbed my palms into my eyes, pushing a couple of stray tears away when the door handle moved. I pulled my covers up a little higher, I was still sitting in my hospital gown. My eyes eagerly locked on the door as I saw my beautiful, red-headed best friend walk through as she threw herself at me, her arms round my neck.

"God, I have been worried sick." She sighed. "Honestly, what the hell happened?" She let me go before pulling the chair next to the bed closer to me, resting her feet on my lap as she slouched down on the chair.

"Comfortable, are we?" I teased.

"I am actually, I'm not hurting you though, am I?"

Panic laced her voice as she went to move.

"You're fine." I smiled and blew her a kiss.

"How drugged up are you?" Her eyebrow arched, her hands resting on her stomach.

"Oh, pretty fucking drugged. God, I am starving, I am waiting for the nurse to come round. I haven't eaten since yesterday," I said loudly, my stomach grumbling.

"Want me to go and see where the bitch is?" she said, laughing.

"I'll give it another ten, if she ain't here, I'll push the button."

"So, Conor is sitting in the waiting room, looking pretty fucking hot, if I do say so myself. He looks sad though, like really sad. Not sure if something has happened between him and Chase. They aren't even looking at each other." She rolled her eyes.

"Oh shit, really? Wonder if Chase sensed how Conor was being with me?" I shrugged before taking a sip of water.

"What do you mean? Did something else happen?" A confused look spread across her face as her eyes fixed on mine.

"No. Just that he rode in the ambulance with me and wouldn't leave my side until he practically didn't have a choice. He held my hand for as long as he possibly could as well." My lips turned up at the corners, forming a small smile.

"What? So he was there, when it happened?" she asked, reaching back and pouring herself a glass of water out of the jug on the side.

"Yup, he took me to ballet, didn't he." I mumbled as I nibbled my nail. "Then I thought he was going to drop me off and go home, but he didn't. He sat and watched me, Robyn, like, eyes on me the whole time. Then I went to practice my routine and fucked it up the first time as I couldn't focus, cos he was there, but I needed to, I needed to be able to overcome it. Which is what I did. I literally kept my eyes on him the whole time, then I went into my final leap of the routine when I felt the snap. I don't even know how I did it, it wasn't like I hadn't warmed up. I warmed up, I have practiced this routine so much, so I just don't know what happened, I just..." My voice stopped when I realised I was crying.

"Oh, Darce, darling, please don't cry," she soothed as she took her feet off of me, then stood from the chair, sitting next to me on the bed, wrapping her arms around me and squeezing.

"Maybe I deserved this?" I mumbled through the tears.

"Darcey! Don't you dare say that. You did not deserve this. These things happen. It's sad and horrible and unfortunate, yes, but it wasn't deserving," she said abruptly, shaking her head before resting her chin on the top of my head.

We sat like that for a while, I didn't want her to let me go.

"Hello, only the nurse, dear," an older lady called out as she let herself into my room. "You hungry?"

"I'm famished." I sniffed.

Robyn slid off the bed and sat on the chair again, her eyes on the nurse.

Nurse Cora walked over to me, smiling at me as she topped my water up from the jug.

"Sit forward, darling," she urged me. I sat up slowly, shuffling forward, pain shooting through my leg, making me cry out.

"You okay?" she asked as she fluffed my pillows.

"Mmhmm, just moved a bit too quickly," I said as she took my shoulders and pulled me back onto my pillows.

"What can I get you to eat?" she asked.

"Can I just have some honey on toast, please?"

"Of course. Tea?"

"Please, milk and two sugars," I said sweetly.

"Can I have one as well, please?" Robyn asked.

"No. It's for patients only, there is a hot drinks machine just down the hallway." She smiled at Robyn before walking out the room. I started giggling.

"What a bitch," Robyn cursed. "Right, well, I suppose I'll be back in a little while. Going to hunt the drinks machine down." She rolled her eyes as she stood from the chair. "Do you need anything?" she asked as she got to the door.

"No thank you."

"Okay, hun, see you soon." She waved, closing the door.

I slowly slid myself down the bed slightly, pulling the covers up to my chest when I heard the door go. I let out a low groan, throwing daggers at the door when I saw Conor standing there, his hand still gripped on the handle.

"Sorry, should I go?" he asked, hurt apparent in his voice.

"No," I whispered, shaking my head. He turned slightly as he walked in and closed the door behind him quietly.

"How you feeling?" he asked as he sat in the chair Robyn had just been in. He sat with his legs opened, his elbows resting on them and his index fingers pressed into his chin. His intense green eyes boring into mine.

"Not bad," I admitted, shrugging my shoulders up a bit. I ran my fingers through the ends of my hair before twirling it round my finger.

"I'm glad." He let out a sigh of relief. He took a moment, rubbing his lips together. "You've not left my mind," he said quietly, making my heart skip a beat. He sat up in the chair then scooted his hips forward, so he was sitting closer to the edge of the bed as he reached for my hand, running his thumb over the back of my knuckles.

"What did the doctor say?" he asked changing the

subject. He genuinely wanted to know. His eyebrows were pulled together, his stare intense.

I inhaled deeply, my chest felt like it was crushing having to think about it all again. "Erm..." I muttered, my eyes batting down to my hand in his. "Well..." I started, taking another deep breath. I didn't want to cry.

"The surgery went well, yay," I said a little too sarcastically, a smile forming before disappearing as quickly as it came. "But he can't say how I'm going to heal..." I trailed off, pulling my eyes from our hands and meeting his stare.

"He can't say if this means my dancing career is over..." As soon as the words were off my tongue, my bottom lip dropped, trembling. My eyes brimmed instantly as the burn crawled up my throat. He tightened his grip on my hand.

"I'm fine, I'm fine." I let out a little laugh, smiling. "It's just been a tough, long day," I admitted, my smile fading, my eyes moving down to our hands again.

He stood from the chair, leaning over me, his thumbs wiping my tears away, then placing his hands either side of my face. His lips were close to mine, his eyes burning into me intensely as he pressed his lips onto my lips, covering mine as he kissed me delicately, teasing his tongue which I accepted, my tongue stroking his.

Our kiss was slow, intimate and intense. My belly flipped and fluttered because of him, my heart swelling and exploding deep in my chest.

He pulled away, planting soft, light kisses on both of my cheeks, kissing where the tears were. He fluttered his eyes open as he looked down at me.

"Baby girl." His nickname fell from his mouth, his voice low and husky.

"Am I interrupting something here?" I heard Robyn's voice boom through the room.

"No." His voice was clipped and harsh. Conor dropped his hands from my face, snaking back as he walked towards Robyn and pushed past her.

"Okay then," she said before shrugging her shoulders. "I guess moody Conor is back."

"Guess so." My voice was a little higher than a whisper.

My heart was thumping so fast in my chest, my skin on fire, my lips tingling from his touch. I craved it, I craved him so badly.

He was my addiction, my drug and my release all in one.

He was my high. A high I wanted again and again. I could never get enough of him. I never wanted to have enough of him.

Shit.

It hadn't even been twenty-four hours since mine and Conor's first kiss, and I had fallen so hard for him. I didn't even care. I wanted to scream from the rooftops that I had a crush on Conor fucking Royce, a crush so intense that it scared me.

He made me feel things I didn't even know were possible.

He had imprinted on me, stealing my soul and capturing my heart.

I wanted the whole world to know just how deeply I felt for him.

He was my everything.

And going by what just happened, he had fallen for me too.

I hoped.

CHAPTER 11

CONOR

I bolted out of her hospital room, crashing past Chase and his family as I ran for the exit.

"Conor," I heard Chase call after me.

I couldn't stop.

My heart was thumping so hard and fast in my chest, I thought I was going to have a heart attack.

I needed air, I couldn't breathe.

She clouded me, made me hazy.

But fuck, did I love it.

I knew she was sweet, I knew I would be addicted to her from just one taste and now I want more.

So much fucking more.

I looked up at the exit signs as I carried on running towards them. I was scared, I had never felt this deeply for someone. Last night was the first time that I had ever managed to get close to her, to just have that moment that

I craved. The moment I had craved ever since I laid eyes on her in her kitchen.

The warm spring air hit me, I dropped my hands to my knees and bent down, taking a few deep breaths, letting the clean air penetrate my lungs.

I felt like I was suffocating in there.

I have put on this front, acting like I don't care, pretending and hiding from my feelings, but I can't anymore.

I am so fucking scared.

Scared of how much I love her.

I knew she was too good for me, so pure, but I didn't care.

I wasn't going on without her.

I needed her, in every single way possible.

She was mine.

"Conor," I heard his voice booming behind me. I stood up and turned slowly to face him.

"Chase," I said quietly as I stared down at him.

"Why were you running?" He crossed his arms in front of his chest, glaring at me.

"Needed some air." I shrugged, my walls coming back up. Being defensive and arrogant was my best trait.

"Really? Or did something happen with Darce? I told you to stay away from her, you fucking promised me," he shouted as he stepped towards me, pushing me on my chest.

"Don't do that, mate," I warned.

"Why not?" he snapped, aggravating me as he pushed me again.

"Because you'll regret it."

"Oh, will I, big man? Regret fronting out Conor fucking 'king' Royce, will I? You may have been king in high school, but that's about it. Don't fucking forget what my family have given you." He stepped towards me once more, this time I stepped with him, our foreheads together, our teeth gritted and our eyes trained on each other, I felt like they were going to pop from my sockets.

"I am fully fucking aware of what your family have done for me, so don't throw that in my fucking face." I was now shouting at him, my blood boiling, my temper rising but I wouldn't hit him. That's one promise I could keep. I would never lay a fucking hand on him.

But his sister on the other hand, I couldn't help the smirk that came on my face.

"What you smirking at, prick?" He grabbed my T-shirt, bunching it at my chest and pulling me even closer to him, my head dropped back slightly, the smirk still apparent.

"Can't tell ya, buddy," I teased him, antagonising him, goading him.

"I'm warning you, Royce."

"Warning me on what exactly? I haven't done anything wrong," I said coolly as he let go of my T-shirt.

"I don't believe you. What has happened between you and Darcey? You didn't have a good word to say about each other, then after her party, you are best mates?" he said agitated, his face going red where he was getting angrier.

"We turned a corner." I shrugged.

"Stop being a prick, just talk to me, man, for fuck's sake," he begged.

"Okay," I said quietly, dropping my head so my eyes were on my trainers. "I love her, man." The words slipped off my tongue. I lifted my head slightly, my eyes meeting his. "I'm in fucking love with Darcey."

Chase stepped back, his mouth dropping open. "Love?" he stammered. "How can you love her? You fucking hate her. I heard about all the shit you did to her in school, I didn't get involved because I knew you didn't mean it, and she would've given it back to you when she was ready. I was never worried. But love? Fuck," he said, sitting on a planter that was by the hospital entrance.

"Shit," he muttered as he turned his face up to me. "Have you told her?"

I scoffed before laughing. "Have I fuck. She hates me. I'm not stupid. Yeah, we kissed but I think that was more just a 'caught in the moment' type of kiss."

My eyes going wide instantly when I realise that I told him that I had kissed his baby sister.

"You've kissed her?" he shouted, standing up from

the planter and bowling himself over to me again.

Shit, here we go.

I didn't have time to react as he swung his fist, punching me in the side of the face, my jaw clicking as he did. My head felt like it was spinning on my shoulders.

"Fuck," he shouted, waving his hand around.

It took me a moment to register what the hell had just gone on. I bent down, spitting blood out of my mouth and running my tongue round all my teeth to make sure they were all still there. That was a blow and a half.

"Shit, sorry, Conor. I saw red, it was just a reaction. Shit. Hit me back, come on. I'll let ya, just hit me the fuck back," he kept on at me, in my ear, like an annoyance. I stood up, fronting up to him. He was tall, but I towered over him.

"You're going to let me, are ya?" I jibed at him.

"Yeah, come on, just do it," he responded, rolling his shoulders back and cracking his neck from side to side. I moved my face close to him, so our noses were nearly touching.

"Nope." I shook my head. "Even though you were going to let me, thanks and all, but I'm alright. I think we're even. I kissed your sister, you punched me." I laughed. "That was a good punch though, I deserved it." I winked at him then slapped him round the face playfully.

"Come on, let's get inside. We can discuss this later," he said, wrapping his arm around my shoulders as we walked towards Darcey's room.

"I never thought I would see the day that Conor Royce was in love, thought there was more chance of hell freezing over." He laughed, and I laughed with him.

"But, Conor, mate," he said as he stopped before we got to the waiting room, his face serious, his stare intense. "You break her heart, I'll break you. Do you understand me?" he said. "Promise me."

"I promise you, mate." I nodded.

And I did.

This was one promise I wasn't going to break.

I was going to love his sister for eternity.

CHAPTER 12

DARCEY

Two days later and I was home. God, it felt good to be home and in my own bed. You don't realise how much you miss it.

I was on crutches, my leg being kept straight constantly by the tight, restricting gator that I had on. I was grateful I wasn't in a cast.

My dad came up behind me as I got to the bottom of the six steps that took us to our front door. He hooked his arms under mine with the help of Chase and Conor as they lifted me to the entrance hall of our home.

Robyn ran up behind me with my crutches in hand. They placed me down gently as Robyn came beside me with my crutches and handed them to me.

"Thank you," I muttered to all of them and hobbled my way through to the kitchen.

My mum had flicked the kettle on, the whistling

indicating it was boiled echoed through the airy space. I stood in front of the sofa that was in the snug area of the kitchen, the sofa pushing into the back of my knees as I let myself drop.

"Darcey," my mum exclaimed, running over to me and tutting. "You should have asked me for help."

"I'm fine." I rolled my eyes, already feeling agitated. I had to be in this for eight weeks.

"Tanner," my mum shouted down the hallway. "Can you grab the sofa foot stool and bring it in here, please? Darcey needs to put her leg up."

I watched as she walked back over to the kettle, pouring all of us a cup of tea.

I threw my head back when I saw my dad and Conor lifting the poxy footstool.

"I'm fine, seriously," I mumbled.

"Just do as you're told, Darcey. You know what your mother is like. Go along with it for an easy life." My dad winked at me, a smile forming on his face. He was right, it was easier to please her than fight against her.

Conor wrapped his fingers delicately round my ankle and lifted my leg slightly, placing it gently on the foot stool.

Robyn slumped down next to me. "How you feeling?" she asked, patting my bare thigh that was sticking out my shorts.

"I'm fine." I huffed. "You?"

PROMISE ME

"I'm grand, thank you."

My mum interrupted us by handing us our teas and laying out a plate of biscuits. I wrapped my fingers round the hot cup, blowing it before taking a sip.

I started to relax, the rest of my family all quietly talking amongst themselves, apart from Conor. He was just listening, his eyes on me. He made my heart beat so fast, I felt like I had a drummer in my chest. His stare was so intense, it scared me. But scared me in a good way.

I can't read him and that annoys me. I normally can gauge what people are thinking, but not him. He's closed off. He isn't letting anyone in.

I cleared my throat. "I'm sorry for being a bit off with you all." My voice came out small and timid. "It's just been a lot to take in."

"Darcey," my dad said, his voice smooth. "You don't have to apologise. You're allowed to be angry, sad, hurt. It's normal under the circumstances." His eyes flicked to me.

"I know, I just feel bad," I mumbled, tapping my fingers on the side of my cup. I felt like shit and I was tired. I just wanted to get into my bed.

"Would anyone mind helping me up to bed, please?" I felt like an annoyance to them. "I'm just exhausted and need to sleep. Start afresh tomorrow." My lips curled at the corners as a small smile graced my face.

"I'll take you," Conor said before anyone got a chance

as he shot up from his seat, walking over to me. He lifted my leg and placed it gently on the floor before moving the footstool back slightly. He bent down, wrapping his arms round my waist, and pulling me up to my feet. Robyn pushed the crutches into my hand as I made my way to the kitchen door that lead to the hallway.

"Thanks for everything, guys." I nodded at them, nibbling my bottom lip as I hobbled down towards the stairs.

It took me ages to walk down the marbled hallway that led to the entrance hall, Conor by my side the whole time, his hand on the base of my back, helping to guide me. I stood at the bottom of the stairs, looking up at my next hurdle and groaned.

Before I could ask for help, Conor leant down and grabbed me round the waist, putting me over his shoulder so my leg could stay straight. I couldn't help giggling, but I was terrified.

"Conor don't drop me," I begged.

"Baby girl, I would never drop you." His arm tightened round my waist as he climbed the stairs then walked down the hallway and into my bedroom, laying me down gently on my bed. My breath caught as I took in his scent before he stood back up.

"Thank you," I whispered.

"No problem. You comfortable?" he asked, his eyes looking down at me, his hands pushed into his pockets.

"Sort of," I muttered.

"What can I do to help?" His hands were now out of his pockets and pushing through that thick, brown hair of his.

"Can you pull my pillows up slightly and then take one and prop it under my knee, please?" I said softly, my eyes watching him.

I could never get enough of him.

"Of course." His voice was low and husky. He came up and stood close to the bed, reaching for my pillows and pulling them up behind me. His hands moved to my shoulders as he gently eased me back.

"Better?" he asked.

"Much." I smiled up at him, his green eyes glistening at me. My heart felt like it was dancing in my ribcage. Something had shifted between us and he felt it too, I know he did. I always had a crush on him, even when I hated him, but this was deeper than a crush.

This was so much more.

He leant across me, grabbing a big, square cushion that was beside me, his tee riding up his body slightly, showing his toned, tattooed stomach. My eyes widened at the sight, my mind wandering to what all of him would look like.

My lips parted as my heartrate quickened. He lifted my leg slowly, his fingers gripping round my ankle, his eyes penetrating mine as he placed the cushion under my foot, before he stood up and stepped back, away from me.

"Anything else, grunge?" he teased.

"Stay." My voice coming out was more of a plea then an ask.

"I suppose I could do that." His tongue darted out, running along his bottom lip before he pulled it between his teeth, his breath shallow and fast. He knelt on the bed, crawling up and sitting himself down next to me, his beautiful face turning to me.

"Thank you," I mumbled before nibbling on the inside of my lip.

"You don't have to thank me, Darcey…" he trailed off. "But I could do with another kiss, seeing as we were interrupted in the hospital." His eyebrows raise, his eyes darting back and forth from mine.

My heart skipped in my chest, the butterflies fluttering deep in my stomach.

"I suppose I could do that," I said smiling, mimicking him from earlier.

I leaned my body into his. He wrapped his arm around my shoulders, giving my shoulder a squeeze as his large hand came up to my face. His thumb brushed against my cheek. Our connection was getting stronger, I couldn't deny the pull much longer.

A desperate ache for him was apparent in my belly.

"You're so beautiful, Darcey," he whispered, bringing his lips towards mine.

I fluttered my eyelids closed, biting my lip before he pressed his plump lips against mine. His mouth covered mine as his tongue edged into my mouth, waiting for me to accept him, which I did, eagerly.

His tongue danced with mine as our kiss grew stronger, a moan leaving my mouth. He moved onto his knees, breaking our kiss for a moment. His hungry eyes drawled down my body, his breath hitching before he crashed his lips back onto mine.

One hand was firmly still on my face, his other hand was on my good leg, his fingertips trailing up slowly. My skin tingled with need and want.

He stopped when he got to the hem of my shorts, pulling away from me, his eyes looking down at where his hand was, my eyes following his. It wasn't long before his eyes were looking at my lips, then darting to my eyes. He was waiting for the go ahead to trail his fingers further. I let out a whimper as I pushed my lips to his, his fingers wrapping round the hem of my shorts tightly, his breath harsh through his nose on my face.

The ache had now moved from my belly, down between my legs. It was a surreal feeling. Everything was new; his touch, even being touched at all like this, I had never experienced anything like this before. He slid his fingers from my shorts as his curious hands delved into them, his finger brushing over my sensitive spot through my knickers.

"Conor," I whispered, breaking away from him, panic rising inside.

"Darcey, I want you. I want to touch you and own you everywhere." His voice was low and came out more as a growl.

"I've never been touched," I felt myself blush, "Before." I couldn't help but feel embarrassed at my lack of experience in this department.

Conor's hand darted out of my shorts before he placed both hands on my face.

"The thought in knowing that I will be your first in everything, turns me on, so fucking much. But this, right now, isn't the right time. I want to make your first time everything and more. The first time is always a little…" his voice trailed off, a wicked grin on his face. "Shit," he said bluntly. "But, I promise you, it gets better, and I can't wait to show you. Just not now."

He leant down and pressed his lips against mine softly, a quick kiss planted on my lips before he knelt back, sitting on his knees. I didn't know what to say. I couldn't be mad at him for wanting my first time to be special, but I was so ready for it now.

"It won't be much longer for you to wait, I promise," he responded as if he could read my mind. "I don't know how much longer I can keep my hands off of you."

"Chase is going to go mad," I muttered, bending my right knee then stretching it back out again.

"Chase knows," he said, a silly grin spreading across his face.

"Oh my God, no," I said shocked, my hands going to my mouth, my eyes wide.

"Yup." He nodded, his hair flopping on his head where he hadn't styled it.

"When?" I pulled myself up, so I wasn't sitting against the pillows anymore.

"At the hospital, after our kiss when Robyn walked in. I was outside, and well, you know, it just came out." He shrugged his shoulders before untucking his legs from underneath him and swinging them off the bed, before laying on his side and propping himself up on his elbow.

"What did Chase do?" I questioned him, my eyes burning into him.

"He wasn't happy." He laughed. "He punched me, but it's alright, you're his baby sister. I would be the same." His fingers rubbed across my silk bed sheet.

"He hit you? Oh, God, I'm sorry." I winced, I couldn't believe Chase hit him.

"It's fine, it was going to happen sooner rather than later. He needed to know." He nodded, his fingers still running and swirling over my bed.

"I can't believe he punched you." I broke into a small laugh.

"I know, I've seen him lose his shit twice since I've known him," he admitted.

"Oh yeah? When?" I asked.

"The night of your birthday, and the day I..." He stopped, stammering slightly over his words before he continued. "The day I told him about you," he said coolly.

"Well, at least I know he cares about me." I snorted.

"Of course he cares about you. We all do." His hand moved to my knee and gave it a gentle squeeze.

"That's good to know," I joked. "Can't believe I'm in this gator for eight weeks."

"I know it sucks, but at least it'll be off for your prom." He smiled. "Every cloud and all that."

"I suppose that's true. Me and Robyn weren't sure if we were going to go."

"Baby girl," his mouth spoke the nickname I had come to adore. "You're not missing your

prom night. Let me take you." He sat up, linking his fingers as he pushed them out, clicking them.

"Don't be a joker." I laughed out loud at him.

"I'm not. I want to, please, let me take you?" he asked again, his face serious, his eyes burning into mine.

I took a moment, mulling it over. Who wouldn't want to go prom with Conor? I mean, he is a God. Everyone would love to have someone who isn't at school anymore taking them to prom, but Conor Royce was a different league

"I would love that." I smiled at him, he moved closer to me, leaning my head up to meet his craned neck as I kissed him. My mouth was hungry, my tongue darting into his mouth as he groaned.

His hands moved round to the back of my neck, tilting it back as he leant over me, his tongue fast and seductive. He was an expert with his tongue which made me feel uneasy, thinking about how much he must've used it to get this good, but I didn't care. I still couldn't believe I was kissing him, I couldn't get enough of him.

After our serious make out session, Conor dismissed himself, telling me he would be back later. Not going to lie, I was disappointed, but we couldn't hide up here kissing each other.

I looked at my door to see Robyn standing there.

"Hello you." She smiled as she walked towards me, climbing onto my large, high bed.

"Hey," I muttered, muting my tele.

"How's it going? Sorry, I had to pop home and I didn't want to interrupt, you know, like I did before," she said, a deep laugh leaving her.

"Aha, no worries. You would've only seen a full-on snog. I wanted more but he won't touch me... yet," I whined. "Honestly, I am so ready for him."

"I bet, but just take it each day as it comes. Don't let lust blind your judgement."

"Oh, this is more than lust, Robyn. I'm scared this is love. And I have fallen so deeply in love with him."

"Oh shit..." her voice trailed off when she heard the

seriousness in mine. "Boo, you've got it bad." She shook her head before getting under my covers. "Enough Conor talk, put *Friends* back on," she demanded.

She was a bossy little thing.

CHAPTER 13

DARCEY

I couldn't believe it was prom night already. These last eight weeks had been hard, but I was determined to be up and about and less dependent on people. Everyone was amazing though and patient when I had days where I didn't think I could go on. Some days were so much harder than others, it was more the thoughts of what was going to happen in my future. I didn't focus on the right now. I had hospital Monday morning, and I was glad it was after prom.

I just wanted to enjoy my night.

My mum had called a stylist and make-up artist in for me and Robyn, which I was grateful for. I had sort of let myself go a bit being bed-bound for nearly two months. We had my dress made as going shopping was off the cards; last thing I wanted to do was walk around on crutches looking at dresses that I needed help in and out of. The seamstress was brilliant and listened to everything I liked and didn't like.

I decided on a black, A-line gown. I wasn't a girly girl, but you only get prom night and your wedding to go all out, so why wouldn't I go for the full shebang?

I stood and looked at myself in the mirror, smiling from ear to ear at how I looked. The dress had thin black spaghetti straps running over my shoulders that tied round my neck, giving me an open back. The neck-line plunged down into a V which stopped just before my waist, it was a bit risqué for prom, but I loved it.

A satin belt ran around my tiny waist, forming a bow that sat just above the bottom of my spine. The skirt was a long, black tulle overlay which sat over the top of a fitted black skirt that had two thigh splits either side, revealing a little too much skin, but this was all for him. I wanted a reaction from Conor, knowing full well that I was going to get one from him in this gown.

My mum was a bit sceptical at first, but after pleading and giving her my puppy dog eyes, she finally agreed. I was donning my all black converse which I think just took the edge off just how sexy this dress was.

My hair was pulled half up, half down. The hair that was down was styled into loose curls that tumbled past my breasts and sat just underneath my rib cage. My eyes were smoky, but not overly. I had eyeliner on my top eyelids, mascara that made my lashes look so long and thick, my blue eyes shining like crystals, and a light brushing of bronzer making my tanned skin pop even more.

My lips were finished off with a matte, bright red lipstick. I was pulled from looking at myself when Robyn walked in the room.

"Damn, girl, you look hot as hell. Conor is going to lose his mind," she said as she waltzed over to me, taking my hand and spinning me round.

"Me? What about you, you're on fire," I complimented her back.

She was wearing a figure-hugging, bandeau red gown that went all the way to the floor, a slit sitting up her left thigh as she pointed her white converse out and moved it side to side. Her beautiful, red hair was pulled to the side in a low bun. She looked stunning. Chase was a lucky guy.

After I had asked Conor, Chase asked Robyn, which made my heart swell. My best friend and my brother were going on a date, it was so sweet.

My mum appeared in the doorway, taking pictures on her phone before handing us both a glass of champagne. Me and Robyn clinked our glasses together as we took a big mouthful, both giggling to each other.

I walked over to my bed, grabbing my bag. I heard a noise outside which made me move towards my window.

Conor was standing there in an all-black tuxedo, sorting my brothers bow-tie out. Behind them was a limousine with the door open, waiting for us.

A huge smile graced my face as I looked down at him. He was so handsome. My heart was pirouetting in my chest at the sight of him, the hairs on the back of my neck standing up when he looked up at me, a small smile appearing.

I turned from the window and made my way downstairs, holding my skirt with one hand as I tiptoed down the stairs gracefully, calling out for Robyn to come as I waltzed towards him, stopping at the top step outside, the soft summer breeze blowing, my hair being pulled with it gently.

My eyes were on him, looking him up and down as he turned from Chase to face me. His eyes widened slowly, drawing up and down my body, and his mouth opened before he pushed his tattooed hand up to his mouth, rubbing his index finger over his bottom lip before pulling it between his teeth, his glorious lips forming into a smirk.

He rushed over to me, wrapping his arm around me and pulling me to him, bringing his mouth to my ear.

"You look fucking breath taking, how the hell am I meant to keep my hands off of you tonight?" he groaned, setting a fire off deep inside me.

"That's the point, Royce," I teased.

"Oh, Darcey, baby girl," he moaned out.

I dipped my head down, giggling and pushing him away slightly before his lips were on mine, his tongue in my mouth, caressing and massaging mine on every stroke. My arm snaked up round his neck, pulling him into me more. His fingers ran over the material of my skirt and up my thigh, causing my breath to hitch as he pulled away.

He rested his forehead on mine, his breathing harsh and fast. "You, Darcey Sawyer, are fucking delectable," he said, stepping away and taking my hand, pulling me into the back of the limo, smiling at Chase who had a smile like a Cheshire cat when he saw his girl.

After a short limo ride, we pulled up outside the school, nerves started flitting through me. It was bad enough being the loner of the school, but for the loner to turn up with the king, that was something to be gossiped about and glared at.

The limo driver stepped out the car and opened our door, Conor getting out first as he re-adjusted his tux jacket then held his hand out to help me. I put one foot out, my bare leg on show as he helped pull me up, his arm swooping behind me as he kept me close, walking towards the main entrance.

I could feel the burning eyes of jealous girls on me, but I didn't care. I was with him, he was with me. That was all that mattered.

As we walked into the school, he pecked me on the cheek before we had to stand for our photos. We stood to the side and waited for Robyn and Chase to make their grand entrance. They looked so good together. Deep down, I was hoping they would both just admit their feelings for one another and get it over with.

After the photos we made our way through to the main ballroom, the theme being Kings & Queens. Quite fitting seeing as I was with the king of Buck Hall.

"Drink, baby?" he asked as I took in the extravagant surroundings. Glitz and crowns everywhere.

"Yeah, please, champagne." I smiled as him and Chase walked towards the bar.

"How amazing did it feel to walk past those bitches?" Robyn shouted in my ear over the music.

"Pretty amazing." I laughed. "Can you believe we are actually here, with Chase and Conor?"

"I know, crazy. And we were thinking of boycotting it." She shook her head. "So glad we didn't."

"Me too, boo, me too."

Within minutes Conor was back, his arms snaking round my waist as he pulled me into him, his mouth on my ear, nibbling softly.

"I want to take you home." His tone was laced with seductiveness. My belly flipped. I downed my champagne before leaning my head back on his chest, his mouth on my neck as he planted soft kisses down to my shoulder before we lost contact, a whimper leaving me.

"Dance with me?" he said as he took my hand and spun me out, my skirt fanning.

"Always, Mr Royce," I cooed back at him.

PROMISE ME

He pulled me towards him before his hand found its way to my waist again, my arms up round his neck as we danced to The Calling, "Wherever you will go."

The lights dimmed around us, the rest of the room blurred as I stared into his beautiful, green eyes. They hypnotized me. I was drunk off the sight of him. His neck craned down before he kissed me slowly. A slow, meaningful kiss.

As we pulled away, I smiled up at him, his eyes soft and hazy. I just couldn't get enough of him. The chemistry was crackling between us, and I knew he felt it just as strongly as me. I didn't want to be here anymore, I wanted to go home with him. I wanted him, this was the moment I had been waiting for. I wanted him to claim me as his own.

"Take me home," I said breathlessly, I couldn't wait any longer.

"You sure?" he asked, pulling away slightly.

"So sure." I nodded.

He leant down and pecked me on the lips before breaking our contact and grabbing my hand, pulling me out into the main hallway.

"One minute," he said as he took his phone out. I'm assuming he is texting Chase to tell him we are leaving. He placed his phone back in his suit trousers and took my hand, lacing his fingers through mine as he pulled me outside and into the rain.

Normally, I would have refused to walk out in it, but I didn't care.

He stood reluctantly for a moment. "We can wait for it to stop," he said quietly.

"No chance." I laughed, pulling on his arm as we ran down the steps and into the carpark where we were waiting for our ride. I stood, arms wide letting the rain pour down on me before I stopped to look at him, the tension between us too much as he crashed his body into mine, putting my arms around his neck and lifting me effortlessly, his mouth finding mine.

My hands moved to his hair, tugging hard. It was like an animal that had been caged for the last few years was finally released, and I couldn't stop. It was taking over me, and I loved it. Our kiss was raw, passionate and filled with so much heat. The apex between my legs was aching, I needed him.

Our kiss broke when we saw the limo pull up, but he didn't put me down, he walked me over with my legs wrapped around his waist.

The driver opened the door, not even looking at us as we slid into the back, my hungry eyes on him. He had my red lipstick smudged all over his mouth, but I didn't care, it just made the want for him even more intense.

Once the limo started moving, my eyes were on him, full of need. My back was towards the door of the limo, one leg on the floor, the other bent on the seat. My skirt pooled between my legs, so my bare thighs were exposed.

He always looked hot, but soaking wet, his hair loose and flopped over his face, just made him even hotter. All these new feelings were confusing. I was still trying to catch my breath from our kiss, my soul was on fire from him, my heart like a drum in my chest.

His eyes moved from mine down to my heaving, wet, chest. A small growl left his throat as he pounced on me, nestling himself in-between my legs as his hungry mouth was on mine, his tongue darting in and out fast. He sucked my bottom lip in before sinking his teeth into it, then pressed his mouth to my neck as his kisses started to slow, it was like he remembered that this was my first time, but he got caught up in the moment.

He moved his expert lips to my collar bone as he placed soft, butterfly kisses along then trailed them to the other side. He pulled his head up, his eyes boring into mine.

"Darcey," he whispered.

"Conor," his name spilled off my tongue, my voice silky and full of lust.

"I need to get you in my bedroom."

"I know, king."

"Fuck." He sucked in his breath and moved back from me. "I can't control myself around you, baby," he admitted, pushing his wet hair off of his face.

"Good." My raging hormones were taking over.

He darted out the car before the driver had a chance to stop outside my house, grabbing my hand and pulling me out. I couldn't help but smile.

He opened our front door, sneaking in quietly, the television flickering in the lounge. He pressed his finger to his lips, knowing full well if my mum knew we were home, that was our night blown. She wouldn't stop talking about our night, then she would want to know where Chase and Robyn were.

We tiptoed up the staircase, letting out a sigh of relief when we made it upstairs. We stood between both of our bedroom doors.

"You sure about this, Darcey?" he asked, water dripping from his hair.

"So sure," I whispered.

He stepped towards me, his hand round the back of my head, pulling me to him, the other arm round my back as he guided me to his bedroom. The familiar scent filled my nostrils, the scent that reminded me of him.

He kicked the door shut then picked me up and walked me over to his bed.

His room was so dark, light and dark greys covered the walls. He had a big queen bed and a black, metal headboard. He dropped me just before his bed, his eyes beating down on me. He stood in front of me as he peeled his soaked suit jacket off and threw it on the chair by his wardrobe.

His tattooed hands moved to his shirt as he slowly unbuttoned it, revealing his toned, tattooed upper body. My mouth instantly went dry. I ran my hands up his body and pushed his shirt off of his shoulders. Then kicking my shoes off.

He stepped closer to me, his hands running around my neck as he pulled the thin strap, letting it fall down.

He dropped down to his knees, pushing the tulle overlay part of my skirt up round my waist as he planted soft kisses up both of my thighs, his hands moving down and gripping my legs harder.

My eyes batted down to him, his mouth leaving my skin as he looked up at me.

He stood slowly, towering over me, his eyes dark, inviting me in.

I was falling harder for him in that instant.

I pushed my dress down, letting it pool at my feet, my arms spreading across my chest as I tried to cover myself. I was standing in just my black, lacey thong. He shook his head slowly, curling his fingers round my waist as he pulled my arms away gently.

"Don't ever cover yourself up in front of me. You're beautiful, Darcey." His hand was on my chin as he tilted my head up for me to look at him. "Do you understand me?" he said softly.

I nodded.

"Good."

He pushed me back gently, so I fell onto the bed. He knelt in-between my legs, spreading them with his knees before he dipped his head to my neck as he began a soft trail of kisses down to my breast, his hot mouth taking my nipple, sucking gently, puckering it before flicking his tongue over it slowly. I wish I could calm my racing heart.

His other hand glided down my body, his finger running up and down my core, over the top of my knickers. A small moan escaped my lips and I threw my arms over my face, embarrassed.

His head popped up. "Take your arm away," he said, a small smile on his face. "Do you trust me, baby girl?" he asked, his face close to me, his eyes staring deep into mine.

I nodded. "Completely," I replied in barely a whisper.

His head moved down between my breasts, his mouth planting soft kisses on my tingling skin as he trailed down towards my pelvis, his fingers following his line of kisses. He slid off the bed, his knees now on the floor, on the rug beneath him, his fingers wrapping round my lacey knickers as he slid them down my legs and off my feet.

His hands now gripped my inner thighs and pushed my legs apart even further. I heard him suck his breath in through his teeth.

Nerves were crashing through me.

Nerves of anticipation.

Nerves of wanting this so bad.

I have thought about this moment over the last few months and I couldn't believe it was finally happening.

I felt his warm breath over my sex before his tongue slowly, slid into my folds. A gasp left my mouth at the sensation that pulsated through me. He did it again, just as slowly, and another gasp escaped me.

I felt one of his hands move away from my thigh as he gently pressed and rubbed over my sensitive bud, his green eyes flicking up to mine as he removed his tongue from the most sensual part of my body.

My wanting eyes watched him, the intimacy so present and strong between us. He glided his finger from my bud, down to my opening.

"This may feel a little uncomfortable, okay? But it's normal. If it gets too much, tell me," he said, his voice low.

His fingertip pushed gently and slowly into me. A louder gasp left me as an unfamiliar sting burned, making me tense.

"Relax, baby," he cooed as his lips kissed the inside of my thigh.

The feel of his lips on me took my mind off of what he was trying to do for a moment. His finger pushed further into me and I could feel myself stretching for him, the stinging and pain easing as his kisses stayed on my inner thighs.

He pulled his lips from my skin, his eyes back on me

as he dipped his head between my legs again, his tongue flicking across my bud, his fingers pushing into me deeply but slowly, pulsing them.

I felt a tickling sensation building in my stomach, my insides clamping round him. His pushes sped up slightly, his tongue still slowly gliding in-between my folds and licking my bud.

"Conor," I moaned, my hands in his hair as I tugged for him to lift his head.

"Have I hurt you?" Panic shot across his face.

"No, no. I'm just… just…" I stammered in a mumble, putting my hands over my face.

"You're getting close to coming, baby. Are you feeling shy?" he said with a smile creeping over his face.

He slipped his fingers out of me, and I instantly missed his contact as he shuffled in-between my thighs, his face now hovering over mine.

I couldn't help but notice a shimmering trail over his lips, my eyes focussing on them.

"That's you, baby. Your arousal." He grinned, licking his lips.

I glowed a crimson red.

"You're shy," he muttered, grabbing my hands and pulling them away from my face.

"Look at me," he said, my eyes obeying his order. "Baby girl, I know you're not going to come from just my dick." He winked. "But I *am* going to make you come, I want you to experience your first orgasm. So lay back, relax and don't be shy. You have nothing to be shy about."

He kissed me softly on my lips, his hands pinning my arms above my head.

"Only move them if you're going to grab my hair." He smiled as he moved down my body and nestled himself back between my legs, his mouth over my sex once more before he glided his finger back in, this time not easing himself in.

A sigh left me as he continued his fast strokes, but his tongue stayed slow like before. He flicked his tongue from side to side before sucking my sensitive bud and then gliding his tongue back down.

The ticklish feeling started again, intensifying quickly, feeling like a wave about to crash down over me. The ache between my legs was building up, when all of a sudden, I felt this overwhelming urge to arch my back and moan his name, my toes curling as the sensation crashed through me, before disappearing completely.

My whole body tingled, his fingers still slowly pulsing inside me, his tongue leaving me. His head lifted, my arousal glistening on his lips, his eyes drunk off of me, his smile so big and wide at his accomplishment, which made me feel amazing.

He slipped his fingers out, pressing them between his lips as he sucked them clean.

"So sweet," he moaned as he laid next to me, my eyes

wandering to the huge, bulge that was busting out of his suit trousers.

"You okay?" he asked gently, kissing my forehead in my post orgasmic state. I felt like I was floating, slowly coming back down to earth.

"Mmm," I said, sleepily.

"Good." He smiled at me as he shuffled off the bed, pushing his trousers down and kicking them across the room, his cock hard and bulging against his tight boxers, my mouth going dry.

I looked him up and down, his glorious, toned body covered in so many tattoos. I wanted to lay and study every single one of them.

He crawled back onto the bed, kneeling in-between my legs, pushing them apart.

"You still want to do this?" he asked with a hint of seriousness in his voice.

"Yes," I whispered.

He took his bottom lip in-between his teeth as he hooked his thumbs at the side of his boxers and pushed them down his thick thighs, his cock springing free. My eyes widened. I tensed up at the sight of it, my mind filled with a thousand questions.

I had to trust him, I needed to relax.

Before he knelt on the bed, he reached over to his bedside unit and grabbed a condom, tearing it with his teeth and placing the wrapper on the side before rolling it down this thick, long cock.

My eyes felt like they were watering just looking at it. He knelt back on the bed, his weight making it dip slightly as he parted my thighs.

"Baby girl, relax, okay? This will be quick, but once I've had you a few times, this will be the best feeling you have ever experienced. Do you trust me?"

I nodded my head quickly. His body lay over me, his body on mine, his weight on top of me. He placed his hands round my face, his mouth moving towards mine as he kissed me, his tongue darting in, dancing with my tongue.

He moved one of his hands, running it down my body before slipping a finger into me, twirling and stretching me. He kept his tongue movements slow, matching his finger.

A burning sensation started again, deep in my stomach, now aware that this feeling was the start of an orgasm building. A slight moan escaped into his mouth which spurred him on. He pulled his finger out, rubbing my arousal over the tip of his cock as he grabbed the base and lined himself up at my opening.

My eyes flicked open, his mouth pulling away from mine.

"Relax, I promise I won't hurt you," he said sweetly, his eyes glistening.

He pushed the tip of his cock into me, my mouth

forming an O as I felt myself stretch, the stinging and burning back again as he continued to edge a bit more of himself into me.

"You okay, baby?" he asked me.

I nodded. I couldn't speak, he had literally taken my breath away as he pushed a bit more of himself in, stilling for a moment, his eyes watching my face.

He looked down at himself as he eased a bit more of himself in, the burning apparent now, a little groan coming out of my mouth.

"Want me to stop?" he asked concerned. I shook my head while holding my breath.

He pushed his hips forward slightly as I took more of him, the burn easing slightly, then in one gentle thrust, I had taken all of him.

He stilled, not moving, letting my body adjust and accept him.

His lips pressed on mine, one of his hands resting on my hip, the other cupping my face as he slid himself out slightly before slowly pushing back in.

I had no control over my feelings. A tear escaped my eye as he continued his slow, graceful pushes into me, claiming me as his own and I couldn't have been happier.

"Feel okay?" he asked me, his voice low, his breathing ragged.

"Mmhmm," I hummed as he picked his pace up slightly. My body stretched around him, taking every inch of him.

After a few more thrusts, the stings had left and it felt different, the small burn apparent again in my stomach. A groan left his throat, his breath being sucked in through his teeth as he bit into his bottom lip, his eyes leaving mine as he leant up and watched himself pushing into me.

"Fuck. Darcey," he moaned, his head tipping back, his grip tightening round my waist as he speared himself in and out of me, his hips thrusting slightly faster.

"Baby girl, I'm going to come so hard for you," he growled as his thrusts became shorter but harder.

"Fuck," he hissed as he found his release, grunting softly as he slowed down to a complete stop, his eyes on mine, so dark and hazy and filled with lust.

"I fucking love you, Darcey," he whispered before collapsing on top of me.

"I love you," I replied, his mouth moving over my lips.

I was his.

Completely and utterly his.

We laid for a moment before he pulled me into him, wrapping his heavy arms around me, not letting me go "you okay?" he whispered in my ear.

"I'm amazing" I whispered back.

He kissed my neck, squeezing me tighter as I fell into a deep sleep cocooned in his arms.

CHAPTER 14

CONOR

I laid there, my heart drumming in my chest. Placing my hand over it as I tried to still it. I rolled my head to the side looking at her, laying there, still naked, her skin glistening.

She was so fucking beautiful.

Her blonde hair fanned out behind her, her crystal blue eyes on me, an adorable smile on her face.

I reached over for her, rubbing my thumb over her cheek as she nuzzled into my hand.

"Morning baby girl, you okay?" I asked, now rolling onto my side, wanting to know how she was feeling.

"Morning" she smiled her beautiful smile at me "I am," she said, rolling into me. My arms wrapped around her, pulling her close to me. I placed a kiss on her nose and breathed in her scent.

She was intoxicating.

Addicting.

"Come with me," I muttered standing up, holding my hand out for her to take.

I led her through to my bathroom, turning the light on. I turned the shower on, letting the water run warm before stepping under it, pulling her under with me.

Her eyes darted down, then flicked up to mine, wide and scared when she looked in-between her legs.

"It's normal," I re-assured her, picking up a flannel and running it under the shower, lathering it with my shower gel. I started at her neck, washing her skin, watching the suds bubble over her.

I dragged it down to her breasts, going over each one delicately before moving it in-between her legs to clean her up, rinsing the flannel back under the shower and putting more soap on it, handing it to her for her to clean me.

I stood out the shower as she swapped places with me before washing me down. She stopped at the tattoo of the girl in the centre of my stomach, her eyes burning into it before bringing them up to mine.

She realised.

Realised that the tattoo was her.

I looked down at her, the water dripping down my face as she stepped closer to me, her arms around my neck as she reached on to her tiptoes as she kissed me.

My tongue pushed in-between her lips as our

tongues entwined with one another. Her hands dropped from my neck as she ran them down my chest, down to my torso then stopped just above my dick.

She pulled her mouth from mine. "Can I do something for you?" she asked, her naivety showing.

"What do you want to do?" I asked, smirking down at her.

"To touch you."

I took her hand and put it on my cock.

"There, you've touched me." I laughed, she let out a giggle and shook her head before wrapping her fingers round me, moving her hand up and down, slowly making my dick twitch.

"Darcey..."

Her hand moved quicker as she got a reaction from me and I groaned at her. I just wanted to clean her, shower her and snuggle up to her.

The desire grew inside me.

I needed her.

I grabbed her wrist, my fingers wrapping around it and pulling her hand away, shaking my head.

I pushed her back against the wall, running my hands under her arse, my fingers gliding across her creases, a smirk on my face before I kissed her. It was hungry and full of want. I lifted her effortlessly and held her against the wall, her toned, long legs wrapped round my waist.

I dropped one hand from underneath her as I grabbed the base of my cock and lined it up at her opening as I pushed my hips into her slowly, taking my time to fill her completely. I rocked my hips into her as she gasped, she was so tight.

I growled as I picked up the pace of my thrusts, a moan leaving her as her head dropped forward.

"Look at me," I growled out.

Her head lifted up as she did as I asked. Low groans were escaping me as I felt myself getting close to my release. She moaned again as I felt her clamp around me.

"I'm going to make you come," I whispered in her ear, my hips rocking into her slower now, taking my time to let her build.

"Conor," she moaned loudly. I crashed my lips to her, and she bit down on my lip as the pleasure coursed through her.

"Conor," she called again, and this time I thrust into her faster and harder as she clamped down around me.

"Fuck," she hissed as her hips started moving with mine, sending me over the edge as I came hard, pumping myself inside her as she came with me.

Her head flopped onto my chest, her breathing fast as I gently placed her down.

I tilted her head back, smiling at her. "Fuck, Darcey." I sighed, pushing her hair away from her face.

"Fuck, Conor," she moaned back at me, smiling her

gorgeous smile.

I swooped her up, carrying her to my bed and dropping her gently before covering her up as I scooted in next to her. I placed my arms over her, pulling her closer to me as I nuzzled into her hair, her body going heavy as she fell asleep in my arms.

-

DARCEY

Robyn came over on Saturday morning and perched herself on my bed as she waited for all the juicy gossip. I sat down next to her, aching in new places but blissfully happy.

"Before I spill..." I smirked. "Did anything happen with you?" I raised my eyebrows at her as I took a sip of my tea.

"No... I wanted it to," she admitted.

I winced. "Not that, you know, I *really* want to know about what happened between you and my brother, but..."

"Ha, don't worry, if something did happen, I would tell you, but I would spare the details." She smiled at me.

"Good to know." I laughed, putting my thumb up at her before I shook my head gently.

"So, come on, tell me about Conor. I want to know *everything.*"

"Well," I said shyly, biting my lip, "I don't even know

where to start."

"Why don't you start by telling me why you skipped out of prom early." Her eyes narrowed on me, her brows raised.

"Because, I couldn't wait any longer, the tension was off the charts and the heat between us was combustible. Honestly, Robyn, it was unreal. Even talking about it now is making my stomach knot." I sighed, taking a sip of tea, trying to calm my mind.

"Really?" she asked, taking a sip of her own tea.

"Yeah, it's mad. I thought what I felt for him was just pure hate and he probably felt the same, but something had to give. Something changed the night of my birthday, he became a completely different person. Then it just went from there..." I trailed off.

"Mate, you are not fobbing me off with that story. This is about the night you had sex with Connor fucking Royce, I want details. I don't want any stone left unturned." A snarky grin was on her face, her eyes boring into mine as she sat waiting, fidgeting on the spot.

"Fine, okay." I rolled my eyes at her, then finished my cup of tea before leaning back and putting it on the side table.

"So, we left prom, as you know. We walked out the hall and it was pouring with rain. Whilst we were waiting for the driver, we had this hot as hell kiss which spurred us on. Once we were in the limo, he literally pounced on me, sliding between my legs. He was so fucking hot. Where his hair was wet, it flopped onto his forehead and he had these water droplets on his face. The look he was giving me told me that if it wasn't my first time then I would have been fucked in the back of that limo, and you know what? I would have let him." I blushed, my eyes batting down to my hands that were playing with my duvet cover.

"Go on." She wiggled her eyebrows.

I leant across and swatted her with my hand. "Anyway…" I laughed. "We pulled up outside, and we had to sneak in the house because if my mum would have heard us then, you know, game over. She would have asked like, a trillion questions. So, yeah, we sneaked upstairs and as we got to the hallway separating the rooms, he asked if I still wanted to go ahead with it." I nibbled the inside of my mouth.

"He was so attentive and caring." I sighed.

"Continue… I want the dirty bits, come on, girl, you're dragging your heels."

"We got to his room, and he took his suit jacket and shirt off, and my God, Robyn, I can't begin to tell you just how fit he is. His stomach is toned, his tattoos cover every inch of him… Well, not every inch." I winked.

"And then he dropped to his knees, pushing my dress up round my waist as he started kissing my thighs. Things got heated pretty quickly. He pushed me onto the bed, made me come with his tongue and fingers. Honestly, I never knew it would feel that good. Then he took off his trousers. Seriously. Robyn. The monster size of his thing." I stopped as Robyn spat her tea all over my bedding before throwing her hand up to her mouth, shocked at what had just come out of my mouth.

"Monster." She howled, wiping the tears from her eyes.

"I was worried it wasn't going to fit." I laughed with her. "But it did... Obviously."

"Monster dick," she spat out, laughing again.

"Oh yeah, one hundred percent." I nodded enthusiastically.

"Did it hurt?" she asked, perching herself up on her elbows as she laid on her front.

"Yeah, it did. But after a while, the pain eases. He was really gentle and took his time. I can't wait to experience him properly, like, with no pain. We had shower sex this morning and I actually came from that, but it wasn't as intense as his mouth and fingers." I blushed again.

"Lucky you." She giggled. "Mate, I can't believe Conor Royce took your virginity."

"I know, me neither." I smiled. "And, Robyn, he told me he loved me."

"He what?" Her eyes widened.

"Yup, once he did his bit, you know..." I shrugged.

"Well, who would have thought it, aye?"

"I know." I sighed a happy sigh, snuggling myself under my duvet.

We spent the rest of Saturday chilling and talking about all things Conor. By the time Robyn went home, she was probably sick of me, and him. But I didn't care, I was like a love sick puppy dog. I couldn't get enough of him. He was on my mind all the goddamn time.

-

Sunday evening was soon upon us. I had just had a shower and washed my hair and was looking forward to an early night. Conor said he was going to come and watch a film with me, and I couldn't wait, I felt so happy.

I put my phone on charge and dropped Robyn a quick message, telling her I would message her tomorrow after the doctors and let her know what was said. I was feeling apprehensive already, but I just had to trust that it was all going to be okay.

Camilla checked in on me every other day. I tried not to think about the exams that I had missed. I would have known by now whether I would have got into ballet college, but I couldn't dwell on it. I just needed to know if I could dance again... That I *would* dance again.

I walked over to my pyjama drawer as I picked out a silk floral nightdress, dropping my towel when I heard a cough at the door.

"Ahem."

I turned to look, and there he was.

My Conor.

His cotton grey shorts swinging round his hips, an oversized vest showing his arms, chest and ribs. He shut the door behind him and walked over slowly.

"You naked for me, baby?" He groaned, his lips pressing into mine, his tongue slipping through my lips.

"I was actually just about to get my pyjamas on." I smiled at him, my hands on his chest as his snaked around my waist.

"Don't get dressed for my sake." He looked down at me, winking.

I shook my head as I giggled. I grabbed his hands from round my back and prised them away as I bent down slowly, my face turning to him to see his reaction. His lip was pulled between his teeth, his hand grabbing his crotch.

I winked at him before standing up and pulling my nightie over my head, pushing it down my body. The length sat mid-thigh, enough skin covered with just enough showing.

"Oh fuck, baby girl." He groaned as he strode towards me, grabbing and picking me up as I wrapped my legs round his back. He placed me on the bed, pushing me towards my headboard and settled in-between my legs.

"Don't fancy a film anymore... Do you?" he asked, kneeling up, looking down at me, his eyes devouring me.

He pushed my knees apart, his eyes moving to my sex.

"Oh baby, I'm going to enjoy every inch of you tonight." He growled before dipping his head between my legs, sending me to seventh heaven.

-

I sat anxiously on the way to the hospital on Monday morning, nerves rattling through me. Staring out the window, my mind wandered back to my weekend with Conor. He was amazing, and he was right, after a few times, it has gotten *so* much better. Not that I have anyone else to compare him too, but I can't imagine it gets much better than this.

I felt a squeeze on my leg and my head turned to look at my mum as I took my headphones out.

"We are here, you ready?" she asked anxiously, I could see the worry in her eyes. She tried to keep strong for my sake, but I could see she was ready to crumble.

"Ready as I'll ever be," I muttered as I hopped out the car, slamming the door shut behind me.

I was hoping it was all going to be okay. Some days I had good days, others were bad, where my leg would completely stiffen up and I would be in agony. But I knew it wasn't going to be a quick fix.

We walked into the hospital as we took a seat in the waiting area. I was tapping the glass on the back of my phone with my nails, trying to keep my mind busy. I felt sweaty and clammy.

This moment, right here, could destroy and shatter my dreams.

"Try not to worry, sweetie," my mum said, swooping my hand into hers. "It'll be okay." She smiled.

I smiled back at her, scared to talk in case my voice betrayed me and I ended up in tears. The lump was apparent in my throat, but I kept swallowing it back down.

"Darcey Sawyer," Dr Cal called out. I stood slowly, waiting for my mum to start walking with me as I grabbed her hand and squeezed it, a small smile appearing on her face.

We walked into his office, him closing the door behind us as he showed us our seats.

"How are you feeling, Darcey," he asked as he took his seat opposite us and laid my file out in front of him on his mahogany desk.

"Not bad." My voice was shaky. "Nervous." I let out a little laugh, my eyes darting to my mum.

"That's to be expected." He smiled back at me. "How's the leg been?"

"Today's a good day," I mumbled, tapping my nails on my phone again as I watched him make notes. "But then I have bad days." I sighed.

"What do you mean, bad days?" His eyebrows pulled together, his pen now resting on my notes, his fingers interlocking as his hands rested on top of my file.

"Pain wise," I said, my voice small.

"Go on."

"Well, some days my leg stiffens and tightens, sort of like a spasm, I suppose. But the pain is unreal. If I'm having a day like that, I can't do much. I'm hoping it's just part of the healing process." My voice filled with hope, but his face shattered that hope within seconds from just his look. I knew it wasn't going to be the news I wanted to hear from the way he looked at me.

"Darcey, that isn't part of the healing," he said with a grimace, and my bottom lip trembled. "But, let me take some X-rays and do a couple of scans, so I can see how the bones and muscle look, then we can go from there, okay?" he said sweetly as he stood from his seat. "Come with me."

He walked past, me and my mum stood from our seats as we followed him into the hallway.

Once my scan and X-rays were done, we walked back into his office to wait. He assured me it wouldn't be long.

My phone beeped, and I looked down to see that Conor had text me.

Hey, baby, any news yet? Miss you. X

I smiled before tapping a reply.

Nothing yet, just had scans and X-rays, so hoping to hear soon. Will call you as soon as I'm out. Miss you too. X

PROMISE ME

I locked my phone, putting it face down on my lap when I saw Dr Cal walk back in.

"Sorry it took so long," he apologised before sitting back down in front of me and my mum.

"Okay, so the X-ray was as I thought, no change." He nodded as he put the X-ray onto his computer screen for me to see. "But the scan..." his voice trailed off as he removed the X-ray and loaded the scan up for us to look at.

"The muscle that had the tear in it hasn't healed as much as we wanted it to. Can you still see the slight tear in it?" he asked as he pointed the lid of his pen to the screen.

I nodded, completely numb, knowing what the next part of our conversation was going to be about.

"This should have healed. And the fact that it hasn't, means that it won't, hence why you get the occasional pain."

"Can she have another round of surgery?" my mum asked.

"Unfortunately not. There is nothing else we can do. The muscle has already been fixed once, we can't do it again," he said, his face full of grimace. "I'm sorry, Darcey, but you won't be able to go back to dancing as a career. The risks are too great."

"So, that's it? My dream is over?" I muttered, my bottom lip trembling, my eyes stinging and my throat burning from the lump.

I had to go.

I pushed away from the desk, standing up and running

from his office, following the signs for the exit.

I couldn't sit there, there was no point.

Nothing was going to change.

I escaped through the hospital doors, taking a deep inhale of the summer air. It took a moment, but my tears started to fall, my heart obliterated.

I felt weak, my legs going from beneath me, when all of a sudden, I was caught. My eyes looked up to see him, my Conor.

That's when I lost it, an uncontrollable sob leaving me, screaming as my body reacted to the news.

My heart obliterated into a million shards.

My dream was over.

CHAPTER 75

DARCEY

The hours rolled into days, the days into weeks, the weeks into months. I was slipping down a black hole that I was struggling to get out of. After the news that my dancing career was over, I felt like my life was over. Everything I had dreamed and wanted for my life was snatched away from me in a second.

I felt like I had a continuous dark, grey cloud hanging over my head and an unbearable weight crushing down on my shoulders, that no matter how hard I tried to shrug off, it just wouldn't budge.

I spent most of the time in my room, Robyn came by every day, and every day she sat next to me on the bed while we watched episode after episode of *Friends*.

She was trying anything and everything to cheer me up, but I just couldn't shake it.

One minute I would get annoyed with myself, lash

out and scream. Then other times, I am so secluded in my own head, I want to be left alone. I want to curl up in a ball and never come out of it.

Conor hadn't left my side either. Him and Robyn have been taking it in turns to watch me, even when I shower I'm not left alone, which annoys me, but I understand why they do it.

I think they are worried I am going to do something when I'm on my own, so they don't want to take any risks. I appreciated them being there, but sometimes I just wanted to be on my own, without anyone babysitting me.

I look at my calendar every day, mentally ticking off the dates. The thirtieth of September was getting closer; closer to Conor and Chase leaving. My heart broke a little more each day. I didn't want them to go, even more so now.

I needed him.

I wanted him to stay with me.

I didn't want him leaving me when I needed him more than the army did.

I was being selfish, I know, but I honestly don't think I can get through this without him.

"Baby girl," I hear his voice.

I am wrapped up like a cocoon in my duvet, I stick my head out from underneath. My long, blonde hair is up on my head like a bird's nest. I stank and was wearing one of Conor's vests that I had been wearing for the last three days. I actually disgusted myself, but I couldn't help it. I couldn't pull myself from my funk.

He climbed onto the bed, pulling at my duvet and wrapping his arms around me.

"You need a shower," he grumbled as he lifted me effortlessly out of bed and walked towards my bathroom. He sat me down on the toilet whilst he ran the shower, holding his hand under to check the temperature.

He gave me a little smile as he walked closer to me, taking my hand and pulling me up to stand. His hands moved to the hem of my vest, then he pulled it over my head. He reached up to the messy bun on my head and pulled at my hairband, letting my hair cascade down my back, to tumble over my breasts.

"You look beautiful," he said as he led me to the shower, nudging me in.

He stood back and undressed himself before stepping under with me. He wrapped his big, muscly arms around my tiny waist and squeezed me tightly. I didn't want him to let me go. I felt safe and loved with him.

"I don't want you to go," I whispered, the water dripping down my face.

"To go where, baby? I'm not going anywhere."

"The army. You go in ten days."

"Oh..." his voice trailed off as he turned me round to face him, his eyes looking down at me, his chocolate brown hair loose and resting on his forehead as I watched the droplets run from the top of his head and down to his nose before falling between our naked bodies. His hands moved to my face, tilting me up to look at him.

"I'll be back before you know it," he muttered.

"Four years is a long time." Sadness laced my voice.

"Darcey, if I knew that we were going to end up together, if I knew that you loved me, I would have never signed up. I would never have let your stupid brother talk me into it. But things were different back then, we were different back then. I can't not go," he said in barely a whisper, the pain striking through my heart.

You could see on his face he was feeling it too. He had no choice, he had to go.

He craned his neck lower as he pressed his lips onto mine, softly trying to show me how much I meant to him.

The tears began to fall, streaming down the sides of my face and becoming one with the droplets from the shower.

He inhaled deeply as he pulled away, his hazy green eyes boring into mine.

"Promise me one thing, Darcey," he mumbled, his voice sounding desperate.

"Anything." My eyes darted back and forth to his.

He took a moment to speak again, his eyes were focussing on mine so hard, as if he was trying to remember every detail about them.

"Promise me you will be strong. I need my Darcey

back. The one I fell in love with.

"I promise," I said, even though my voice didn't sound convincing. I really did want to keep my promise.

"Promise me you'll wait for me" his voice hushed

"always."

-

Today was the day, Conor and Chase were standing outside the front of our house in their combat dress uniforms. I was so proud of them but absolutely heartbroken at the same time.

Me and Conor spent last night exploring and remembering every inch of each other's bodies. I needed the intimacy. We didn't have sex last night. We made love, over and over again. I could still smell him on me, a scent that I never wanted to go. But I knew it was going to. Just like him, he was going to disappear.

Fear crippled me that he wouldn't be back. Sadness and anger consumed me.

Chase hugged my mum and dad, lingering a little longer than usual. My mum was a broken mess, and my dad even had tears in his eyes.

Chase stood in front of me, his grey eyes red and bloodshot, but he still had his beautiful smile on his face.

"I'm going to miss you," I choked out, my throat tight and constricting.

"I'm going to miss you too, Darcey," he said as he bent down, hugging me tightly, lifting my feet off the floor, kissing my cheek.

"Be safe, look after each other," I mumbled as I palmed the tears off my face.

He nodded at me before he went to Robyn. His arms wrapped around her as his mouth covered hers, their kiss was slow and sweet as they said goodbye.

I couldn't say I was shocked at their little outburst of PDA. Then my heart stilled, my handsome, stunning king was standing in front of me. His dreamy green eyes glistening from the unshed tears.

"Baby girl." He just about managed to get my nickname out as he wrapped his arms around my waist and lifted me up, my legs wrapping themselves around him tightly.

"Please don't go." I sobbed, my forehead pressed against his.

"I don't want to go, but I've got to." His voice was low, so only I could hear.

"I can't live without you." I sniffed, the tears still running down my face.

"Of course you can, and it's only for four years. It'll fly." He let out a little laugh as his lips broke into a small smile before leaning in and kissing me slowly.

My heart fluttered in my chest. The contact that I so desperately craved from him shattering in an instant as he pulled away from me. I rubbed my thumb across his face to wipe away the stray tear that was running down his cheek.

"Promise me one thing, Conor." I sniffed, trying to hold it together. The lump in my throat was burning, I felt like someone had stuck a hot iron rod into my wind pipe, my breath taken away from me, my tears threatening to spill.

"Anything, baby girl."

"Come home to me," I whispered through my silent sobs, my arms clinging round his neck. "Both of you."

"I promise you," he said as he put me down, leaning in, kissing me softly. "We've got to go," he said as he let me go

"No, no, no. Conor, no, I'm not ready," I shouted as he started to walk away, climbing into the coach that was sitting in the car park.

"I love you, Darcey Monroe Sawyer," he said as he pressed two fingers to his lips and kissed them, holding them out to me.

"Always my baby girl," he said before walking into the coach, Chase following behind him.

"I love you," I cried out to him as the door shut. The coach started to pull away and move out of the car park. I don't know what come over me, I knew I couldn't stop him, I wouldn't stop him, but I couldn't stop my mind from acting. I ran as fast as I could after him, screaming his name over and over again. My voice was hoarse, my throat burning.

I could see his face in the rear window, his beautiful smile beaming at me, his stunning green eyes glistening, but not with happiness. With complete sadness.

He was feeling broken, just like I was.

I felt my heart starting to break as he got smaller and smaller from my view.

And just like that, he was gone.

I fell to the gravelled floor, my legs completely giving way under me as I gave up, hot tears burning down my face, my eyes blurring as I shouted out his name.

My heart obliterated inside my chest.

I was completely broken.

PART Two

CHAPTER 16

DARCEY

Four Years Later

I locked up my studio and walked to my car, looking at the messages I had missed throughout the day. A little smile graced my face as I saw the day. Thursday. Thursday quickly became my favourite day over the last four years as it was letter day.

The day I got to hear from my king.

We never officially said we were boyfriend and girlfriend, but I knew I didn't want any other man.

I pulled up outside my beach house that I bought a year ago. It was secluded and on the coast with a stunning sea view that I could never tire of. I was only a ten minute drive from my parents, so that worked well for me. I didn't want to move out, I wanted to stay at home with my parents, but I needed to move on. I needed some sort of closure from him.

I spent the first year in his room, sniffing his clothes and duvet cover. Anything to feel closer to him. He left a gaping hole in my heart when he left me. I knew he had to go but anger took over everything. He shouldn't have left, I was in my own dark place and I needed him more than I could have ever imagined.

I slammed the car door shut, smiling to see that Robyn was home also. I ran towards the mail box that sat by the stairs that led to my house, and as I opened it, excitement brewed when I saw a handful of letters.

As I jogged up the stairs, I flicked through the letters, my heart thumping when I saw one for me and one for Robyn.

I put my key in the front door and let myself in.

"Hey, I'm home," I called out, dropping my keys on the table by the front door.

I walked into our airy, light, open-plan kitchen and dining area, dropping the rest of the letters on the worktop, then walking towards the snug at the back of the kitchen. I ran my finger under the envelope and pulled the letter out, unfolding it slowly. A picture fell into my lap as I slumped in the basket chair looking out at the sea.

I started to read.

Baby girl,
What's this, letter 203? I can't believe we are in our fourth year. There has been rumours about us being

deployed for our first tour in the next couple of days, but of course I can't tell you where.

I am hoping that we get leave soon, that we get to come home.

But if the rumours are true, I'm not sure when I will next see you, and that breaks my heart even more than it already is.

How's the dance studio going? I know I always say it, but I am so proud of you. You continued with your dream, but it just took a change of course. You get to teach your love for ballet. Sometimes our lives take a turn and we have no control over it, but I am a strong believer that our lives are mapped out for us and everything that happens is for a reason. Even though we sometimes don't know what the reasons are, they soon make sense.

I would do anything to be home with you, laying behind you, burying my head in your neck and breathing in your intoxicating scent. Darcey Monroe, I don't think you understand just how much I love you, just how much you make me feel. You have knocked me off my feet, baby girl, but in a good way.

Chase is doing okay, he has his good and bad days like us all. But his letters from you, Robyn and your mum keep him going. The days are long, but they seem to slip by in the blink of an eye, which I know doesn't make sense. There is a light at the end of the tunnel. It's close. I know it is.

I wait for your letters, they are my little bit of hope and happiness, my escape from this harsh reality.

If we are being deployed, I'm not sure when I will next get to write you, but let it be known, I'll be thinking about you. Always.

I still have the photo of you that I stole all those years ago from the summer fete. I call you my guardian angel to the other lads. Because you are.

I love you Darcey.
Promise me one thing?
Promise that you'll write back.

I miss you.
Always mine, only yours.
Your king, Conor.

I held the letter close to my chest, wiping away my tears. As I grabbed the photo from my lap, there stood my beautiful Conor, a huge grin on his face, holding my photo. His green eyes glistened in the sunshine, his dog tags low round his neck, resting on a fitted white vest top. I missed just laying on him, my fingers tracing over his tattoos.

I stared out into the calm ocean that was just outside my window when I heard footsteps behind me, a glass of wine appearing in front of my eyes.

"There you go." Robyn smiled. "I thought you would need it."

"Thank you." I smiled at her, folding the letter over and placing it on my lap. "You have one too." I nodded my head back towards the worktop.

Her eyes lit up as she bounced over and grabbed it. "I'll be back soon," she said quietly as she slipped her finger under the envelope and walked towards the stairs.

It's funny, I love getting the letters, I love reading them, but once they're finished, your heart breaks all over again. It's bittersweet.

I stood up from my chair and walked over to the fridge, grabbing the white wine before pouring a large glass for Robyn and leaving it on the side for when she came down. Her and Chase's friendship had bloomed whilst he had been away. I always hoped they would actually get together properly, once he was home.

This was our routine; read our letters separately, cry, drink wine, talk and cry some more until we were so mentally exhausted we had to go to bed.

I woke the next morning, stretching then rolling over, smiling as the sun beamed through my window. My eyes focussed on the photo of Conor that was resting against my lamp. All his letters were in a glass jewellery box. Small enough to take anywhere with me.

I studied his features, even though I knew them so

well. I liked just looking at him and wondered if he did the same as me.

From the moment I woke, up to the moment I fell asleep, he was on my mind, which made me feel like he was safe, as silly as that sounded.

I threw back the duvet and padded over to my white desk that sat underneath my large window. I loved the light in this house. All the walls were white throughout with accents of colours through accessories.

I had long, draping, white linen sheer curtains that were blowing in the gentle, summer sea breeze. I pulled out my chair, looking over the rolling green hills as I pulled out my notebook to write back to him.

King,

Thursdays are my favourite, because I hear from you. We are now on letter 204.

I had a cry after your letter at the thought of you being deployed. I know we knew it was a possibility, but the thought of it scares me, so much.

But each day that passes is one day closer to me seeing you. To me holding you. To me kissing you.

And I can't wait.

I can't believe this could be our last letter for a while. Every time there is a clear night, I walk towards the sea and look up at the stars and think of you, because I know you're looking up at them too.

I still can't believe the last time I saw you was four years ago, the last time I held you, kissed you, smelled you and felt you. You are always on my mind, never leaving for a second. You keep me going.

And when I'm asleep, you invade my dreams, which I love, because I somehow believe that our souls find each other whilst we are asleep, that we get to be together in spirit. And that makes me happy. But my God, baby, I can't wait to be reunited with you for good. Even if it was for a day, that's all I would need to get my fix from you that I so desperately need.

I miss you. So much.

And of course, I promise you.

Promise me one thing?
Promise that you'll come home to me.
I love you.
Your Darcey.
Only yours, always mine.

I folded the letter, slipping it into the envelope so I could get it to the post office today. I normally have to wait at least two weeks before the letter comes back, but the fear was crippling me that I may not get one back anytime soon if he was getting deployed.

I hopped in the shower before throwing on my leggings and oversized vest. I walked downstairs to see Robyn sitting with a cup of tea.

"Morning, hun." I smiled at her as I placed my phone, letter and bag on the worktop.

"Morning." She smiled back at me.

"You okay?" I asked her whilst grabbing my hot cup of coffee.

"Yeah, not bad. Glad it's Friday."

"Me too, film night tomorrow? I feel exhausted," I admitted, taking a sip.

"Tell me about it. Been a long few weeks." She sighed.

"Long few years." I nudged into her. "Hopefully not too much longer. What did Chase have to say?"

"The usual. He misses home, that they are rumoured to be being deployed in the next few days." She shrugged. "I just want them both home."

"I know, me too. Me too." I nodded, finishing my coffee then grabbed my things. "You got a letter to send to Chase? Want me to take it?" I asked.

"No, it's okay, hun. I'll post it when I'm in the city." She smiled sweetly at me.

"No worries, how is work going? Any big names to look out for in the book world?"

"Oh, there's a few. I'll bring you some of the new ones that are due out. I love my job, I basically get paid to read."

"Dream job right there. How's the hot CEO of CHP?" I swayed towards her.

"Carter Cole?" Her eyebrows raised, as she gave them a seductive wiggle. "Oh-so-dreamy and hot. His wife is a lucky lady." She sighed. "Man, if only I was that little bit older, I could have met him five years ago and I could have been his wife. But I can perv over him, it's nice to have a cheeky look when he does come down to the offices." She winked then laughed as she grabbed her bag. "I'll see you tonight, hun, dinner at mum's tonight?"

"Oh, yes. And try and sneak a photo of him."

"Just google him." She rolled her eyes and walked out the door. I couldn't help but laugh at her.

"Google it is. Spoil sport," I muttered to an empty house with a ghost of a smile on my face.

CHAPTER 17

DARCEY

It had been four weeks.

Four weeks and still no letter from him.

That could only mean one thing. They had been deployed to wherever the hell they were. All I wanted was to have one note, one call, one message to let me know they were both okay, that they were both safe.

I tried to keep myself busy, my ballet studio was booming with business and all my classes were booked solid which I was grateful for, but it was hard to concentrate when my mind was constantly with him. Wondering where he was.

I walked into the studio to set up for my first class of the day; my little ballet class. The children were so sweet, I loved their innocence and excitement they had every time they walked into the class.

I played the warm up music, smiling when I heard

the door go.

"Miss Darcey," they called out as they came running in, all wearing their light pink leotards, tutu's and ballet pumps. My heart exploded.

"Hey." I turned round, dropping to the floor and opening my arms as they came for a group hug. "You ready to dance?" Excitement was in my voice as they all screamed.

The morning flew and me and Robyn were at my mum and dad's for dinner this evening. I only had two classes on a Friday as I liked to spend the afternoon with my family. It sort of became a tradition since Conor and Chase left for the army.

I was lazing in the garden, waiting for Robyn to finish work, the sun beating down on my skin. It felt nice to take in the quiet for a moment.

I heard my mum call out to me from the kitchen. "Darcey, there is someone at the door. Could you see who it is please?"

I rolled my eyes as I dragged myself off the sun lounger and walked back into my parents' home, through the kitchen and down the hallway towards the double oak doors. I pulled both handles and opened them at the same time, my heart shattering in my chest when I saw an army sergeant standing in front of me, slowly removing his hat.

I knew what was coming. My legs felt weak beneath me as I screamed at the top of my lungs for my mum. She came running down the hallway, her eyes wide as she saw who was at the door.

"Mrs Sawyer. May I come in?"

She stood aside as she let him through and walked us to the lounge, sitting down next to me. My hands were shaking, my skin cold and clammy.

"The commandant of the British Army has entrusted me to let you know that Chase is missing in action. Him and his colleagues were in a Humvee, driving back to base, when their vehicle was hit by the enemy."

I grabbed my mum's hand, squeezing it as her other hand went up to her mouth as she let out a high scream before sobs fell from her eyes. Panic rose within me as the tears began.

The sergeant continued. "I have also been asked to inform you about Conor Royce. We have you down as his next of kin," he muttered to my mum.

The blow of the news of Chase hit me like ten-ton of bricks, and now we were going to be hit with Conor.

I looked at my mum, she was as white as a ghost, rocking back and forth as she sobbed uncontrollably. My arms stretched around her, trying to comfort her. My eyes darted to the sergeant as he shuffled in his seat, a grimace apparent on his face.

"Conor Royce was also in the same Humvee..."

Before he finished, I howled. An uncontrollable sob leaving me from deep within.

"But when the Humvee was checked, none of the squadron were in there. They are all missing in action. We will be sending a band of troops out," he said quietly, his fingers wrapped round the cap of his hat.

I felt the air being knocked out of my lungs in that moment, my heart obliterating into nothing but shards as they pierced through me, cutting me so deeply.

"We will be in contact if we get any news on Chase and Conor, Mrs Sawyer. I am terribly sorry to have to bring you this news. You will receive a phone call when we have updates."

His mouth pressed into a thin line as he saw himself out. I dropped my arms from my mum's body as I stood on shaky legs, getting to the bottom of the stairs and crawling up until I got to the landing. Pulling myself up on the stair bannister and walking slowly towards Conor's room, everything blurred around me.

An unbearable weight crushed in my chest, a burn scalding my throat, feeling like acid crawling up and dissolving my wind pipe.

I couldn't breathe.

My stomach was in knots of grief.

I pushed the door to his room as I fell to the floor, heart-breaking sobs leaving me. Both of the men I loved with all my heart were missing. The awful thing is that me and my mum will endure this pain again when we break the news to Robyn and my dad.

I can't imagine feeling what my mum is.

I crawled under his duvet and cried. I cried until I had no tears left, my eyes dry but sobs still escaping. I cried until the room went black, and I exhausted myself into darkness.

Remember that black hole I went into four years ago? I was spiralling back into it again. But this time, I didn't have him to pull me back out of it again.

-

I woke the next morning, my head fuzzy. It was just a dream, a bad nightmare.

I sat up in bed, heart palpitations flitting about in my chest when I realised I was in his room, Robyn still asleep next to me wearing some of Chase's clothes.

It wasn't a dream.

This was real life.

We were living this nightmare with no guarantee of when it would end.

I tiptoed out of bed, not wanting to wake Robyn. I felt like I had grit in my eyes, I had hardly slept.

I walked downstairs to see my mum sitting at the kitchen table, staring into the garden. Her eyes were bloodshot and red, her lips cracked, and her nose red underneath where she had been wiping her nose with a tissue.

"Mum," I said softly, pushing my own grief and feelings down, so I could get through a conversation with her.

Her face turned towards me slightly, she was a ghost of herself sitting there.

"Did you get much sleep?" I said, standing next to her.

"No." Her voice was small. I wrapped my arm around her, pulling her into me.

"Let me make you a tea, then go to bed. Even if it's to watch the tele and have some quiet time," I said a little louder, my voice echoing round the room as I walked through the kitchen to put the kettle on.

I heard slow, dragging footsteps coming down the hallway. My dad. Grey, broken and beside himself. My mum stood slowly, wrapping her dressing gown round her tiny body as my dad smothered her with his arms as they both let out choked, silent sobs.

I placed their tea on the dining room table, standing next to them, wrapping my arms round them before leaving the room whilst pushing my own tears off my cheeks. I made my way back into Conor's room, rolling myself in a ball and falling back into sleep.

-

The next few weeks merged and faded into one. It was like Groundhog Day; every day was the same. Waking up, crying, sitting and waiting for the call to let us know our boys were coming home, but each day that passed, we all lost a slither of hope of them being found.

We all walked round in dazes, like zombies. Like passing ships in the night, barely muttering two words to each other.

We weren't living, we were surviving. There was a difference.

We still hadn't had an update on either of the boys, and week five was soon approaching.

I just wanted out.

I just wanted to hear that they were okay, that they were safe and just got lost.

I know that sounds silly, but it's the only thing that kept me going. Having Robyn here helped, but she was consumed in her own grief.

After this happened, she confessed that her and Chase were together and have been since prom night. Of course I was happy, over the moon in fact, but this just crashed and burned over everything I had ever felt.

I pulled the last photo out that Conor sent me, memorizing every detail of him.

His green eyes were my favourite out of all of him.

I missed him terribly.

What I would do to hear his voice call me "baby girl."

One last time.

CHAPTER 18

CONOR

The piercing screams that were coming from the cells next to mine were horrific. I didn't know where I was, how long I had been here, or who was here with me. I just knew it had felt like a lifetime. The days rolling into one.

The rooms were damp, dark and smelt so bad. All I cared about at this moment was getting to Chase, to survive long enough to find him.

I could hardly sleep, but the little sleep I did manage to get was plagued with nightmares. They were always the same, haunting me.

My mind flashed back to the moment it all happened. We were in the Humvee on our way back to base after a day of patrolling the civilian town. As we approached the final stretch, we were flash-banged and then tear-gassed. Every single one of us had a bag put over our head, ropes round our wrists and were thrown into a moving vehicle. We were left like that for two days, only having half the sack moved to have a sip of water before being plunged into the darkness again.

My heart had been shattered into a thousand pieces knowing that Darcey and the family had probably been told by now that we were missing in action or presumed dead. The photo I had looked after for so long had gone too. I missed seeing her beautiful smile, but she was imprinted in my brain, there was no forgetting her. The pain that was impaled through me every hour, of every day was indescribable.

Day number fuck knows.

The screams next door were getting louder and every fibre in my body knew it was Chase, but I couldn't fucking get to him.

I tried, God I tried.

I jumped in my skin, my lifeless, dull green eyes wide when I saw a man masked up, walking towards me, a machine gun swinging round his body, his arm reaching for the sack before he threw it over my head, shouting aggressively in a language I didn't understand as I heard more footsteps marching towards me. I was dragged up by my dirty, sweat-stained tee and forced to move with them.

My eyes darted around in the sack over my head, the tortured screams getting louder. "Conor!" I heard a blood curdling scream that sent shivers down my spine. My heart

thumped when I realised it was Chase.

"Chase!" I screamed out. "Chase, CHASE!" The veins in my neck throbbed as I strained my voice, my blood running cold when I heard a loud gunshot next to me, the screams stopping.

Fuck, no. Fuck, no. Please God, no, no, no.

I felt myself slowly dying inside. I prayed, fuck did I pray, that they didn't just shoot my best friend.

Maybe they shot the ground?

Maybe they missed?

Maybe they did it to scare me?

I heard a heavy door swing open, the men walking with me talking away, with not a clue what they were going on about.

The sun was beating down on my abused skin, instantly burning from lack of sunlight. I felt the warmth, the sunshine hurting my eyes where I had been hidden for so long in darkness.

My legs gave way as someone kicked at them as I tripped, then I was being pushed to the ground, my face hitting the hard sandy floor. I felt my nose crack, but I didn't care. The pain inside me overtook the physical pain I was in.

The sack was removed with force from my head, my eyes darting around me to see if anyone I knew was near me, but they weren't. It looked like we were in a run-down factory. I just couldn't make sense of any of it.

I felt like my eyes were burning to ashes from the intense sun. I threw my arms over my face, trying to shield myself when I felt an almighty blow to my ribs, making me roll on my side before taking another boot to the ribs, then another one to my face.

Spit flew from their mouths, covering me in their saliva.

This was it.

The moment I was beaten to death.

I just hoped my letter made it to her, just hoped that she knew just how fucking much I loved her.

I would wait for her until we met again.

I was rolled over, a stranger staring down at me. All I could see were his hazel eyes as he lifted the machine gun above my head, lining it up right between my eyes.

Squeezing my eyes shut as tight as I could, he muttered something before I heard the gun shot, the pain ripping through me, then another gun shot before everything went black.

My thoughts drifted to her. She was guiding me, guiding me home.

My baby girl.

My Darcey Sawyer.

My thoughts quietened, the noise around me deafening with guns firing all around me before I gave in to my fate.

CHAPTER 19

DARCEY

It had been eight months since we received the news that Conor, Chase and their entire squadron were missing.

Every day I woke up thinking that today would be the day that we heard something, to hear that they were okay, and they had all been found safe and well.

Me and Robyn moved back to our home after spending three months living at my parents, we just couldn't leave, but we knew Conor and Chase wouldn't want us moping around. They would want us upbeat and positive, and we were trying.

I left her a cup of tea on the side as I got ready to leave for a run, it just helped my mind quieten for a bit. I slipped my running shoes on, putting my phone in my arm sleeve as I ran down the stairs and onto the pathway, slipping my ear phones in and playing Second Hand

Serenade, "Fall for you," as it reminded me of Conor; the night of my eighteenth he was listening to it.

Spring was blooming everywhere you looked, and I just hoped that Conor and Chase could see just how beautiful it was, wherever they were.

By the time I got back, it was mid-morning. I only had afternoon classes today, and Robyn would have already left for work. I opened my front door and made my way to the shower; the sweat was dripping off of me. I walked into the main bathroom, turning the knob on the shower before walking into my bedroom and pulling out my leggings and one of Conor's tops.

I walked over to my desk, running my finger tip along the edge of the glass box where I stored his letters. I had one more come after the one I sent. I sent one back but never had a response. I was too late.

I opened the lid of the box carefully and pulled the letter out, reading it again, trying to piece my broken heart back together.

Darcey, baby.

We are moving out in a couple of days, so I don't know when you will next hear from me.

I just wanted you to know how much I love you, and I will always love you. Until the day my heart stops

PROMISE ME

beating.

I have loved you from the moment I saw you in your kitchen when you were fourteen.

I have loved you in secret, and out loud.

Loving you out loud is my favourite.

You complete me.

If I make it back home, promise me one thing?
Promise you'll marry me.
Please.

Always yours, only mine.
Love Conor x

I recited my response to him, out loud, as if he could hear me.

"I promise.
It's always been you.
Only you.
Promise me one thing?
Come home, I need my groom.
Only yours, always mine.
Love Darcey."

The tears sprung to my eyes, my voice hoarse. I struggled

to swallow, I felt like I had swallowed sandpaper.

I read his letter every night before bed, it just doesn't get easier. I folded the letter and placed it on top of the others before closing the box, shaking my arms and hands, trying to shake the shiver that was crawling over my skin before walking towards the shower to wash my tears away.

Once my ballet dance classes were over, I came home and sat on my sofa, watching Friends and drinking a bottle of wine, waiting for Robyn to come join me.

Seven o'clock rolled around and she walked through the door, looking dead on her feet.

"Hey," she called out as I heard her bag hit the floor, and the dragging of her feet down the hallway. "I don't know how much longer I can keep up this travel to London." She sighed as she flopped down on the sofa, putting her feet on my lap.

"Rough day?" I asked, handing her the glass I got for her earlier and pouring it with wine.

"Not even a rough day, just a long day. Just been one of those weeks," she huffed before

taking a big mouthful of wine.

"We all have those days." I patted her foot, smiling at her. "Tomorrow's a new day, and one day closer to us hopefully seeing Conor and Chase." My smile faded before I quickly plastered it back on again, the tears threatening to come. I didn't want to blink, because if I did, the tears would fall again.

I couldn't keep putting myself, and Robyn through this.

PROMISE ME

This was becoming a regular occurrence; drinking wine, moping, crying, drinking more wine.

I woke Friday with a banging headache, me and Robyn stayed together. We got ourselves so worked up over everything, I just didn't know how much more we could take.

My parents were going through hell, and I just wanted to take it all away from them. Take their pain as well as my own.

I felt awful, and I cancelled my class today. I just wasn't up for it.

I convinced Robyn to take the day off too, she was burning the candle at both ends. It took some doing but I did it, selling it that we could lay on the sofa all day and binge all the *Twilight* movies. Who doesn't love a glittery vampire and a hot man-turned-werewolf?

By the time we were finished, it was time to go to my mum's. As much as I loved going there, I hated it as well. Seeing your parents so broken and unable to soothe them was just too much sometimes. They were desperate for answers. My dad looked like he had aged about ten years, he went grey overnight. His crystal blue eyes, like mine, were dull, lifeless. I missed his glisten, his sparkle.

My mum had given up. She hardly came out of her bedroom. My dad was breaking but he had to be strong for both of them.

We eventually got out our pyjamas and got dressed, heading down the stairs to the car, and heading to my parents.

When we got there, we let ourselves in.

"Mum… Dad?" I called out as I put my bag and trench coat on the chaise lounge in the hallway, Robyn following suit.

I walked into the kitchen first. Neither of them were in here. I walked back down the hallway and into the lounge to see my mum asleep on the sofa, curled into a ball, clinging onto a photo of Conor and Chase.

My heart broke on the spot, falling out of my chest and into the burning acid of my stomach.

I walked through the lounge, to the back of the room, to see my dad standing, vacant, looking out onto the garden. I walked quietly over to him, wrapping my arms around his waist and snuggled into his back. His hands covered over mine before he choked out sobs.

I decided to order us a Chinese, my mum wasn't in no fit state to cook and I just wanted to make sure they had both eaten. Once it arrived I served it up, pouring us all a glass of wine. Me and Robyn walked the food through before taking our seats on the plush sofas. We were never allowed to eat in here, but mum had given up with her rules and with how house-proud she was.

My dad took his plate from me, my mum taking hers from Robyn as we both sat down and begun eating when my dad placed his plate on the floor, as he stood up and walked towards the television, pulling the drawer open that sat underneath as he rooted through the DVD's.

I knitted my brows together, throwing Robyn a confused glare when I saw him pull out the old video camera from the back of the deep drawer and plug it into the back of the television before clicking play.

It took a moment to come on, but when it did, it was videos of a young Chase and Conor, playing in the garden. My dad smiled weakly, picking his plate up and sitting down next to my mum. He leant over and planted a kiss on her cheek as she sat, her eyes fixated to the screen before palming her tears away. We sat eating in silence as we enjoyed hearing their voices and seeing them, even if it was only through a television screen.

Once we were finished, I cleared the plates and walked through to the large kitchen, Robyn following behind me.

"God, I am tired." Robyn sighed.

"Me too, it's mentally exhausting, isn't it?" I said as I rinsed the plates in the sink before loading the dishwasher. "Think we should just stay here tonight, save driving home," I suggested.

"Fine by me, as long as I can go to bed soon." She laughed quietly.

"Go to bed now, I'll finish off down here. I can't switch off just yet." I smiled at her as she placed the cutlery and wine glasses down, pulling me in for a tight hug before she disappeared upstairs.

I washed the glasses up and left them on the draining board. I would never be forgiven if I broke one of mum's crystal glasses. I put the cutlery into the dishwasher and switched it on. I turned the kitchen light off, the low humming of the dishwasher keeping me company for a while, whilst I stood in the kitchen, looking at all the photos on the fridge, smiling at the happy memories.

My eyes moved to the one from prom night, of me and Conor. His arm wrapped round my waist, him pulling me into his side. I still remember how he clung onto me so tightly, as if he was afraid I was going to run away. His smile was everything, he lit up any room he walked into.

I was so desperate to hear his voice, see his beautiful face in person. Photo's just didn't do him justice.

I let out a deep sigh before walking upstairs to his bedroom, closing the door behind me and stripping out of my clothes. I pulled his drawers out and grabbed a mustard-yellow T-shirt, slipping it over my head, bringing it to my nose and sniffing. A small smile spread across my face, his smell lingering faintly, making me feel whole inside for a moment.

But that was it, a small moment of feeling full and content washed away by a tidal wave of grief and loss.

By the time I finally fell asleep, it was early morning. The constant battle with my thoughts was too much to switch off. As each day went on, our hope diminished that bit more. My mum was calling the army every day, just to see if she could get a little update, but nothing. They were so tight-lipped about anything and kept telling her that they would contact her when they had news. She was starting to fear the news would never come.

We all were.

PROMISE ME

I woke at nine, after a few hours' sleep. I felt like death. My eyes were dry, bloodshot and felt like they had dirt embedded in them. I dragged myself out of bed and towards his shower. I just wanted to be as close to him as I could.

After my shower, I slipped my clothes on from last night, folding the mustard tee up and putting it back in his drawer.

As I walked towards the staircase, I heard the sound of a male voice. My heart raced in my chest, my ears thumped from the rush of blood. I flew down them, seeing the sergeant that delivered the news just over eight months ago, his hat off, a look on his face that I couldn't quite gauge.

I darted my eyes from my mum, to my dad, and then to the sergeant, listening to the blur of words that were coming out of his mouth, seeing my mum fall, my dad grabbing her as I heard the screams shatter through me.

CHAPTER 20

CONOR

Eight Months Ago

I jolted awake, eyes wide and panicked.

I was scared, my heart thumping in my chest, bouncing around my ribcage, not being able to calm it.

I looked down at my hands. I had tubes coming out of me, bandages wrapped round my chest and torso. The distant beeping becoming more apparent to me now.

I was in the military hospital.

I turned slightly, wincing at the burn and shooting pain that shot from my stomach up to my chest. The pain was caught in my chest, causing me to clutch at it, gasping for breath as I reached for the nurse button, hitting it as fast as I could.

I felt like I was having a heart attack, the pain crushing.

An older nurse walked in. "Good to see you awake,

Conor, I'm Nurse Maria." She smiled down at me as she clicked the call button off.

I couldn't help but look at her confused. Damn I *was* confused.

"My chest, I think I'm having a heart attack." My voice was panicked.

"Where is the pain?" she asked as she walked towards me, her voice calm. I pointed to just under my heart then moved my hand to the middle of the chest.

"You're not having a heart attack, darling." She smiled her warm eyes at me, "It's trapped wind. Try and move a bit, I'll get you something to help shift it."

"What happened to me?" I managed to muster as I shuffled up the bed slightly, wincing at the pain that seared through me.

"I'll get the doctor, darling," she said as she poured me a cup of water from the jug and placed it on the table that was now sitting over my hospital bed.

"Have a drink, only sips though please," she said kindly as she walked towards the door. "The doctor will be in soon." She smiled, closing the door behind her.

My heart hadn't slowed at all since being awake, I was trying to piece everything together and the last thing I remembered was Darcey. She was the last person I saw when my eyes closed. I was pulled from my thoughts when I saw a female doctor walk in, smiling down at me.

"Conor," she said, her voice smooth and kind. "How

are you feeling?"

"Confused," I admitted, rubbing my hands together slowly then pressing them back into my chest, palming my skin in small, circular motions.

"That's normal for someone who has woken from an induced coma."

"Coma?" I scoffed, shaking my head. My eyes burned into her.

"Yes Conor. You've been in an induced coma for about two weeks," she replied softly as she came to sit on the edge of my bed, her face soft. "You took two bullets through the chest, which impaled you and left through your shoulder blade." Her voice was quiet now, her eyes darting back and forth to mine.

"You lost a lot of blood, the bullet hit a main artery. If it wasn't for the rescue team being there when it happened, you would have died."

"The rescue team..." my voice trailed off. *Died? I could have fucking died. Shit.*

"Yes, the general lieutenant is outside, waiting to speak to you. Are you in pain?"

"My chest is tight, I have an awful crushing pain. And I'm just sore." I slowly pointed to my chest and shoulder.

"That would be the trapped wind," she said, confirming what nurse Maria said a few minutes ago. The doctor continued, "Where we had to operate to stop the bleeding, it can cause trapped wind because we have to move around in there. And the soreness is from the wound. I'll get the nurse to bring you some painkillers and I'll top your morphine up," she said as she stood, readjusting my drip and changing the bag over before walking to the door. "See you soon, I'll be back round tonight." She closed the door behind her.

A coma?

"Royce," I heard the lieutenant snap as he walked through the door. "I'm lieutenant Tyrrell."

"Lieutenant Tyrell," I muttered, holding my hand up to salute him.

"Drop your hand, boy," he said, his voice quiet as he came and sat next to me. "How are you feeling?" His eyes darted from my chest to my eyes.

"Confused," I muttered again, feeling slightly agitated that I had to repeat myself. "Have you told my family?" I asked, the question paining me. I know they weren't my biological family, but they were all I had. All I wanted from a family.

"No, not as yet. And we won't until you have made a full recovery," he said sternly, his eyebrows pulled together slightly.

"But they won't know I'm safe." I sat up slowly.

"They know you're missing, that's all they need to know at the moment."

I went to argue but it was pointless. I wouldn't win this.

"And Chase? Where is he?" Panic rose in my chest at the memory flashing through my mind of the gun shot when I heard him scream my name. Tyrell's eyes left mine and shot down to the floor, focussing on his feet.

"We still haven't found him." His eyes shifted to mine.

My eyes stung with tears, my throat tight and constricting. "How could you have not found him?" My voice was raised and hoarse.

"I can't discuss that with you." He shook his head. "I need to know he's safe," I argued back.

"And when we know, I will tell you," he said defensively.

I couldn't help but eye roll. "Am I allowed to know what happened to me?"

"Of course." He placed his hat on the bed next to him. "When your team went missing, the first thing we did was assemble a squadron to where the Humvee was found. It took us a month to track you down, using maps and drones to see what was around. We found a redundant factory that we were getting a few infrared images from. When we got there, that's when we first saw you. You were laying with a machine gun to your head. I gave the order for them to shoot, but as they pulled the trigger, the enemy retaliated, but with a stroke of luck, we managed to shoot him first, the bullet hit him but as his arm dropped, he pulled the trigger, sending two bullets through your chest. We only found you, Parker and John. No sign of Chase, Ryder or Sam." He shook his head.

"Were Parker and John okay?" I asked quietly, trying to process everything that had just been offloaded to me.

"Parker, yes." His voice was now quiet. "John, unfortunately not."

I wiped a stray tear from my face at the news we had lost one of our own.

"Rest up, Royce. Once you're feeling up to it, rehab and counselling will be arranged," he said as he stood up, putting his hat on.

"Can I make a call?" I asked, desperate to hear Darcey's voice.

"No, not at the moment," he said before walking out the room, not giving me a chance to answer him.

Anger bubbled inside me, my stomach twisting in knots, my eyes stinging as the tears began to fall again.

I felt broken.

I just wanted to go home.

I woke the next morning, the nurse placing breakfast on my over-bed table.

"How are you feeling this morning?" she asked me, smiling as she put the plate down.

"Sore." I sighed.

"Once you've had your breakfast, I'll come back and

remove your dressing and check you over." She nodded before walking out of the room.

My eyes looked down at my toast and cup of tea, a small groan leaving me. The toast tasted of cardboard, the tea like cat piss. Not that I knew what cat piss tasted like, but still. I didn't understand why I couldn't call home to let them know I was okay. It's more Darcey, she must be going out of her mind.

I didn't even get the chance to see if she replied to my last letter or not.

I pushed the toast away after only managing a mouthful when the nurse came back in.

"Not hungry?" she asked.

"No." I sighed heavily.

"You need to eat."

"I'm not hungry." I rolled my eyes, shrugging my shoulders. I heard her tut and let out a sigh, but I ignored her.

"Okay, let's get these dressings changed," she muttered to herself, washing her hands under the tap before walking over to me. "Sit forward please," she said as she slipped her gloves on.

I winced as I moved forward, her fingers fumbling on the string that was tying my gown together, undoing it and pulling the gown down my arms before pushing me back slightly. My eyes looked down, the dry blood and ooze that was sitting on the white, cotton dressing made my stomach go. Not because I was squeamish, but because it just made it all real. It hit home.

I tossed my head back into the pillow, staring at the ceiling, letting out a deep sigh.

"You okay?" she asked as she started undoing the dressing, her voice showing her concern.

"Yeah, fine." My voice was soft and quiet.

"I like your tattoos," she said, hearing the smile in her voice I pulled my head forward, looking at her, smiling back at her.

"Thanks."

"You're welcome, do they have any meaning?" she asked as she continued undoing the bandage.

"Some do, some I just had done for the sake of it." I shrugged.

"Do you regret any?"

"No, not a single one." I tilted my head, taking a deep breath as I felt her peeling the bandage away from my skin.

"What's your favourite one?" she asked me. I think she was trying to keep me distracted, and it was working.

"This one," I replied, my voice cool and calm. I looked down and pointed to the one of Darcey before smiling.

"She's beautiful," the nurse cooed.

"You have no idea." I nodded.

After five minutes, the dressing was off. She walked

it over to the orange bin in the corner of the room before coming back over and looking it over.

"How's it looking?" I asked, anxious.

"Not bad, still a bit oozy but that's normal. We changed it a few times whilst you were asleep but maybe a bit of air will do it good." She nodded to herself. "We will get you up in a bit, stretch your legs," she muttered as she walked over to my file, jotting down her notes.

My curious eyes wandered down to my chest and to the bullet holes sitting above my left nipple. How they didn't go through my heart, I would never understand. But then it hit me, it was her. My guardian angel. I was meant to return to her.

I wanted to touch them, but I couldn't. Trying to get your head round being shot twice was something I couldn't explain. I was lucky. I was one of the lucky ones, I knew that.

My mind was swirling with questions. What if the rescue team didn't show up? The bullets would have gone straight into my skull, killing me instantly.

"Okay, Conor, I'll be back in about an hour. Can I get you something else to eat?" the nurse asked as she stood by the hospital door, pulling me from my dark thoughts.

"No, thank you." I smiled weakly at her. She bowed her head before walking out and closing the door behind her. My head fell back, my eyes heavy, my chest crushing. It was all too much.

PROMISE ME

-

A week had passed, and I felt a lot stronger already. My therapy started this week. I didn't want to talk to a stranger, but I knew I had to.

I was being moved from the hospital and into a rehabilitation centre for God knows how long. There had been no update on Chase, and no update of when Darcey would be told that I was okay.

Maybe they were holding out for news on her brother before letting me home?

I really didn't know.

I had a small bag of my clothes brought over from base which I was taking with me. I sat on the edge of my bed, my letters from Darcey were also in that bag, along with the one she sent me after we were deployed. Smiling, holding back the tears, I read it in my head.

I promise.
It's always been you.
Only you.

Promise me one thing?
Come home, I need my groom.

Only yours, always mine.
Love Darcey x

"I promise you.

I do.

I will be home."

I whispered to the letter, it's the only promise I could keep.

She asked me to look after Chase, and I couldn't do it.

I broke my promise to her.

I felt like a disappointment.

How could I face her if something has happened to him? She would never forgive me.

Fuck, I could never forgive myself.

I looked up to the door when I heard it open to see the lieutenant walking towards me.

"Royce," he said abruptly. I stood, saluting him before grabbing my bag and walking towards the door. I ushered past him and stood in the hallway, waiting for him.

"Give me your bag," he instructed. I handed it over to him. "You need to take it easy," he said as he started walking beside me.

"I know, I know," I huffed. "I just want to go home."

"I know you do, soldier, but I need you better first. You can't go home. Not yet, it's too soon," he said with a grimace.

I stopped for a moment, clutching my chest, taking a

few deep breaths. I felt breathless all of a sudden.

"Everything okay, Royce?" lieutenant Tyrrell asked, gripping my shoulder.

"Yeah, just a bit breathless," I admitted.

"Don't rush. Take it easy. We've got all the time in the world."

We didn't.

I wanted this over.

Completely over.

CHAPTER 21

CONOR

"How are you feeling?" Dr Harper asked me, her hazel eyes penetrating through me.

"Good and bad days, I suppose." I shrugged as I lay on the couch in her clinically white office.

"That's normal, Conor. You have been through a lot in the last five months. But you have also come such a long way from when I first met you." She gave me a reassuring smile.

"I don't feel like that," I admitted, picking the skin on the side of my nails.

"Talk to me. Why don't you feel like that?" she asked, putting her leg over the other one so they were crossed. Her long brown hair was tucked behind her shoulder, her head bowed as she started to jot down notes. The notes. I hated the fucking notes. I hated being documented, being judged.

PROMISE ME

Her eyes flicked up to mine, and she pushed her black, thick framed glasses up her nose.

"It's the nightmares. The not having closure on Chase." I shook my head.

"Tell me about the nightmares," she said, her pen scratching on the paper. It was eating at me.

"The screams are the worst, and they are always Chase's. I know that sounds silly, but I am trapped in the dark, damp room. It stinks. I am dirty, hungry, broken. It's always the same. I hear the men walking towards my room, then I hear Chase call me, screaming for me. I run to the door, banging, pleading for them to let me out, pleading for them to let me see him. Just to make sure he is okay. Just so I can keep my promise. My promise that we would both come home." I shook my head "But I can't. The door is opened, and I am shot through the chest by someone in a mask with golden, hazel eyes. I fall on the floor as I'm gasping for breath, the air being pulled out of my lungs. I can still hear Chase, but now he is begging me to help him, begging for me to get to him and bring him home. I hear their voices again. But I can't do anything now, I can't respond." My heart is beginning to race in my chest, the blood pumping through me so fast I can hear it in my ears "I am bleeding out on the floor, everything around me blurring out when I hear another gun shot and I am thrown into darkness." I sniff, fidgeting on the couch then I take a breath before I carry on.

"Then there is light, the light that is Darcey. It's always Darcey. She is standing there, looking down at me, the sun shining behind her beautiful face, her blonde hair blowing softly in the wind. She is smiling at me, holding her hand out to help me up." I smile "We are on a beach, she whispers the words, 'I love you,' then she is gone, she is fading and moving away from me. But I can't move. I can't run after her. I go back to bleeding out in that dark, damp room before my eyes close again, but this time when I wake, I am in the hospital. The dream continues on loop, constantly, until I open my eyes. When I do finally wake up, I am sweaty, my throat sore from the screaming, I'm assuming. I am just exhausted with it all. I am broken. I want this over, I want to go home and get out of here."

My heart is racing just talking about it. I can feel a cold sweat coming on. My eyes dart round the room as I grab the glass of water on the table next to me, drinking it as fast as I can.

"Conor, these dreams are normal. You have had a very traumatic experience that no one should ever have to go through. It is being made worse by the fact that you don't know what has happened to your best friend. You are being kept in the dark. Also, you're not allowed to go home and see your family, and I couldn't imagine being where you are now. But, we will get through this together, we will get you home. You said about keeping a promise... Promise to who?" she pried, no writing this time, just a sincere question.

"To Darcey," I said quietly.

"You haven't broken that promise, have you," she said, her eyebrows raising, not sure if she was asking me or telling me.

"Well... I have to an extent. Because I am safe, but he isn't. I will be going home, he may not," I admitted, my eyes looking at the ceiling.

"But you can't let your recovery slow down because of a promise you haven't broken. You are being too hard on yourself," she said softly.

That was the final strike.

My blood boiled.

I had no control on my temper.

"TOO HARD ON MYSELF?" I screamed at her as I stood from the couch, my fists balled, grabbing my glass with my water in it and throwing it across the room.

"I HAVE BROKEN MY PROMISE. I BROKE THE PROMISE TO THE GIRL I HAVE LOVED SINCE I WAS SIXTEEN. MY QUEEN. THE GIRL I AM SO DEEPLY IN LOVE WITH IT SCARES ME. DON'T BULLSHIT ME WITH YOUR THERAPY SHIT."

My teeth grit, my veins pop in my neck.

I hear the siren, the siren that she had pressed because I have just lost my shit.

She stood slowly. "Conor, you haven't broken anything. Go back to your room, cool off. We will continue this tomorrow." Her voice is cool and calm.

I look behind me as I see two male carers waiting to take me back to my cell. My box room with a shitty view. I drop my head in disappointment. One step forward, ten back.

"Take your medication with your lunch," she said as I walked out the door like a scolded child. "It'll help."

I turned my head and looked over my shoulder at her. My eyes apologizing for my behaviour.

I saw her mouth, "it's okay," with a hint of a smile on her thin lips.

I focussed on the airy, light hallway in front of me and walked towards my room. My anger slowly leaving my body as I got further away from her office.

I was slightly relieved when the meds kicked in, my heart rate slowing down completely, my rage non-existent. I hadn't a clue what they were giving me, and in this moment, I didn't care. They were helping.

I laid there, stretched out on my bed, staring at the white ceilings, my eyes fluttering between sleep and the dream world. I just wish it was the dream world and not hell where my mind kept taking me.

I just wanted it to all be over now, but I feared it wouldn't be. I feared I would be haunted for the rest of my life.

A few hours later, I woke to find Dr Harper sitting on

the edge of my bed, her eyes gazing down at me, her smile soft.

"Hey, Conor." Her voice was quiet and calm.

"Hi," I muttered as I rubbed the sleep out of my eyes.

"How are you feeling?"

"Better," I said, slowly sitting up.

"That's good, the medicine helped then?" Her smile appeared again.

"They did." I nodded. "Will I have to be on these for life?" I was terrified of the answer.

"No, just until the nightmares get better," she said. "Just until we can clear your mind a bit."

She scooted closer to me, taking my hand in hers. "We will get there, you have already made such great progress in the last five months. I am really proud of you Conor. Get some rest, we will discuss tomorrow." She patted my hand, then stood from my bed as she walked out the room.

After dinner, I reached under my bed and pulled out a tin box.

My box full of letters from Darcey.

I opened the lid, smiling as the scented paper filled my nose from her perfume that she sprayed on each of her letters. I read every single one, like I did most nights, just so I could feel close to her.

It was dark by the time I had gone through most of them, when I saw my dog tags sitting at the bottom of the tin. I picked them up, running the steel beads through my fingers, letting out a snort at how much had changed.

Before I met Darcey, this was my life, my dream. It had always been this. But since meeting her and falling for her so fucking hard, this wasn't what I wanted anymore. I just wanted her. She was my dream, my home.

I dropped the dog tags into the tin, putting the letters over the top and closing the lid before sliding back under my bed.

I laid down, letting my thoughts take over my calm mind, I wanted to stop them, but I couldn't.

-

I woke up, the nightmares plagued me once more. I feared they would never stop, only hoping that they stopped once I was home with Darcey.

Home, where I was safe.

It was four in the morning. I slid out of bed before dropping to the floor and doing my two hundred press-ups, then my hundred sit ups. I needed to keep fit, active. I walked into the bathroom, stepping under the warm shower, trying to relax my tense muscles. I always felt tense. Even when I felt calm, relaxed, I was still tense.

I wanted to go for a run, but I was scared that if I did leave and run, I wouldn't come back. Not that I could go anywhere, it was like a prison. No one left, no one came in apart from who needed too.

I had another therapist session this afternoon. I

wasn't looking forward to it at all, but if I had any chance of getting out of here, then I needed to do them and not lose my shit like yesterday.

But it's so hard when they get in your head, spitting shit out to you to make you doubt yourself. I knew what I felt, I knew that I had fucked up. I didn't need her telling me I was wrong. I knew I wasn't wrong. But I needed to play by the rules.

Play by the rules to get the fuck out of here and back to my girl.

My baby girl.

My little grunge.

CHAPTER 22

DARCEY

Present Day

"They've been found," I muttered as I approached my mum who was being cradled by my dad.

"Yes. But as I was just saying to your mum, when we found Chase a few weeks ago, he was in a very bad way, and still is in a very bad way. I can't say much more than that, although he won't be home for a while, he is safe. I thought it would bring you some comfort." He nodded slowly at me before his eyes moved back to my mum who was sobbing in my dad's arms. I didn't know if they were tears of joy or tears of fear.

"And Conor?" I asked. "He is okay?" My eyes stung from the tears that were glassing my eyes over, I was trying so hard not to let them out just yet.

"We have him too. He is better. Took us a while, but we got there," he muttered softly, a small smile gracing his face.

"When will he be home?" My voice sounded desperate, Robyn was now standing in ear shot.

"I can't say at the moment, but it will be soon," he said as he stepped back towards the front door, turning his body to face my parents. "Mr and Mrs Sawyer, we will call weekly with updates on Chase. But you can relax, he is safe. It will be a long road, and we don't know when he will be home, but I hope you will all be reunited soon." His voice was soft, his face hardened but his eyes showed the emotion that he was feeling. But then maybe it was just a show? This was his job, telling broken families the devastating news that their loved ones have been lost or injured. The unbearable weight on his shoulders must be crippling.

I was back in the room when I heard the front door shut, my mum's sobs loud as she gripped onto my dad. The rush of relief washing over me, us, that both our boys were safe.

They were coming home.

We didn't know when, but they were coming home.

That evening we headed back to our house, back to some normality as such. We thought it was best to leave my mum and dad alone for the evening, give them some space to process everything.

The knotting feeling in my stomach, that I thought would ease when we knew they were safe, was still firmly there, but I think that was because of the unknown still. We didn't know what lay ahead for us or them.

I couldn't stop thinking of Chase and what he must have been through, and why he couldn't come straight home. My heart hurt at thoughts that were running through my head at a hundred miles an hour.

It had just gone eleven o'clock, and my mind was wired. I couldn't sleep.

I got out of bed, throwing on my dressing gown over my nightie and getting into my car. I went into auto-pilot, driving to my parents. I pulled in the driveway, parking my car in front of the side-gate before walking towards it, pushing it gently.

I stood in the garden for a moment, just looking at my surroundings when I started walking deeper into the garden, making a bee-line for the pool house. I pushed the brown, glass door open, the smell of chlorine hitting me, burning my nostrils, but instantly filling me with comfort.

Memories flooded back of my eighteenth birthday. I don't know what I was thinking, flirting with that bartender, putting myself in that situation. I was so naive and stupid.

It was the thrill. The thrill of getting under Conor's skin.

I wanted his attention, even when he was bad. Even when he was awful to me and made me cry, hating him with everything I had. But I still wanted his undivided attention on me at all times. I was a brat.

I felt anger bubbling inside me at my stupidity. That night could have ended very differently, but as if he knew, my guardian angel was there to save me. Running to my rescue like a knight in shining armour, or more like a knight covered in tattoos and rocking Doc Martens.

God, he looked heavenly that night.

I sat down on the side of the crystal, turquoise pool, letting out a deep sigh. I hitched my dressing gown up my thighs as I dipped my feet into the heated pool, instantly calming. I kicked my feet gently, listening to the sound of the water clashing with my skin, smiling at the noise.

I just wanted to see Conor, to hold him and kiss him.

My mind wandered to the one evening before he left for the army.

It was a warm summer night. We came in here, stripping down to our underwear and diving into the cool pool. I came up for breath, my eyes watching as he swam over to me, snaking his arms around my waist and pulling me into him.

He pushed his lips onto mine, a spark coursing through my veins. His hungry hands round my back, unclipping my bra and throwing it over the other side of the pool, a wicked smile forming on his face.

I instantly wrapped my legs round his waist as he moved to the edge of the pool, my back being pushed up against it. His fingers wrapped round my thong and pulled them to the side before he pushed his own boxers down. No words were spoken, the passion and intimacy were too much.

He lined himself up against my opening, pushing into me, hard and fast.

I gasped, the sensation was something I couldn't even describe.

His hips slowed down as he pushed deeper into me, his hand grabbing my hair and tipping my head back before he started nipping at my chin.

"Oh," I moaned quietly.

"Feel good, baby?" he asked, his breath on my skin.

"Mmhmm," was all I could muster.

When he stilled completely, a whimper leaving my mouth as he pulled himself out, then grabbed my arm as we swam over to the steps. He climbed out, kicking his wet boxers off of his feet, holding his hand out to help me get out the pool. As I stood, dripping wet, he lifted me up and walked me over to the rattan furniture set that was in the corner, dropping me down softly as he knelt between my legs.

He leaned down, nipping my ear, pushing his lips against it.

"Turn over," he ordered.

I closed my legs, then rolled myself over. He leant across my back, his hands running down the side of my wet body as he gripped my hips, pulling them up so my arse was in the air.

"Fuck, you're stunning," he moaned out as he ran his finger down my bum and slipped it straight into me, circling slowly as he stretched me. I groaned, pushing myself up on my arms, my back arching as I turned my head to look over my shoulder, biting my lip as I looked him up and down.

I had never wanted someone so much in my life.

He reared up behind me, his hands sliding from my hips to my bum, pushing my cheeks apart, his breath sucking in through his teeth.

"Oh, baby, you are so fucking perfect. And you're all mine. Every little piece of you. Do you understand?"

"Yes," I whispered. I was aching for him, my sex felt heavy. I needed him inside me. "Conor," I moaned out.

"Yes, baby girl?"

"Fuck me." My voice begged him. All I heard was a growl before his hands grabbed my hips tightly as he pushed himself into me. I moaned loudly at the contact.

His hips were slamming into me hard and fast, not slowing his harsh, relentless movements and I didn't want him too. I needed this, I needed him to claim me.

The familiar tingling spread from deep in my stomach as I felt my orgasm building, fast. I couldn't slow it. I wanted to, I didn't want this to end. This feeling of him inside me, pushing me to my pool of pleasure.

"I'm going to come," I cried out as I dug my nails into the cushions of the sofa we were fucking on, my back arching as I clamped down around him, tightly.

"Oh, fuck, baby, yes, baby. I'm coming." I cried out I felt as I milked him of everything he had. His grip tightened on my hips as he found his release, his breathing fast and ragged. I looked at him over my shoulder, his head was dropped, watching himself still slowly pulsing in and out of me. He stilled, taking his hands off of my hips and trailing his index finger up my spine, causing goose-bumps to swarm over my body. My hairs stood up on the back of my neck.

"I fucking love you, Darcey, I can't even put into words just how much. I don't feel like my words could even do my feelings justice. I love you for infinity, forever and always. Only mine, always yours," he said softly as he pulled away from me, wrapping his muscular arms around me and pulling me down onto his lap before his lips pressed against mine softly.

I pulled away, nibbling my bottom lip with my teeth, my eyes focusing on his plump mouth. I loved his mouth. Fuck, I loved all of him.

"I love you, and I know exactly how you feel because I have been worried that I can't muster up the words to tell you just how deeply I love you. I just want you to know that it's always going to be me and you. Whatever happens. You are never going to be without me, and I am

never going to be without you. Even when things are set out to break us and pull us apart, just know that I will never give up. I will never let that happen. Because you, Conor Royce, are my destiny, my soul mate, my forever. And I will always be yours. Only yours."

He ran his hand round the back of my neck before he pulled me back against his lips.

I sighed. I felt like we were being tested. Once he was home, I was never letting him out of my sight again.

The silence was what I was needed. The pool lights dimmed the glass pool house, giving it a calming feel. I must have been sat here for at least an hour when I heard my phone beep. I grabbed it out of my dressing gown pocket, the screen hurting my eyes it was so bright. It was Robyn, asking where I was. I smiled before I text her back, telling her I would be home shortly and that I just needed a bit of time-out as I couldn't sleep. She replied telling me to be safe and she would see me in the morning.

I slipped my phone back in my pocket, taking a deep breath as I watched the still water. I could have stayed here all night, but I needed to go home, I needed to sleep and let the events of today sink in.

Every day I would wake up now, apprehension filling me as to whether that day was the day that Conor came home. For good. I didn't know if he was going to sign up for another tour, I hoped he wasn't, but I would never stop him.

He wouldn't stop me chasing my dreams, so I wouldn't stop him from doing his. I begrudgingly stood up from the pool, slipping my wet feet into my flip-flops before walking into the garden and closing the pool door behind me, walking to my car. I plugged my phone in and played Second Hand Serenade, "Fall For You," softly through my speakers, reminding me of my King.

Always my King.

The weekend flew past, which I was grateful for in a way, but it was also another two days with no word on Conor or Chase. I sat in the snug overlooking the calm sea when I heard Robyn walking into our kitchen.

"Morning," she said, sluggish and quiet.

"Hey," I mumbled into my coffee cup as I turned to look over my shoulder, giving her a small smile. "How did you sleep?" I asked as my hands cradled my cup.

"Shit." She groaned. "You?"

"Shit."

"I'm exhausted though," she wailed as she added her milk before her hot water to her tea.

"I know, babe, we will sleep when our bodies need it. At the moment there is too much going on." I sighed as I took a mouthful of my black coffee.

"I just want them home," she said as she sat down in

the other corner of the snug, putting her feet on the windowsill that overlooked the sea.

"Me too. And they will be. It's just been made worse as we haven't been told when. But we need to remember they are in the best place…" my voice trailed off. "I hope." I sighed.

"Oh, don't say that," Robyn whined at me.

"I'm sorry, I didn't mean it like that, it was just my brain," I said quietly. "I'm sorry." I gave Robyn my best puppy dog eyes.

"I know, you don't need to say sorry. It's just all a bit much," she admitted, staring into her cup.

"I know," I whispered, standing up and walking over to her before wrapping my arms round her shoulders and hugging her tightly. "We are all feeling the same. Hopefully we get an update soon," I said as I let her go then walked my cup over to the sink and rinsed it out before putting it in the dishwasher.

"I'm going to get dressed for work. You going in today?" I asked as I stood in the doorway between the entrance hall and the kitchen.

I heard her let out a deep sigh before she responded. "No, not today." She shook her head.

"Okay, babe, if you need anything then let me know. I need to go and keep my mind busy. I would love to stay with you, but my mind would run away with me and my anxiety would peak. I've only got half a day anyway, so I'll be home about two." I smiled at the back of her head, her eyes not leaving the sea.

"Love you," she muttered as I walked out the room.

"Love you too," I shouted out as I walked up the stairs to get ready.

I made my way to the dance studio. I had my older girls and boys today, all preparing for their exams. These classes were always bittersweet for me. I loved seeing the kids I had taught from their younger years about to take their exams, but I also got envious because I remember when it was me and how my dream got taken away from me. I love what I do, don't get me wrong, but it was never what I had planned, and I learned that life doesn't always go the way you want it, and I am okay with that.

Everything happens for a reason.

Now, I get to teach the dance that I love so passionately, and to see your students go on to do massive sell-out shows, and get into the royal ballet, is just phenomenal. I am in awe of them and feel like I get to live the dream I so cruelly missed out on through them.

I park outside my dance studio, locking my car and walking into my building. I set everything up and get the music ready, when I saw them walking in.

"Morning, guys," I called out as I sat on the floor to stretch. I still liked to join in where I could, when my leg allowed it.

PROMISE ME

"Morning, Ms Sawyer," Blaire called out, Thea, Florrie, Charles, Nate and Vaughan walking in behind him. They dropped their bags in the corner, all sitting down to kick their trainers off and slip into their pumps. They had chosen to do Odette's dance from Swan Lake. It was a popular dance, but it was a classic. And the judges loved a classic.

We had two weeks to get them to where they needed to be. I had every faith that they would all smash it and pass with flying colours.

"Okay, class of twenty nineteen, step up to the barre, please," I said as I clapped my hands to get their attention from their chitter-chatter. "Guys, come on. You have two weeks, don't get distracted now." I laughed as I played my playlist.

"First position and straight into a plie," I called out as I slowly walked up and down the room, watching their every move, watching to see if they put a step out of place. That's all it would take. One step out of place, or one wrong move. Fuck, even missing a beat on your chosen track was enough to get you thrown out of your exam. And I didn't want that for these kids, they were too good.

CHAPTER 23

CONOR

Present Day

I couldn't believe today was the day I was going home. I didn't know if Darcey and the family had been told that I was coming home today or not. I hadn't been told much to be honest, so I assumed that they hadn't either.

I was sad that I wouldn't be going home with Chase, but he was in the best place. But yet, that still didn't make it easier. I felt guilty for going home without him. We started this journey together and now we were going home separately. I wanted us to end our journey together. I would never get the images out of my head of how he looked when he was found. They haunt me. They will always haunt me.

His screams were the worst. He wasn't the Chase I knew. Of course he was in there, but he was so deep down inside his own body, I was scared they would never get him back, but I was assured he is making progress. I went to see him this morning, to check on him and tell him that I'll be waiting for him. He was coming back, slowly. There were glimpses of the real Chase there when he spoke, when he reminisced with me about our life before the army.

It had already been decided that Chase would not be re-joining the army for another tour, and I agreed. He belonged at home with his family and Robyn. He told me on the bus that him and Robyn were trying to make a go of things and that she was nervous that Darcey would hate the idea.

I remember laughing at him and telling him not to be stupid, of course Darcey wouldn't hate the idea. I told him that she would love nothing more than her best friend and her brother to be together. He still didn't believe me.

I packed the last of my items into my duffel bag, placing my tin of letters on top of my clothes, smiling as I looked down at them before doing the zip of my bag up. I wanted to show her every single letter that she had wrote to me. I sat on my bed, my duffel bag on my lap as I sat anxiously waiting to be told that we were leaving.

I was called into the lieutenant's office yesterday morning, along with the therapist. Harper was called in to tell Tyrell that she was happy with my progress. I was off of my meds and had been since a month ago. I did hit a bit of a darker patch, but Harper caught it just at the right time, which I am forever grateful for. I am just hoping she can fix Chase like she fixed me. She needs to. I needed my best friend back, Zara and Tanner needed their son back, Darcey needed her brother back and Robyn needed the love of her life back and safe.

I hardly slept last night, I was full of anxiety and apprehension. I felt like I had a balloon in my chest that was slowly inflating until the tightness got so bad, my heart started racing, palpitations making it seem as if my heart was on a pogo stick, jumping all round my damn ribcage. The knot in my stomach twisted continuously, making me feel sick. My palms were sweaty, which I couldn't control. My breathing ragged and harsh.

I was terrified.

What if she had moved on in the last eight months? It's not like the army had kept in touch with her or the family as such. She may have thought I was never coming back. I don't think I could take it if she had found someone else, she was the one for me. She promised me that she was only mine.

Mine.

And I was always hers. No one else's.

No one else could compare to her, it was always her.

The realisation hit me. I couldn't be mad though, could I? If she had moved on, she had every right to. I couldn't stop her.

PROMISE ME

You can't help who you fall in love with.

How can I stop her from being happy? I couldn't bear to think about it, but it's something I may have to accept. And if she has moved on, I would do everything in my power to get her back. I couldn't live without her. She was the reason for my existence. The reason for me waking up in the morning and breathing. She was all I wanted, all I needed.

I felt like my brain and heart, the devil and the angel on my shoulder were playing tennis, batting their different thoughts around.

Tyrell cleared his throat. "You ready to go home, Royce?" A small smile graced his aged face, his grey hair cropped and short, fully-clothed in his uniform, the same as me.

"I am," I said, standing up from the bed and placing my beret on my head before putting my duffel bag over my shoulder and walking towards him.

"You did your country proud, son," he said as I stood in front of him and saluted him. His arm reached up to his head as he saluted back to me. I waited for him to drop his arm before I dropped mine, then bowed my head as I followed behind him.

I didn't know where I was, and how long it was going to take me to get home, but the day was finally here.

I was going home.

The drive was long, and quiet. So deathly quiet. I kept wanting to spark up a conversation with Tyrell, to ask him about his home life and family, but I couldn't quite pick up the courage. I felt like a shadow of myself, not quite sure if the old Conor was ever coming back.

"Where am I dropping you, son?" His eyes pulled off the road for a moment as he stared into mine.

"Err, just drop me in the high-street. I'll find my way," I mumbled.

"Do you not want to go home?" he asked, confused.

"I do, I've just got to do something first." I smiled at him before my eyes batted down to my duffel bag that was on my lap, my fingers clenching tightly to the ends of it.

"Not a problem." He nodded. "Do you think you'll sign up for another tour?" he asked, this time keeping his eyes on the road.

"I'm not sure yet, how long have I got to decide?" My voice was small and quiet, my heart thumping in my chest.

"A few months. Normally, you would be re-registered automatically, but because you were injured, it is your choice," he said bluntly.

"And if I decided that I didn't want to re-register at this time, and then say, six months later I wanted to re-join, what happens then?"

"You can re-join. Now you have been in the army, you can re-join anytime. If there is a position available of course, then yes, you can." He smiled.

PROMISE ME

"That's good to know," I mumbled. It was good to know I had options in case Darcey didn't want to know me anymore.

The rest of the journey was again, in silence. My nerves started when I saw the sign for Sidmouth, we were so close. So close to being reunited.

"Is anywhere along this road okay for drop off?" Tyrell asked, his eyebrows raising under his hat.

"Yeah, anywhere please. Just stop here, it's fine," I said as I released the grip on my duffel bag as the car started to slow before stopping completely.

"Thanks for everything. Tell Chase to get better, we all need him home," I muttered as I opened the passenger door, my army boots touching the kerb.

"Will do. Take care of yourself, Royce. I'll be in contact in the next few weeks to see what you want to do in regard to re-signing up," he said as he reached his arm over and squeezed my shoulder. "If you get into any bother, or need anything, then please, don't hesitate to contact me."

"Thank you again." I smiled at him as I exited the car, throwing my bag over my shoulder before shutting the door.

I stood, watching Tyrell drive away, down the high street. Once he was out of sight, I threw my duffel bag over my shoulder then made sure my beret was sitting correctly.

I looked down at myself in my duty uniform, taking a deep breath as I started walking up to where her shop was. I knew she was in there. Wednesday was her busiest day.

My heart was thumping so loudly in my chest, it was like someone was beating a drum. I felt tingly, a cold sweat coming over me. I swallowed down the lump that was creeping up my throat as I approached her shop.

I stood at the half-white, frosted window, smiling at the sign.

Darcey Sawyer's Ballet School.

I dropped my duffel bag at my feet, my eyes leaving the sign and now looking straight through the window for her.

It was time to see my Queen.

-

DARCEY

I locked the office up at the back of the studio, then turned the lights off. This was the worst room. There were no windows which made it so dark. I hated working with a light on when it was daylight outside.

My last class had finished for the day. I had back-to-back lessons all day, so was grateful when four o'clock rolled around. I closed the door behind me and walked out to the main dance studio area. I grabbed my ruck-sack with my clothes in. I was meant to be getting changed but I couldn't be bothered. I was so tired.

I looked down at my black lycra leggings and converse. I had my leotard on underneath but threw a cropped jumper over the top once I finished dancing. This studio needed to be cold, so as soon as you stopped dancing you felt it.

I looked in the big floor-to-ceiling dance mirrors. I looked like a wreck. I needed a shower. My long, blonde hair was pulled up into a tight ponytail, my face pale and clammy. I sighed, putting my bag on my back and taking my phone off charge, my eyes on the screen seeing what I had missed.

As I walked through to the front of my studio, I felt a familiar feeling wash over me, the hairs on the back of my neck standing, goose-bumps smothering my skin. The feeling of someone's eyes on me, and I knew exactly who's eyes they were.

My eyes darted up from my phone, looking out of the half-frosted window, when I saw him.

Conor was home.

My lost king had returned.

CHAPTER 24

DARCEY

I winced when I heard the bang of my phone hitting the dance studio floor. My heart raced in my chest.

Were my eyes deceiving me or was he really here? I was frozen to the spot, the fear that he wasn't real, that he was just a figment of my imagination.

No, he was really here. Standing proud in his army uniform, his beret sat on his chocolate hair. He looked even more handsome than I remembered.

I saw him move slightly, his eyes not leaving mine as I walked towards him, the excitement and nerves combusting inside of me. I picked up the pace as I ran at him. He was in the doorway as I jumped into his arms, wrapping my legs so tightly around his waist I thought I was going to crush him before looping my arms around his neck and cuddling into him, my face burying in his neck as I breathed in his scent.

PROMISE ME

It took a moment before the tears began to fall, my sobbing uncontrollable as I clung to him, not wanting to let him go ever again. His arms tightened round me, a whisper leaving his mouth.

"Baby girl." He sounded choked, squeezing me even harder and kissing the side of my head. I didn't realise just how empty I was without him. Part of me was missing while he was gone, and now I felt whole once more. Nerves ripped through me, it had been so long since I touched him, felt him and kissed him. I was overwhelmed and consumed with my love for him. I was instantly drunk off of his scent.

"You're home," I wailed, pulling my head out of his neck and moving my hands from around his neck to his face, resting them on the side of his head, my eyes darting back and forth over his beautiful face, taking in every part of him. I was absolutely petrified that he was going to go and never come back again. My eyes pierced through his stunning green ones, our connection zapping through me, the rush of love coursing through my veins.

"I'm home. For good," he mumbled before he pushed his lips on mine, our tongues intertwining. Our kiss was hot, heated but sensual. Four years and eight months since I last kissed him, and I didn't want him to stop. I felt my insides alight with the passion that I had for him.

He pulled away, a small whimper left my mouth as he did, his green eyes burned into mine.

"Fuck, Darcey," he choked out. He let me down slowly, my hands still on him, not wanting to lose my contact from him for a second.

"You're home," I muttered again, my eyes glassy. My heart was galloping in my chest. I couldn't believe he was standing here in front of me.

My king was home.

I had so many questions, but I didn't want to ask him yet. I just wanted to take him home, shower him and feed him. I debated taking him back to my parents' house, but I didn't think it was right. I needed to talk to my mum, dad and Robyn. Do it gradually. It would be too much for all of them at the moment.

We all just want Chase home, and having Conor come home without him would just rub salt into the already gaping wounds. I dropped my hands from his chest as I placed my forehead on his heaving chest. After I moment I moved, my eyes darting down, following my arms before I bent and grabbed my phone off the floor, frowning at the cracked screen. Brilliant. I unlocked it and messaged Robyn, letting her know that Conor had come home and that we needed to talk and that I would call her tonight.

I took my backpack off and slipped my phone in one of the side pockets before slipping my arms back through the straps. Conor just stood there, a ghost of himself. It unnerved me.

PROMISE ME

Where was my cocky boy?

I let out a little sigh, looking down at my feet and kicking my shoe. It took me a moment to pull my eyes back up. I felt shy, nervous and scared.

Fuck was I scared. God knows how he was feeling.

I reached out and took his hand, gripping it tightly as we walked towards the front of the shop.

"Let's go home." I gave him a small smile, his face mirroring mine before he followed behind me as I walked to the car. I took his duffel bag off of him; it weighed a ton, but I wouldn't let him take it off me even when he protested. My lips curled slightly as I saw a flicker of my old Conor coming through. My heart burst.

I lifted the boot of my mini before slipping his bag in and slamming the boot down before walking round to my side of the car, Conor still standing on the kerb.

"Get in the car," I said gently, opening my door and sliding in, hoping he would follow. Luckily, he did.

"You okay? You've gone a bit vacant," I asked as I started the engine, slipping the gearstick into first and pulling away after looking over my shoulder as I drove down the road.

"I'm fine. Just all a bit surreal. I feel weird being home, like I don't deserve to be here," he said quietly, his fingers locked together, his eyes on his feet in the footwell of the car.

"Of course you deserve to be here." Sadness now

laced my voice.

"I don't." He shook his head before his beautiful, broken green eyes flicked up to me. I could feel his intense, sad stare on the side of my face. I pulled my eyes from the road and turned to face him.

"Don't ever say that," I said a little more harshly than I would have liked but I couldn't help it. I know he has been through a hell of a lot, but he should be grateful that he was home and that he was safe.

"Conor, please listen to me," I said as we pulled up outside my house. "Don't ever feel like you don't belong or deserve to be here. You deserve to be here like all of us. You can't think negatively." I sighed. "I hardly ever thought negatively when we got told that you and Chase were missing, and we stayed hopeful because we all knew that you were coming home. Even though we didn't know when, we knew you would come back to us. And you did. Well, one of you did, and Chase will be right behind you when he is ready." I nodded, then wiped the stray tear that I hadn't realised had escaped.

"Conor, please, I need you to be strong. I need you to realise you were saved for a reason. I can't have you self-doubting everything. I know you feel bad, I know you feel like you should be taking Chase's place. But you're not. You're home with us. With me. All our lives are mapped out for us, we have no control over them. So please, just realise how lucky you are to be home and safe." I smiled at him.

I felt awful for being so harsh but he needed to know that he was sent home for a reason. "Let's get indoors, I'll put the kettle on and we can chat," I muttered as I opened the door of my car, walking round to the boot and grabbing my backpack and his duffel bag. I felt him next to me, close. He took the bag off of me, throwing it over his shoulder before stepping back onto the kerb.

"So, this is you then?" he muttered, his eyes shooting up and looking up the winding stairs to my little bit of heaven.

"Yup, lovely, isn't it?" I smiled as I started climbing the stairs, him close behind me. I unlocked the front door, dropping my back-pack on the side table as we walked in. I would go through it later, but at the moment I had more pressing matters to deal with, someone more important.

I walked through to the kitchen, my eyebrows knitting when I didn't see him follow me. I walked back towards the hallway, he was standing just inside the front door, his eyes looking around my home.

"You coming in?" I asked gently, pulling him from his thoughts.

I felt my heart crack as I focussed on him. He looked like a lost child. All I wanted to do was guide him home and make him feel safe, but I just had to trust that he would be back with me soon. I didn't want to rush him, but I was also terrified that I was going to make him worse, push him away and lose him completely.

I wanted to help him, heal him and love him. It was going to take time, and I was prepared to put the work in.

My mind started ticking about work, I was going to have to call some favours in and see if I can get some cover for a couple of weeks. I feel awful because of exams, but I would still be there on the side-lines cheering them on.

I walked closer to Conor, taking his bag out of his tight grip, putting it at the bottom of the stairs in the hallway before grabbing his hand softly and leading him through to the kitchen, then walking him over to the little snug that overlooked the calm sea, hoping that would help calm his busy mind, even if just for a moment.

"Sit there, I'll make you a tea," I said, leaning down and pecking him on his lips. My fingertips ran along his shoulder and across his back as I walked over to the kitchen to make him some tea. Tea always made everything better.

My mind was hectic, racing and going over the same questions again and again. I put the spoon in the sink before taking his drink over to him, his eyes turning up to mine. His beautiful green eyes were tormented, broken and bloodshot. I sat down in the other corner of the snug, putting my feet on the edge of my chair and bringing my knees to my chest, resting my hot cup of tea on top of them, my eyes on him the whole time, his eyes out at the sea.

"How could you ever leave here? It's so peaceful and tranquil," he said, still not breaking his gaze from the calm, glistening ocean.

"I have to, I don't want to, but I have to for work." I laughed softly. He just sighed before staring back into the never-ending sea.

"What can I do to help you? I feel helpless, I'm rendered useless…" My voice trailed off.

"You can help me by giving me you," he muttered in a low growl, his eyes drawling up and down my body.

"Me?" I asked dumbfounded.

"Yes, you. I need you. I want you. Please," his voice was desperate.

"Okay," I whispered as I stood from the snug, taking his cup before putting it on the breakfast bar behind us then walking over to him, standing between his legs.

"Shower," he said bluntly, but his eyes were dark and hooded. He needed his release and I was going to give it to him.

"Shower," I muttered back to him before grabbing his wrist tight and dragging him.

"Come on, Royce, let's get you washed." I winked at him as I lead him towards the bathroom upstairs.

I wanted to cleanse his soul. Help him start over.

I will get my king back.

I had to.

CHAPTER 25

DARCEY

I walked him upstairs and stood outside my bedroom, dropping his hand as we got there. I pushed open my bedroom door and stepped in when Conor spun me around, picking me up and carrying me over towards my bed as he pushed his lips onto mine, slipping his tongue between my full, cushioned lips. I took him greedily, stroking his tongue with mine. My hungry mouth wanting so much more.

"Darcey, fuck," he groaned as he pulled away. "I am going to do my nut in about three seconds from you just kissing me," he muttered, dropping me down and pushing me on the bed. "I need to make you come, because as soon as I'm inside you, I am going to lose it so quickly. It's been four years, baby girl, and it's only you. I need you. But I need to make you come so fucking hard that when we do fuck, you'll still be riding your orgasm," he growled as he stood over me, his eyes so dark they intimidated me slightly.

He unbuttoned his army jacket before discarding it on the floor. He was wearing a tight, white tank-top. His tattooed arms rippled under his hard muscles. My mouth instantly dried, my knickers soaking wet. His dog tags were hanging down his chest. He looked so hot.

I didn't care if he stood there and come over me, I could combust just looking at him.

He shuffled out of his cargo trousers and kicked them over with his jacket before he knelt in-between me. My greedy eyes snaked down his body as they focused on his hardness. I sat up, shuffling myself to the edge of the bed as I pushed his boxers down to his thick, toned, tattooed thighs.

My eyes lit up at the sight of him, his arousal beading on his tip already. I looked up at him through my lashes, moving my mouth towards him and taking him deep. His delicious groan vibrated in his throat, his head tipping back as he took a chunk of my hair. I slowly moved my lips to his tip, giving it one flick of my tongue before pushing my plump lips back over him, when he shouted out, "Fuck."

He thrusted his hips into my mouth, pushing himself down the back of my throat as he came, hard. I took him out of my mouth, wiping the corner of my lips with my ring finger before licking the tip and smiling up at him.

"Fuck, Darcey. What was that? Was that even a minute?" he laughed as he pushed me back on the bed. "My turn to taste you."

He hooked his fingers round my tight, lycra leggings, pulling them down my legs, a small groan leaving his throat as he licked his lips looking down at me before pushing my black ballet leotard to the side, exposing me. A wicked smile spread across his lips before he pulled his bottom lip between his teeth and sucked in his breath as he dipped his head between my legs, running his tongue along my core, making me moan.

His tongue glided in my folds before he sucked hard on my sensitive bud, sending a pulsing sensation through me. He lined his finger up at my soaked opening, removing his hot mouth from me for a moment as he pushed his finger deep inside me, slowly pumping it then covering me with his mouth again as he continued flicking and sucking over my bud.

I felt myself building, I wanted him inside me so bad. I didn't care if he came as soon as he touched me, I needed him. I needed him close.

"Fuck me," I moaned as I fisted his hair, his green eyes batting up at me before he shook his head, his tongue following which changed the sensation, making my legs tremble.

"Please," I whispered, his delicious moan agreeing with me. He slipped his finger out of me and knelt up on his knees as he pushed his finger into his full lips and sucked it dry.

"Tastes like honey, so fucking sweet," he murmured, my arousal evident on his lips. He grabbed my cropped tee, pulling me towards him so I was sitting up. Grabbing the hem, he pulled it over my head and threw it behind him, then he ran both his fingers under the straps of my leotard, gliding them down my arms.

I hooked my thumbs inside the side of the leotard that I was wearing and shimmied myself out of it, now completely naked and ready for him. He grabbed his vest, yanking it over his head. The sound of his dog tags clicking together as they hit, before sitting back on his chest, pulled my eyes to them. I noticed his bullet scars, my heart instantly breaking and hurting.

I didn't have a moment more to think about it as his hand came down between my legs, pushing me towards my headboard so I was sitting up against it. He pressed his thumbs into the inside of my thigh, hard, which caused a pinching sensation, but I didn't care. Pushing my legs further apart, my knees dropped to the bed, so I was completely exposed to him.

I looked down at his cock bobbing and how hard it was again. He crawled over me, his hand grabbing round my hip and dragging me down slightly. He took his hand from me and held the base of his cock as he lined himself up, a whine leaving me at his contact. I was already clamping down. He pushed himself in slowly, just the tip at first. He threw his head back, a growl leaving his throat, his eyes squinted shut.

"Fuck, I've missed you," he said. He stilled for a moment, then looked down at me, pushing himself in a little bit more to begin with, stretching me in the most delicious way. He stilled again, giving my body a moment to adjust to him after so long. He slowly pushed his hips towards me again, pushing himself deeper and this time not stopping until I took every, glorious inch of him.

My body stretched completely for him, only him, claiming him once more.

I heard him hiss as he started thrusting into me. I forgot how good he felt, a moan of appreciation slipped out between my lips.

He sped up, hitting into me harder, the sound of our skin hitting against each other. His hand flew to the headboard, tightening his grip as he ploughed into me, hard and fast. His breathing became ragged.

"Oh, baby girl, fuck, you're so tight. Come for me, baby, come for me," he called out.

I felt my walls clamp round him as he continued, I was so close to him pushing me into heaven.

"Oh, Conor," I cried out, my hand flying to his dog tags that were dangling down in front of me, wrapping my fingers around the ball-chain and pulling him closer to me, so his forehead was resting on mine as I felt that delicious wave of pleasure swarm over me before the cool chill that followed crashed over my body as I came, my toes curling as my orgasm rocked through me. My moans spurred him on as he came inside me, my name rolling off of his tongue.

We laid in each other's arms, only my thin bedsheet over us, my head on his chest, my fingertips walking up his tattooed stomach, slowly trailing to his chest. His lips were on my head, kissing me softly. I pulled my head up, my eyes going to his scars. My gentle fingertips running slowly over them, his eyes looking down at me.

"You okay?" he mumbled.

"Do they hurt?" I asked, turning my eyes up to face him.

"No, baby." His head shook softly, his chocolate brown hair flopping onto his forehead, his hand pushing it back. My eyes started glassing over, I couldn't believe he had been shot, I can't believe he could have died. His hand moved to my face, his thumb and finger grabbing my chin gently, tipping it up to face him. His lips covered mine, kissing me softly before he pulled away, his hand still in place.

"Don't be sad, I am here. I am safe." My eyes batted down, closing as a tear escaped. "And Chase will be home soon too." His mouth was back on mine. "I promise you," he muttered.

Once I had composed myself slightly, I lay my head

back on his chest, listening to his steady heartbeat. "Shame we didn't make it to the shower," I groaned.

"Oh, baby," he said seductively. "We have all the time in the world for showers."

A small smile graced my lips. Bits of old Conor were starting to show, only slightly, but it made my heart sing knowing that he was still in there, deep down.

"I missed you so much, don't ever leave me again," I muttered, my voice small. My fingertips played with his dog tags.

"Darcey, I am never leaving. Ever." He sighed. "And I can't even begin to put into words how much I missed you." His voice was quiet. "It's my demons, I'm scared they'll never go away."

I leant up on his chest, taking his hand and bringing it to my lips before kissing the back of it. "We will get through this; the demons will go. It'll just take time. Small baby steps." I smiled at him, leaning towards him and pecking him on his lips.

"So, Mr Royce, any hot army nurses I need to worry about?" I asked, wanting to change the subject.

"Only Nurse Maria. She was smoking." He winked at me before laughing. A pang of jealousy shot through me instantly at the thought of him being with someone else. No, he wouldn't have. He wouldn't do that to me. He must've sensed the panic or saw it on my face.

"Oh, baby, I am joking! Maria must have been in her

sixties, very happily married. Can't say she didn't fancy me though but didn't take her as much of a cougar." He chuckled. "I told you, always yours. Do I need to know anything?" His eyebrows raised.

"Only yours," I muttered. "Always. I couldn't even think about anyone else, it has always been you, it will always, only be you. I love you."

"I love you too, with all my heart. I need you more than you know right now." He sounded desperate.

"I will be here, right by your side. I'm not going anywhere, Conor. Not now, not ever. I promise you. It's me and you, forever and always. You have my heart and soul, just promise me I have yours back."

"Baby girl, you don't even have to ask. I promise you, you have my heart and soul. Always yours, only mine." His beautiful smile was big, his teeth on show. I could never get over how beautiful he was.

I leant into him, kissing his fully tattooed covered neck. "I love you so much," I whispered.

"I love you more, now, how about that shower?" he asked.

"Sounds amazing," I chimed back at him as I went to sit up before he wrapped his arm around me and pulled me back into him, covering my mouth with his.

After our shower, we sat in the lounge as we both cradled hot cups of tea, his arms snaked round me, pulling me close to him.

"When are we going home?" he sighed, knowing it was going to be mixed emotions.

"Whenever you are ready." I took a mouthful of my tea. "Just let me know and I will call them."

"How about tomorrow?" he asked as he placed his tea on the coffee table.

"Tomorrow could work. Friday evenings became our thing when you were gone. I'll drop Robyn a call in the morning, let her know. I've got to pop into work, just to fill in some last bits of paperwork for the dancers doing their exams, so why don't you come with me? Should be no more than half an hour." I smiled at him, placing my tea on the table next to his.

"Sounds perfect," he muttered as he snuggled into me, the sun setting in the distance. "I love this house."

"I know, it's amazing, isn't it?" I sighed. It really was. We were tucked away, sitting pretty on a hill with not much around us apart from the beach and the sea. It was all I needed. I was hoping being here, away from everything, would help him heal. Help him recover.

We spent the rest of the evening watching tele. Every time I went to speak about what happened, he clammed up, refusing to answer me and just saying, "Not now, later."

I didn't want to push it, but I also thought it may help if he did just speak about it, even if it was just little snippets.

We climbed into bed. It was a warm evening, so I had the window open slightly as we got a cool sea breeze through. Conor wrapped his arm round me, pulling me towards him as he spooned me, kissing my neck and whispering, "As much as I want to taste and touch every single inch of you, then make love to you, I am beat. You'll have to wait until the morning."

His teeth grazed along my earlobe, my stomach knotted, the apex between my legs aching to be touched by him. I went to respond but I heard his soft snoring in my ear. My eyes looked over my shoulder to see him sleeping like a baby, his chocolate hair fluffy and resting on his forehead.

I wanted to kiss him, smother every part of his body, but he needed to sleep. God knows when he last had a decent night's sleep.

I held onto his arm that was wrapped round me, squeezing it slightly before my own eyes fell heavy.

I woke, startled, jumping out of my skin.

My heart fell through my chest when I heard screaming coming from beside me.

"NO, NO, PLEASE. STOP. CHASE, CHASE, I'M COMING. NO, NO NOOOOOOO."

I rolled over, panicking. Conor was on his back, saturated in sweat.

"Baby," I said softly, his eyebrows pulled together, his eyes squinted shut.

"Conor, it's okay... Conor," I said a little louder this time, nudging him slightly.

His eyes sprung open, wide and panicked. His breathing was fast and harsh as he sat up on his elbows. He looked round the room, then down at his clothes before his pained eyes found mine.

"It's okay," I soothed as I took his hand, trying to calm him.

"Baby," he mumbled in a sleepy haze as he took me in his arms, pulling me into him and holding me tight before he crashed back out again.

My heart was thumping in my chest, like a drum. I couldn't stop it.

He must be so haunted. I didn't even know where to start when it came to helping him.

I was now wide awake whilst he was sleeping like a baby. I reached over, straining myself to grab my phone off the bedside unit, unlocking it and searching on how to help.

There was no way I could go to sleep now, I had to do everything and anything I could to help him. I couldn't have the man I love in so much pain. It didn't help that Chase wasn't here, and by the sounds of it, he is in a worse way than what Conor is.

We would start by talking, that's what we were going

to do tomorrow.

    Talk.

    It's the best thing for him.

    He needed to talk.

CHAPTER 26

CONOR

My heart was pounding when my eyes sprung open, my knuckles white where I had been clinging to the sheet underneath me, my body soaked from sweat.

I turned my head, her eyes were on mine, full of worry and sadness. She was sat up, her back against the headboard, a cup of coffee sitting on her lap. She looked tired, the small bags under her eyes puffy and dark, whilst her eyes were bloodshot. She still looked absolutely stunning though, she really was the most beautiful woman in the world.

And she was mine.

"Hey." My voice was small, slightly embarrassed.

"Hey, you," she mumbled as she turned to face me.

"You okay?" I turned on my side, my elbow propped up, so my hand was resting on the side of my face.

"I am, but I'm worried about you, Conor. You were

in a state last night. The screams were heart-wrenching. I've been looking it up and you need to talk. Small baby steps." She smiled her perfect fucking smile at me.

"I don't need to talk," I snapped, throwing the duvet off me. "That's all I've done for the last eight months," I shouted as I climbed out of the bed, looking for my bag.

Why didn't I unpack last night?

I saw it sitting over by her window. I rummaged through it and pulled a pair of jogging bottoms out and top, pulling it over my head and slipping into my trousers.

"Conor," she said calmly, "I just want to help you." Her eyes were on me, not moving. She intimidated me.

"I don't want your help. I don't *need* your help," I hissed at her.

I grabbed my phone and wallet off the nightstand and stormed out of her bedroom. My chest constricted, my eyes blurred. I felt like I couldn't breathe.

I forced my feet into my trainers, walked out the back door and down towards the beach. My anger was rising from deep inside, I needed to walk it off. As soon as I was outside, the fresh air filling my lungs, my mood started to calm.

I looked behind me at her house and saw her standing on the balcony at the back, watching me, not saying a word.

Fuck.

I contemplated going back, but I didn't want to. Not

yet anyway. I didn't want to fight with her, but I felt like I was suffocating.

I didn't know where I was going. I just knew I needed to walk it off.

I took my trainers off as I walked along the shoreline, the cold sea nipping at my toes. I was completely cool now.

Darcey had text me, telling me to take my time. I felt like a complete arsehole snapping at her like that. I knew I had issues, I knew I had to sort them. Don't get me wrong, Dr. Harper helped, so much. She bought me back from my darkest place, but now it was time to open up and talk to Darcey. I knew talking would help. You can't help but instantly feel better and feel the humungous weight lift that crushes me daily.

It doesn't help that Chase isn't here. I want him home with us all.

I am anxious about going home today, I can't help but feel that Zara and Tanner will be heartbroken that I am the one that is home and not Chase. I know they see me as one of their own after I basically moved in, after my mum overdosed and my dad fucked off.

I still remember the day, it was a Sunday. *I had come home from The Sawyers. I didn't normally come back, maybe once every two weeks. I don't know what made me go home that day, maybe it was a sixth sense? I*

PROMISE ME

opened the door to the shithole, a stench of gone-off milk and rotting food making my stomach turn.

I had a shitty childhood. An only child, my mum was more interested in her drugs and my dad used to like beating me down when things didn't go his way. He worked, he tried to provide, but after my mum had me, she just couldn't keep up the clean life that she had before me. She was an addict as a teen, my dad thought he could be the knight in shining armour and save her, which he did. For a while.

She fell pregnant with me, she was lonely and hit a new time low which caused her to relapse. It was the norm for me, seeing my mum taking pills and jacking up every day before she laid on the sofa, passed out from her poison. That's the only way I remembered her. She wasn't the loving mum who couldn't wait for me to come home from school and ask me about my day. I never had playdates. I was lonely, being an only child and not having many friends. I put everything into school, which is why I was a gifted student that got into Buck Hall.

I was the shiny new toy, and I wasn't going to go unnoticed anymore. I was going to leave my mark, my stamp.

Then I met Chase. He was the first one to say hello to me, the first one to make me feel welcome. I decided there and then that we were going to be friends forever. He was too good for me to lose. He helped me when no one else could. I was angry all the time, I liked being a dick around the school. I could do whatever I wanted, people were intimidated by me.

Then I met Darcey. God, I loved her from the first time I laid eyes on her. She made me feel complete, the half that I was missing. But I couldn't help being mean to her, because she was my kryptonite. And I didn't want to show anyone that, especially her.

I was an addict for Darcey Sawyer. I didn't want to fall for her, but I did, so fucking hard. All I knew how to do was push her away, but not completely. No. I had to ruin her school experience because I wanted to be on her mind twenty-four-seven.

I left my mark on her.

I was always going to redeem myself, make me the perfect guy. I always knew I was going to be with her, I just needed to bide my time for her to realise that she wanted to be with me too.

I sighed as I sat on the shoreline, throwing pebbles into the ocean. My mind drifted back to the day I found my mum.

My dad was at work on a double shift as a security guard. I walked into our dingy, dark lounge to see her sitting on the sofa, a needle still in her arm. I didn't even need to go and feel for her pulse, I could see she was already dead.

PROMISE ME

My heart broke right there and then, falling to the floor as I sobbed for the loss of my mum. Part of me felt glad that she had moved on, was free from her demons, but the other part was distraught that I had lost her.

Yeah, okay, she was no mum of the year, but I knew she loved me. Somewhere deep down. Once I had stopped crying, I called my dad, telling him. He didn't return home until three hours later, stinking of booze as he kicked the door down. I was still on my knees on the wooden floorboards of our lounge, anger seeped out of me as he just walked past her.

I stood up, I remember feeling so strong, but I was so scrawny and little at that point, but I think the grief and anger inside me pushed me towards him. I screamed at him as I punched him in the nose then swung for him again, hitting his jaw. He fell back, wiping the blood from his nose as he came for me, laying into me, punch after punch.

I didn't care at that moment, I didn't care if he killed me.

I fell to the floor, my nose and lips bleeding, yet he didn't stop. He began kicking me in the stomach, spitting and cursing at me when relief swept over me as I heard the door open. The ambulance and police crew arrived. I had called them about half an hour earlier. I didn't know my dad was going to be here, but was glad he was, because now I could get out of this hell-hole.

I was ushered out by a friendly male police officer who sat me in the back of one of the ambulances as I was checked over. My eyes were throbbing, and my ribs were sore, but I was okay. I asked the officer if I could make a call. He smiled and handed me his phone as I dialled the only number I knew. Chase's.

Zara flew down with Tanner, by this point social services had been called as I was still a minor. I didn't hear the ins and outs, but I was taken with Zara. She was my guardian. In every sense of the word.

I wiped my eyes; small tears had escaped as I reminisced about my broken past.

I pushed myself off the ground, slipping my trainers back on before walking towards the high street.

I didn't know where I was heading, I just carried on walking.

I found myself standing outside a motorbike shop in the town. God knows what bought me here, but something did. I pushed the door open, my eyes looking around the room to seek out which one I would buy. I noticed a black Ducati Monster in the corner.

I did my bike license when I was nineteen, not sure why, seemed like the fun thing to do. The young salesman walked towards me, smiling as he saw my interest in the bike.

"Good morning, can I help you?" he asked.

PROMISE ME

"I'll take that bike, please."

A couple of hours later, I was driving down the beach towards Darcey's house. I didn't even know if she would still be there or whether she was at her dance school.

Plus I needed to apologise.

I parked the bike outside the back of her house as I ran up the steps. I tried to open the patio door, but it was locked. Shit.

I looked at my phone, it was nearly midday. I ran back down the stairs and hopped onto the bike, moving to the road and making my way to her studio. My thoughts rattled, trying to think what I was going to say to her. I didn't want a big elaborate speech, but I wanted to say more than sorry.

My heart was like a jackhammer when I saw her car parked outside. I pulled up behind it, pulling my helmet off and placing it on the seat before climbing off the bike and walking towards her studio.

I stood outside, taking a deep breath before walking through her door, my eyes searching for her. A small smile graced my face when I saw her standing in the corner, her eyes on mine.

I walked towards her, my strides big so I could get to her quicker. I stood in front of her, towering over her and taking her face into my hands, my lips hovering over hers.

"I am so fucking sorry," I mumbled before covering

her lips with mine.

Pressing my lips on hers, not wanting to move, I heard a chorus of, "Oooooooo," from her students, but I didn't give a shit. I turned my head over my shoulder and smirked before looking down at her again.

"Forgive me?" I pleaded.

"Always."

"Always?" I muttered.

"Always." She smiled up at me.

"Promise me, promise me you will always love me."

"I promise. Promise me you will talk to me more," she said in a whisper.

"I promise." I nodded at her. "You nearly done?" I asked, taking my hands from her face.

"Nearly. How did you get here?"

"I bought a motorbike." I laughed, "I'll wait out front for you. Don't be long." I winked at her, her mouth slightly open but I didn't give her a chance to respond. I turned on my heel and walked towards the door to my motorbike, swinging my leg back over the tank and sitting, waiting for her. I bought her a helmet too. I unhooked it from my handlebars and held it on my lap.

I wanted to go for a ride. I decided we would go to the beach outside hers and I will try and answer her questions. Then I need to shower and brush my teeth. I literally shot out of bed in my mood and ran for the door.

But I can't run anymore.

PROMISE ME

I need to be able to open up and lay all of me on the table.

I trust her. I need her to trust me.

I wanted to get some of this pent up hurt out before we went back to her parents. That's going to take a whole new level of strength for me to get through, but with her by my side, I can get through anything.

CHAPTER 27

DARCEY

I walked out of the studio to see Conor sitting there on a motorbike.

What the fuck.

"Erm, what's this?" I laughed, slightly hysterically, I thought he was joking. They scared the hell out of me.

"It's mine." He beamed his perfect smile at me.

"There is no way I am getting on that." I shook my head, laughing louder now as I started walking towards my car and unlocking it. I felt his arms snaking round my waist, pulling me towards him.

"Come on, live a little. I won't drive fast," he mumbled into my hair before pulling me to face him. "Trust me," he whispered before placing a kiss on my lips.

"I do trust you." I nodded, placing my keys into my back-pack, walking slowly over to the bike, taking my black open-face crash helmet off of Conor, his face smiling like a Cheshire cat. I swung my leg over the seat of the bike, shuffling back as Conor climbed over and settled in the seat before putting his own crash helmet on and starting the ignition to his new toy.

I clung to him as he looked over his shoulder before pulling away and heading to our unknown destination.

I pulled a face when we drove past my house, confused as to where we were going. He drove down the big hill, taking us towards the beach. I thought he was going to stop in the car park, but he didn't. He kept going.

Driving along the shoreline, I was mortified. Luckily, the beach wasn't packed, but there were still people sitting, enjoying the afternoon sunshine. He carried on driving slowly in the shallow sea until we reached a quiet cove. Stopping the bike, he kicked the stand out, getting off and taking his helmet off, placing it on the tank. Taking my hand, he helped me, my legs shaky. He held his hand out, taking my helmet off of me and placed it on the seat next to his.

He took my hand, rubbing his thumb across the back of my knuckles before walking me towards the sea, plonking himself down on the shoreline, tugging me down with him.

"Why are we here?" I asked, my eyes wandering round the deserted cove.

"I want to try," he mumbled, looking down at his trainers as he kicked them together, knocking the sand off.

"Try?" I asked.

"To try and talk."

"Oh," I said, taken aback. "Conor, we don't have to do this. I didn't mean to pry earlier, I know you will talk when you're ready." I nibbled my lip.

"I want to." He nodded, his eyes still not looking up at me, they were still fixated on his trainers. I puffed my cheeks out, grateful for him wanting to open up, but worried it was going to be too much for him.

"I'm sorry again for earlier." His tormented eyes now coming up to mine.

"Conor, please. It's fine. I shouldn't have pushed." I shook my head.

"No, it's not fine, Darcey. What if I lost my shit so bad that I hurt you?" His eyes brimmed.

"You would never hurt me."

"You don't know that," he snapped, a little harsher than intended, his sorry eyes flitting to mine straight away. I reached out for his hand, trying to give him a reassuring squeeze.

"It's okay." A small smile broke out across my face.

"I never want to hurt you," he choked.

"You're not going to hurt me, promise me?" I said as a bit of light heartedness, trying to get him to smile by using one of our lines.

"I can't promise you. I broke my promise when it

came to Chase. Fuck, I couldn't even keep that. I couldn't keep him safe." His head bowed, his hands going to the side of his head as the tears began to fall.

I hurt. I hurt so bad for him, but I felt like there was nothing I could do. I was helpless. I linked my arm through his bent one and pulled him towards me.

"Babe, you didn't break your promise. You couldn't keep him safe, he couldn't keep himself safe. You couldn't even keep yourself safe. But he is safe now, he is where he needs to be to get the help he needs. He is a strong man, he will get through this, as will you." I smiled again at him.

"But I'm not fixed."

"You have been through so much, you can't expect in eight months for someone to click their fingers and it all be okay again. You had a traumatic experience, but you got through it. You're here with me, you're home." I leant across and kissed him on the cheek, wiping his tears with my thumb. "You've got this."

He blinked at me, pulling his lip between his teeth.

"What's going on in that pretty head of yours?" I asked, scooting that bit closer to him.

"Everything. You, us, Chase, my parents... Just a whole lot of shit."

"Fill me in. With everything. We aren't in a rush, we haven't got anywhere to go," I whispered.

"We are meant to be going home, to your parents."

"They'll understand." I smiled, grabbing my phone

out of my backpack and texting my mum to tell her we would be a bit later than expected before slipping my phone back away.

Conor took a deep breath before telling me all about his childhood and his parents. My heart broke right there for him and all that he had been through. No wonder he was such an arsehole when I met him.

I was pulled from my thoughts when he continued speaking.

"Then I got to live with you, and your wonderful family. They took me in when I didn't think anyone would. I felt like I was given a second lease of life." A tear fell from his eyes again.

I went to speak but then he started again, and I didn't want to stop him.

"And yet, I feel like I have been given a third life, and Chase has been left behind. What if he dies? What if he gives up? I have been there, Darcey, I nearly gave up. But every time I thought about doing it, I saw your face. Every. Single. Time. You're my guardian angel, do you know that? Darcey, baby girl, you're everything to me. Don't ever leave me, don't ever stop loving me. You are my reason for getting up every morning. I couldn't go on without you."

I climbed over into his lap, my hands going to his face. His red, bloodshot eyes penetrated into mine before his head bowed, his eyes closed.

PROMISE ME

"Conor, I am never going to leave you. I love you, more than you could ever know. Don't give up on me, don't give up on us and don't give up on yourself." I tilted his head up to face me. "I am so in love with you, in all your forms. Don't ever doubt it," I mumbled before leaning down towards him, kissing him, lingering a little longer, pushing my tongue between his lips.

I wanted to kiss all of his pain away.

His arms wrapped around me, pulling me closer to him, his knees bent up so I was falling closer. Our kiss heated, our tongues entwining with each other as a moan left me. He pulled away, breathless.

"As much as I want to fuck you, I don't want to do it on a beach," he said, smirking at me, a glint of the old Conor coming through.

I smiled back at him as he lifted me effortlessly off of his lap, standing up himself and re-adjusting his jogging bottoms to try and hide his erection. He grabbed my wrist, pulling me towards him as his lips crashed onto mine fiercely, my heartbeat racing.

His hands snaked around my waist, pressing his body up against mine so I could feel how hard he was. I felt his smirk on my lips before his hands ran under my bum, squeezing before he lifted me up, my legs automatically wrapping themselves round his waist.

I wanted him so bad.

He walked me over to his motorbike, his lips still

locked with mine as he placed me on the small seat of the bike, pushing himself between my thighs. His hands moved round my face and cradled it as he placed his lips over mine, softer this time.

One of his hands roamed down the little curves I did have before slipping in-between my legs, his finger running down my core slowly through my leggings, causing my breath to hitch. I forgot how good his touch was.

He pulled his hand away from me as it moved back to my face, his lips hovering over mine as his tongue slowly came towards me, running across the inside of my top lip before slipping into my mouth and kissing me slowly, our tongues caressing each other tentatively. I moaned into his mouth, his grip tightened round my face.

"Let's go home," he mumbled. "Before I fuck you on this bike."

I didn't care where he took me, as long as I got to be with him. He pushed away from me, grabbing his helmet and pushing it over his chocolate hair, then passed me mine as I slipped it on. He started the ignition, kicked the stand away and dropped it into gear as we started making our way home, along the beach.

The ache inside was getting too much, the vibration of the bike was enough to nearly send me over the edge after Conor's little tease. A sigh of relief left me as I saw my house nearing in the distance.

PROMISE ME

He parked outside when I realised I had left my car at the studio. *Shit.*

I hopped off the bike, taking my helmet off and linking my arm through the chin strap. My hungry eyes watched him as he did the same.

"My car is still at the dance studio," I grumbled.

"Will it be okay there tonight?" he asked as he took the key out of his bike.

"Should be, maybe we can grab it on the way to Mum's?" I mumbled.

He didn't say anything else, just grabbed my hand and pulled me so hard and fast up the steps to my house. If he pulled me any harder, I was scared my shoulder was going to pop out of its socket.

When we got to the top of the stairs, I pulled my back-pack off quickly and searched for the keys. The want was getting too much, and I knew he felt it too. He was fidgety, plus his tight, grey jogging bottoms gave it away. A small smile crept on my face and I pulled my bottom lip between my teeth as I unlocked the front door, pushing it open and dropping my bag at my feet.

Conor was close behind me, slamming the door behind him. His eyes were dark and hazy as he looked me up and down. A shiver ran down my spine as he stepped towards me. He pushed me towards the stairs before his lips pressed into mine, his mouth hungry, moving down to my neck as he started tugging at my oversized vest, pulling it over my head and discarding it to the floor.

He nudged me gently onto the stairs as he dropped to his knees, kneading my aching breasts before pulling them out of my constricting sports bra and taking one into his mouth, sucking and licking whilst groaning. He sucked hard before letting it pop out of his mouth, blowing his warm breath onto it.

His eyes burnt into me. "Fuck." He moaned as he took a deep breath. "Upstairs," he growled. I did as I was told and stood shakily as I walked up the stairs, him following close behind me. I looked over my shoulder, his hazy eyes were full of want, his lip between his teeth again.

I stopped for a moment, my eyes trailing up and down his body, I wanted to see every bit of him. I took the final climb up the last three steps, his fingers wrapping round the back of the band of my leggings, pulling me towards him. His hand snaked round me and splayed over my belly, his mouth on my neck, nibbling my earlobe before I felt his plump lips press against it as he whispered, "I am going to fuck you, again and again, and again," before letting me go and walking me into the bathroom.

I wanted him now, I didn't want him to shower. I didn't care.

He closed the door then walked towards me, his eyes looking down at me as he grabbed the bottom of my sports bra, lifting it over my head, throwing it in the corner of the room. He sucked in a breath as his eyes focused on my naked chest, his breath ragged. He hooked his thumbs in the side of my leggings, pushing them down, bending as he helped me step out of them.

His lips were on my thighs, planting soft kisses, making his way up to my sex.

"I want you," I moaned in a hushed voice, desperate to feel him inside me.

He stood back over me, his arms by his side as it was my turn to now undress him. I took his T-shirt off first, my eyes darting across his toned, tattooed body. He turned me on so much. I loved that he was literally covered head to toe in tattoos, my favourite one being the one of me over his stomach. I placed my hand over it, gliding it down his abs slowly as I grabbed the waist of his jogging bottoms, pushing them down, smiling when I saw how hard he was.

We both stood for a moment, admiring each other's bodies. It was literally a few seconds before he threw himself at me, pushing me into the walk in shower. My hand reached out as I turned the tap to get the water running, a spurt of cold water shot out, making Conor hiss before the warm water cascaded over us, a smile on his face, his hot fucking lips on mine, kissing me harshly, the hunger showing with his forceful tongue.

He grabbed my bum hard before smoothing his hand down the side of my thigh and grabbing just under my knee as he pulled it up and wrapped it round his waist, his other hand on my chin, tilting my head back as his mouth moved down to my neck and collar bone before making its way back to my lips. This time, his teeth taking my bottom lip as he gently bit down, sucking on it before releasing it as his other hand ran back up my thigh, under my bum cheek, his finger teasing at my opening, circling the tip round and round, driving me crazy before slipping it in and slowly pumping it in and out of me, his eyes on mine as he watched me.

"I'm addicted to you," he groaned as his pulses sped up, hitting me deeper.

He slipped his wet fingers out, bringing them up to my lips, pushing his fingers into my mouth, a wicked grin spreading across his face as I sucked them dry. He dropped my leg, turning me round and pushing my back for me to bend forward. His hand glided down in-between my thighs, spreading them open before they found their way to my hips.

He lined himself up at my opening before pushing in harsh and fast, my body accepting him as he stilled for a moment. A deep groan left his throat, my eyes looking over my shoulder at him. His hair soaked, sitting on his face, the water dripping down to his nose, falling between us.

Everything about him was a turn on. His eyes darted up from the floor, burning into mine as he slowly pulled himself out to the tip, then pushed himself hard into me. The sound of his skin hitting mine was delicious. My hands were pressed against the tiled wall, supporting me as he continued his slow pull out, and his hard thrusts into me.

"Fuck me harder, Conor," I moaned out, tipping my head back.

One of his hands gripped tightly round my waist, whilst the other found my messy, blonde hair, grabbing a handful and pulling me back towards him as he thrust hard and fast into me, building me up for my climax. He didn't slow down, he kept the harsh rhythm which my body needed.

I needed him.

All of him.

"I'm close," I whined as he squeezed my waist, groaning and hissing. I felt myself clamp round his cock as my body got closer.

"Fuck, oh, Conor," I cried out loudly. "I'm going to come."

A delectable moan came from my lips as I came undone for him. He continued to hit into me hard.

"Fuck, Darcey, Fuck," he growled out as he emptied inside me. I pushed myself off the wall, turning round to face him.

"Feel better, stud?" I licked my lips as I pushed my body up against his wet body, his cock still hard.

"So much better." He smiled as he kissed me, his hands running under my bum and lifting me up, my legs wrapping round him as slipped himself inside me again.

I could never get enough of him.

CHAPTER 28

DARCEY

After our sex filled afternoon, we had to get ready to go to my parents. I felt apprehensive, so God knows how Conor was feeling.

As I pulled my jeans up, I watched him get dressed, his face soft but his eyes filled with nerves. I hoped him opening up to me a little bit today at the beach helped him, I knew it wouldn't instantly fix him, but by him trusting me to talk, or vent, must help him feel better.

I grabbed a tee and threw it on before pulling my hair into a pony tail. Where I hadn't dried it because of our shower fun, it was wavy and slightly frizzy, and I couldn't be bothered to do it. I slipped into my Doc Martens and walked towards Conor who was doing his jeans up. He looked up at me, then batted them back down to his body, pulling his long tee out of his jeans where it tucked itself in before readjusting it.

I took his handsome face into my hands, bringing his eyes to mine. "I love you." A smile spread across my face.

"I love you, grunge," he muttered back, leaning down and kissing me, a small smile breaking on his face as he used my old nickname.

"I love you. Let's go, my parents are expecting us."

We walked down to my car, the evening was pleasant. As we walked towards the dance studio, Conor linked his fingers through mine, bringing my hand to his lips and pressing a soft kiss on the back of it.

"Thank you for today." A little smirk appeared on his face.

"Don't need to thank me," I said quietly, tightening my grip on his hand.

"I do." He nodded, his head bowing down slightly, his eyes narrowing on my car in the distance. "I'm so scared," he admitted, his voice quiet but shaky.

"Of what?" I stopped walking for a moment, turning to face him, my face tilting up to look at his.

"That I am going to fuck this all up. I'm scared I am going to lose you. I am scared that I'm not going to get over this…" his voice trailed off, his hand slipping out of mine before he pushed them both into his back pockets.

"Baby, I promised you. Promised that I would be by your side, promised that I would always love you. You promised me as well, remember? Only yours, always mine." I took his hand back in mine and squeezed it.

"But I keep breaking the fucking promises." He sighed.

"You haven't broken any, Conor. You need to stop beating yourself up so bad over Chase. He is safe, baby, he is being taken care of. There was nothing you could do to stop what happened. I bet he is feeling exactly the same with everything that happened to you." I sighed.

"Conor, you are amazing. Beyond amazing. You will get through this because I am going to help you. Little steps at a time. It will take time, it will be a long road, but we will get there. Promise me one thing," I muttered our line.

"What?" His lips twitched, trying to mask his smile.

"Promise me you won't give up on yourself, promise me that you won't give up on us." My eyes narrowed on his beautiful, big green eyes. I could never get over how handsome he was.

"I promise you," he muttered before placing his hand on the side of my face, cupping it. I leant into it as he craned his neck down to kiss me. "Always yours, only mine."

I heard Conor let out a deep sigh as we pulled into my mum and dad's gated driveway.

"It'll be okay." I gave him a reassuring smile.

I pulled up outside the stairs that led to the front doors. I got out, Conor was by my side instantly. I took his hand in mine as we started walking towards the door. When we got to them, he pulled me into him, kissing the side of my head.

"I love you," he mumbled. "And I've always hated those lion door knockers."

A laugh left him as I knocked.

"Me too." I let out a small giggle, then I side-eyed him, checking his expression. His eyes were darting round the front door, his hand squeezing mine while his foot tapped on the stone of the stairs.

We stood waiting for someone to open the door. I had a key, but didn't want to just let ourselves in.

I smiled when my mum swung the door open, her eyes on me, then Conor, as she let go of the door and threw herself at Conor, sobs leaving her as I watched her crumble into his chest. He dropped my hand, looking at me for what to do. I just smiled, knowing he would know what to do.

He wrapped his big, toned arms round my mum's petite frame and cuddled her, holding her tight. His head bowed as he rested his mouth on the top of her head before his own tears escaped.

My heart broke right there.

I walked past them and into the large hallway, taking a deep breath as I continued down into the kitchen where I saw Robyn and my dad sitting with a cup of tea.

"Hey," I said softly as I walked in to sit next to them

on the sofa.

"Hey, darling," my dad cooed as he leant across and kissed me on the cheek. "Tea?"

I shook my head.

Robyn poked her head round my dad, her face wary. "Where is Conor?" she asked.

"With Mum." I smiled at her, letting out a deep breath.

"All okay?" she asked.

"Yeah, think they're just having a moment." I nodded.

"How is he?" my dad asked me as he put his arm behind me on the sofa.

"Not great, not sleeping and having vivid nightmares. One minute the old Conor shows himself, but he soon reverts back to his haunted self." I sniffed. "It's really sad. He is full of guilt and regret because he is home and Chase isn't." I wiped a tear from my cheek.

"He shouldn't feel guilty," Robyn said quietly.

"I know, I told him that. But he is fighting his own demons. Fighting his thoughts and guilt. He feels like he let me down, let us down. He keeps saying he broke his promise," I said quietly.

"What promise?" Dad asked.

"When we said goodbye, I said for him to promise that they both come home." My bottom lip trembled as I tried to fight the urge to burst into tears.

"And they both didn't come home…" Robyn trailed off.

I bit my lip and nodded, my eyes filling with tears as I palmed them away, but they started to fall when I heard my mum and Conor walking towards us. My head turned round, looking at both of them, their eyes red and their faces blotchy from the tears.

Conor's face dropped when he saw me crying, he ran to my side.

"Baby girl, why are you crying?" he said quietly, scooting towards me.

"I'm okay." I smiled, his face not buying my bullshit. "Honestly, I'm okay."

I lifted his arm up and snuggled underneath it, sitting as close to him as I could, his scent filling my nose.

"Hey." Robyn smiled at Conor, giving him a small wave. He smiled back at her, holding his hand up.

"Good to have you home, son," my dad said as he leant over me, patting Conor on the leg and giving him a wink. Conor darted his eyes down to his lap, and I felt him inhale sharply.

"Glass of wine anyone?" my mum called out.

"Please," me and Robyn said in unison.

"Yes please, babe, just finishing my tea," my dad replied, taking his last mouthful.

"Conor?" my mum asked, her eyes focused on him.

PROMISE ME

"Just a small one." He nodded before his eyes came back over to me.

After a couple of glasses of wine, we were sitting in the lounge. I was cuddled back into Conor on one of the sofa's, and he seemed a bit more relaxed now he was here. Hopefully the wine would help him sleep a bit better tonight.

"Conor, tell me to piss off if you don't want to talk about it, but, what was the army like?" Robyn was sitting at the other end of the sofa that me and Conor was lazing on. My eyes went wide, boring into her. Panic started rising in my chest, I'm sure you could see it thumping out of my chest like you used to see on Looney Tunes.

"Yeah, it's fine," he said flatly, rubbing his lips together before shuffling up the sofa, taking me with him.

"At first it was exciting, it was the unknown. The training was hard and gruelling, but it was fun. Kept you busy, kept you from missing home twenty-four seven. Don't get me wrong, you missed home all the fucking time." His eyes darted to my parents. He may be twenty-four, but he was still respectful.

He gave them a playful smile, his eyes twinkling at them. My heartbeat had slowed, another sign that old Conor was still very much present, he just needed coaxing out of his black hole. Slowly, gently, patiently.

His eyes flitted back to Robyn, his hand rubbing my

thigh slowly as he continued speaking. "But after a few months, the excitement fades and the thought of not coming home for four years really hits you. Getting the letters from Darcey, and Chase getting them from you Robyn," his voice quivered, "They made our weeks... Fuck, I can't even explain how they made us feel. I couldn't do the feeling justice even if I tried." He shook his head, squeezing my thigh.

"We were quite lucky to not get deployed for four years, but again, excitement fills you, adrenaline kicks in. You're fighting for your country, and what an honour that is. But then the nerves kick in, you get scared. You don't sleep, you're on edge all the time. Your friends get injured or even worse killed..." his voice dropped off, his eyes closed, his brows furrowed.

"Some weren't lucky enough to come back home." His eyes opened slowly, hazy and glassed.

I turned my head to face him, gripping onto his hand. The conversation needed to stop, he was doing so well.

"Robyn, how's work going?" I said quickly trying to change the subject and not get him to disappear again.

"Yeah, okay, really busy, which is good. They've put a vacancy out for a new security, not sure if it's for the business or Carter, but he sent an email yesterday." She shrugged, picking the bottle of wine up and filling her glass, holding it out towards me. I took it off of her and poured some into mine and Conor's glasses.

"Could you get me his number?" I heard Conor's gruff voice.

"Carter's?" Robyn asked.

"Yeah." His voice was a little smoother this time.

"Yeah, I'll text Laura, she is in human resources. I'll get her to send the job description and his number." She smiled as she pulled her phone out.

"Thank you," he muttered, a small smirk appearing on his face.

"Be good for you to get into a job, Conor," my dad piped up, filling his own glass up.

"Yeah, I need to work. Can't sit at home all day. I'll drive myself insane," he said before taking a mouthful of his white wine.

"Can we stay here tonight?" I asked. "I've had too much to drink now." I smiled at my mum, batting my eyelashes.

"You don't have to ask, Darcey." She tutted and rolled her eyes. "Your room is still made up, as well as Conor's," she said, taking a mouthful of her drink.

"You kept my room?" Conor asked, slightly shocked.

"Of course we did. It's your room." My mum smiled at him, her eyes warm as she looked in his direction.

"Thank you," he said quietly. "Do you mind if I go up there now?"

"Of course not, Conor, darling. This is your home.

You don't have to ask, ever," my mum responded, trying to reassure him.

"Can you come with me?" he asked as he stood up, his wine glass still in hand.

"Sure," I said as he held his hand out for me to take, which I did, gladly. His eyes lit up, a ghost of a smile appearing on his handsome face.

"Thank you for everything, thank you for making me feel at home," he said to my parents and Robyn.

They all smiled at him, waving at us as we started to walk out the lounge. I looked over my shoulder at Robyn, waving my phone at her, then blew a kiss to them all before we disappeared upstairs.

He walked cautiously down the hallway, a small laugh coming from him. "God, all the memories are flooding back."

"Yeah? What ones?" I asked.

"The one where I came into your room, having a little tease. Fuck, Darcey, I wanted you so bad." He stopped, turning to face me. His hands were in my hair as he pulled my face towards him.

I smirked. "You wanted me so bad that you went to fuck Marie straight after?" My voice was a little harsh.

His face dropped, his eyes wide as they darted back and forth from mine. His hands were now either side of my face. "Only because I wanted you so bad, but I couldn't have you. Please, don't throw that in my face."

PROMISE ME

My heart dropped, I physically felt it drop out of my chest and into the pit of my stomach.

"I'm not throwing it in your face, I was just playing around," I said quietly, moving my face closer to his, our lips so close to touching. He didn't respond, he pressed his lips into mine as he kissed me harshly. He broke away, grabbing my wrist and dragging me into his bedroom, slamming the door behind him.

CHAPTER 29

CONOR

Walking into my room was strange, everything was as I left it. I felt comforted and normal.

It was home.

I took a moment just to take everything in around me. I was still shocked that they had kept my room, I thought they would have turned it into something else. I felt her walk up behind me, wrapping her long arms round my thick body, squeezing me, resting her head between my shoulder blades.

"You know, I spent most of my time in this room when you went away," she mumbled quietly. "It made me feel closer to you."

My hands were now peeling her arms from my waist and pulling her round in front of me. I could stare at her beautiful face all day.

"I'm glad you stayed in here," I said softly as I

wrapped my arms around her and pulled her close to me, kissing her on the forehead. I loved her so fiercely, it petrified me. She captivated me in ways no other soul would.

"Me too." She smiled at me. "You okay with staying here tonight?" she asked as she sat on the edge of my bed.

"Of course." My voice was small.

"I just didn't fancy getting a taxi home," she admitted as she leant back on her elbows, her eyes running from my head to my toes.

"What you looking at?" I smirked at her.

"Some hot as fuck man in front of me, who I'm hoping will come and show me some love." Her eyebrows wiggled before her tongue darted out and licked her lips.

"He is a lucky son of a bitch." I laughed, feeling my cock twitch, my lips spreading into a smile as I headed over to her, grabbing her round the neck, not too tightly, and pushing her back gently as I knelt in-between her already parted legs.

My fingers stayed firmly wrapped round her delicate throat as my lips pressed against hers, her tongue dancing with mine in a hot, sensual way. My free hand roamed down her body, fiddling with her jean button and undoing her zip as her hungry hands pushed them down her thighs before finding their place in my hair, grabbing and tugging as she pulled me closer to her.

Her scent intoxicated me, I was getting my fix from

her. My fingers curled round her knickers, pushing them to the side as they explored, gliding up and down her folds before slipping inside her, pushing in deeply and pulsing them in slowly, hitting her sweet spot over and over. Her sweet fucking moans escaped her, driving me to continue pleasuring her.

I couldn't get enough of her, she was all I needed.

All I wanted.

I needed to be inside her.

I pulled my fingers out of her, licking them dry before standing up but keeping my eyes pinned to her. I ran my hands through my hair, tousling it and making it loose from its usual side parting, letting it fall down onto my face. I lifted my tee over my head, then ripped my jeans from my legs, kicking them across the room.

I watched as she sat up, lifting her own T-shirt above her head and throwing it off the end of the bed. She was such a fucking sight. Absolutely stunning and breath taking.

And she was all mine.

Only mine.

Always mine.

I grabbed her thighs, pulling her down to the edge of the bed as I fell to my knees in front of her, like a king does to his queen.

She was my queen.

I hooked my tattooed fingers round the hem of her

black knickers, taking them slowly down her tanned, toned legs and pulling them off at her feet, bringing them to my nose and inhaling the scent from them, my eyes going dark and hazy, lighting the fire deep within.

I couldn't help but growl as I pushed her legs as far apart as I could, my hands gripping firmly on her inner thighs as I dipped my head and pushed my tongue into her soaked folds, lapping up her arousal before sucking and nipping at her sensitive clit.

Her moans became louder as she sat up and rested on her elbows before looking down and watched my tongue make her fall to pieces. Her hands were in my hair, fisting and grabbing as she pulled me up towards her lips, kissing me passionately, her tongue stroking mine as her hungry hands made their way to my tight boxers, releasing my aching cock from its vice.

Her tiny hands wrapped round me as she slowly started pumping her hand up and down. I leant down, my breath harsh as I took her bottom lip in my teeth and nibbled on it. I took her hand from me and sat down next to her on the edge of the bed, leaning over and grabbing her round the waist, pulling her onto me, a smile gracing her pretty face.

I reached up and pulled her hair out of its ponytail, watching as it fell around our faces. I reached up, twirling a strand round my fingers, my eyes watching her for a moment. I moved my face to her neck, my lips pressing against her soft skin, her head tipping back, exposing more skin for me to kiss and nip.

I ran both hands down her sides, gliding them under her peachy bum and lifting her slightly so she was on her knees, her legs either side of me. I grabbed the base of my cock, lining it up with her as she slowly slid down onto me, a gasp leaving her as I filled every bit of her. I grabbed her hair, pulling her head back so I could kiss and nip at her neck again as her hips started thrusting. She was so tight.

She clamped down around me as small whimpers left her mouth. I trailed my lips down to her breasts, taking her right one into my mouth, sucking and licking her nipple, her hips moving faster. She pushed her arms back and rested them on my knees, my mouth missing the contact instantly as I moved closer to her to take her pert nipple back between my lips, letting my tongue roll round it.

My eyes moved down to her riding my cock, watching myself move in and out of her as I started thrusting my hips up to her, hitting her harder and with more force. She took her bottom lip between her teeth, trying to hold her screams as he kept her sex-drunk-eyes on mine. I ran my thumb across her bottom lip before pushing it into her mouth as she sucked it then bit down on it, as I hit into her faster.

"Shit," she moaned as I moved my wet thumb and glided it between her legs, rubbing her clit. I was so close, but I was trying to hold off until she was ready to come.

She let go of one of my legs and ran her fingers through my hair before grabbing a fistful, her head dropping slightly, pants leaving her.

"Look at me, baby girl," I said in a low voice.

Her obeying eyes looked deep into mine, her head now tipping back slightly, her lips parted as her moans continued leaving her.

"I'm so close," she cried out.

I stood up with her, turning round and dropping her to the bed before flipping her over on her front. Her arms went down as her arse stayed in the air, giving me a fantastic view of her. I stood close behind her, my hands on her hips as I thrust into her hard and fast, hitting her sweet spot over and over again.

I tipped my head back as a hiss left me, her muscles clenching down around me.

"I'm going to come," she moaned out. I reached forward, grabbing a handful of her hair again and pulled her up, her back arching as I pushed deeper into her as she hit her peak, moaning and crying out my name as she came, pushing me over the edge, filling her as I reached my own orgasm. I stilled for a moment, us both catching our breath before we collapsed on the bed in a post orgasm haze.

She was the remedy I needed to get better, to get through this.

To become me again.

After half an hour of us laying naked on my old bed, Darcey stretched up then stood and walked over to my old dresser. My eyes were on her the whole time. I couldn't help but watch her every move.

Her hips sashayed when she walked, her long golden hair down her back. Her bum was toned and peachy, her thighs thick but toned. She was perfect.

She bent down, her eyes looking over her shoulder and winking at me. I was hard for her once more. She grabbed a couple of my oversized old vests and some long cotton shorts and walked back over to the bed. She threw a set to me before slipping into the set she had grabbed for herself.

There was something about her in my clothes that made her look even fucking hotter than she normally did.

I sat up, pulling the shorts on first, then pushing my head through my vest and pulling it down. She climbed back onto the bed, swinging her legs over my body as she sat on my lap, smirking down at me as I laid back down.

"I love you, Conor Royce."

"I love you more, Darcey Sawyer."

"Hmm, I don't know about that." She giggled, her laugh so sweet.

"Oh, I do." I nodded, smiling at her.

"I was thinking, I want a tattoo," she said out of the blue.

"You do?" I asked surprised. She nodded at me, a silly grin back on her face. "Of what?"

"Not quite sure yet, I have a few ideas." She nibbled on her bottom lip

"I think that's great, I'll take you to my guy," I said, wrapping my arms around her and

pulling her down onto my chest. "I might get my nose pierced tomorrow," I muttered into her hair.

"You'll look even fucking hotter than you do now," she said, lifting her head up off my chest, looking at me.

"Will I now?"

"Oh, yes." She nodded eagerly. "How about another tattoo?" she asked.

"Hmm, not sure, maybe. I have one in mind though, but I won't get that until we are married." I winked at her.

"Tell me what it is," she pried.

"Not a chance." I shook my head laughing. "It's a surprise."

She sat up pouting, crossing her arms in front of her chest, pushing her boobs together, making a perfect cleavage that I just wanted to bury my head into.

"Don't sulk, princess, it'll be worth it," I reassured her.

"Even better than the one you have of me on your stomach?" Her eyebrows raised.

"I don't think so, nothing will ever top that one." I laughed before pulling her back down to me.

"Anyway, enough about that," I muttered as I held her close to me. This is where I wanted to be.

Always with my Queen by my side, until the day I die.

I woke from a peaceful slumber, the first night in the last eight months that I haven't had a nightmare, and it was all because of her.

I rubbed the sleep from my eyes, then looked down at her sleeping in my arms. Where she belonged. Always.

I could literally look at her all day, everything about her was perfect. I didn't move, too afraid that I would wake her. I must have laid staring at her for at least an hour. I didn't even know what the time was, I didn't care. I didn't want to move from this spot.

I heard a sweet moan come from her as she started to stir, opening her eyes slowly, her eyes fluttering softly, her lashes sitting on her cheeks when she closed them for a moment before her striking blue eyes were on mine.

"Morning, king," she cooed.

"Morning, my queen." I leant down, kissing her on her forehead. "I love you."

"I love you." She smiled at me, stretching her arms up, a smirk leaving me when I saw her pert nipples straining against her vest.

"How did you sleep?" she asked sleepily, rolling on her side so she was resting her head on her elbow, trailing her fingers up and down my tattooed body.

PROMISE ME

"Like a log." I beamed at her, my eyes glistening. "I feel so good, first night I've not been haunted by Chase's cries." My voice was quiet, my throat tight.

"That's good, baby," she said softly. "Talking helps, eh?"

"And the good sex." I nudged her. "But, no, I agree, the talking really helped. I am going to get there, I promised myself that I would try and get through this, but I need you by my side. Forever."

"Conor, I am never leaving you. How many times do I have to tell you that?" She smiled at me, leaning across to kiss me. My hand ran around the side of her face as I held onto her cheek, my heart hammering in my chest.

We got up and showered before making our way downstairs for breakfast with the family. I saw her blush as we walked towards the dining table, she was obviously concerned that they heard her last night. I couldn't help but smile from the thoughts of her moaning my name last night. It was one of my favourite sounds.

"What are you two doing today?" Robyn asked Darcey.

"I'm getting a tattoo," she said, her eyes instantly flitting to her mum and dad, my eyes darting down to my lap. Her mum's face was a picture.

"You're what?" Zara shrieked.

"Getting a tattoo," Darcey said confidently this time.

I looked up, Robyn's eyes on mine, mine on hers as she was trying to hide her smile, her tongue pushing into her cheek as she played with her food.

I daren't look at her parents, I knew what they were thinking.

"Why would you want to permanently scar and ink your skin?" Zara said, this time her eyes wide as she focused on me, her shocked eyes batting up and down my body.

"It's art," I said, smiling at her.

"I don't know why you chose to literally cover every inch of you in tattoos, Conor." Zara's eyes were now on her eggs, pushing her fork round her plate.

"Well, not *every* inch is covered," I muttered back, my eyes on Robyn then moving to Darcey when I heard Robyn snigger, Darcey's hand squeezing my thigh hard under the table.

"Conor, you have them on your head, your neck, your body, your back, your arms, hands and legs. There isn't one bit of skin that isn't covered, well, apart from your feet." She shook her head. "And I'm hoping a small, other area." She went a crimson red.

"It's not a *small* area," Robyn piped up, bursting into tears of laughter, Zara not amused. Tanner's eyes kept popping up from his newspaper occasionally eyeing us, but he wasn't interested. Good man.

"Anyway," Darcey snapped, her eyes on Robyn,

before being back on her mum's. "It's only a small one, it's got meaning." She smiled. "And Conor is getting his nose pierced," she slipped in. I threw her a look, rolling my eyes. *Here we go.*

"Conor... Really?" Zara said placing her knife and fork down on her plate, her elbows on the table as she rested her chin on her clasped, closed hands.

"Yup." I rolled my tongue round the top of my mouth.

"Tattoos, ear piercings in places I didn't even know you could pierce. You're a walking, talking colouring book." Zara's lips pursed then spread into a smile as she let out a small giggle.

"And what a mighty fine colouring book I am." I chuckled as we finished our breakfast.

A small piece of me started feeling like myself again. I knew I had a way to go, but it was a start.

A wonderful start.

CHAPTER 30

DARCEY

We sat in the tattoo shop, nerves crashing through me. I was nibbling my nail, not sure whether I wanted to go through with it.

"You okay?" Conor asked as he clasped my hand.

"Mmhmm," I said, not wanting to talk as my voice would betray me.

"It'll be fine." He smiled, reading my thoughts.

"What was your worst one?" I asked.

"Ooo, tough one," he said rubbing his chin with his free hand. "My fingers hurt." He laughed. "Also, my under arm. That's painful, oh, and the elbow." He nodded.

"What does it feel like?"

"The way it feels for me is either a constant bee-sting or someone dragging a lit cigarette across your skin. It does sort of go numb after a while, the worse bit for me is the shading. But you're only having a little one, right? So won't be too bad." He winked at me, kissing me on the cheek. "Can I know what it is yet?"

"Nope." I shook my head when this tall, tattooed man came out, staring down at me. I tightened my grip on Conor's hand.

"Conor, man." Tattoo guy walked over, shaking his hand. "How are you? Long-time no

see."

"Yeah, it's been a while, hasn't it, Jack?" Conor muttered.

"What we tattooing today? You haven't got much skin left, and I wouldn't want to tattoo that pretty face of yours." Jack chuckled.

"Ah, you're funny," Conor jibed. "But it's not actually for me, it's for Darcey," he said, looking at me as I stood up, him standing with me.

"Tattoo virgin?" Jack asked, looking me up and down.

"Yup." I sighed.

"It'll be fine, it can't be that bad. Look at your boyfriend." He winked as he walked through to his room. I swallowed hard, I felt sick.

"I do want a piercing though," Conor said as we entered the room.

"Yeah, not a problem, I can do that now quickly if you want?" Conor looked at me and shrugged "it's up to you angel."

"Can we start my tattoo first? Is that okay?" I asked, my voice so small and quiet it was nearly a whisper. I knew if I didn't do it now, and let Conor go first, I would back out of it, for sure.

"Of course, blondie, let's get started. Where are we doing it?" Jack asked.

I lifted my cropped white tee slightly, exposing my left rib, running my finger just under my side boob, so it sat on my first rib.

"Here, please."

"Not a problem." He nodded. "And what you having done?"

"A small infinity symbol, then after it, in a nice italic writing, *promise me, only yours.*" My eyes flitted up to Conor's. His eyes were glassy, his expression unreadable, but I knew he was happy. I couldn't help but smile at him, feeling instantly better that he now knew.

"Okay, let's do this, shall we? Lay on the bed, blondie, undo your bra and pull your tee up under your armpit, please," he asked as he started filling the tattoo gun with black ink.

I saw Conor's eyes go dark when he mentioned about removing my bra, he was by my side within seconds, holding my hand tightly and kissing my knuckles, then his eyes were watching Jack's every move.

PROMISE ME

I heard the needle start up, my heart jackhammering in my chest, my eyes focused on Conor's beautiful green ones.

"Okay, blondie, here we go," Jack muttered as he placed the needle on my skin, my heart slowing slightly. Conor was right, it felt like someone was dragging a burning cigarette over my exposed skin.

A few times I winced as the pain was more unbearable on some parts, but Conor was amazing. He let me squeeze his hand so tight that his fingers went white, and he didn't once complain. I don't know how he sat here the whole time, getting his entire body covered. It felt like the longest half hour ever, but the gun noise finally stopped.

My eyes were on Conor the whole time, he spoke to me the whole time, keeping my mind busy. My skin felt sore from the constant wiping of the tissue on my skin.

Conor helped me up and walked me to the mirror, a massive smile spreading across my face. It was amazing. I couldn't stop staring at it.

Jack scooted over on his stool as he put some cling film over it and secured it with tape.

"My man will run you through how to look after it." Jack smiled at me. "Right, big man, what am I piercing?"

"My nose, both sides. Also, fancy tattooing me? Only if you have time?" Conor asked. I looked at him confused

"Anything for you, mate, what bit of skin do you have

free?" Jack laughed a deep chuckle. Conor lifted his fitted white T-shirt up, revealing a bare piece of skin running from his armpit down to his waist, in-between his stomach and back tattoos.

"Here." He smiled at Jack.

"Not a bother, what am I doing?"

"An infinity sign, then, *promise me, always yours.*" His beautiful face lit up, his smile so big my heart broke. He looked so happy and free.

"Matching tattoos, cute kids." Jack grinned as he filled his gun up with ink. "You know the drill, big guy, take a seat."

Conor sat down this time, me sitting down next to him and being there for him, not that he needed me. He picked my hand back up, holding onto it as his tattooing started, his lips back on my hands, planting soft kisses over them. "I love you."

"I love you, so fucking much," I mumbled as I stared into his open soul.

We both walked hand in hand back to my car, smiling like Cheshire cats. Our smiles so big, I couldn't believe we had matching tattoos, and he looked even hotter with both sides of his nose pierced. The want I felt for him was unreal.

I got in the car, his hand creeping in-between my thighs, my denim skirt riding a little higher where I had sat down. His finger stroked my sweet spot through my knickers. I faced him, shaking my head as I started the car.

"Not now, Mr Royce, let's get home" I teased, blushing as I pulled away. "So you're going to call Carter?" I asked as we made our way back home.

"Yep, need to work. Need to earn money for me and you." He smiled.

"I think working will do you good, when you calling him?" My eyes darted over to him before turning them back to the road.

"When we get home." He nodded. "The sooner the better, I need to keep my mind busy. As soon as I'm quiet, my thoughts begin, and I drown," he admitted, nibbling the side of his mouth.

"I get that, baby." I nodded back at him. "It'll do you good. I am so proud of you." A smile appeared on my face. I really was.

We pulled up outside my house, locking the car and walking up the stairs. My legs were aching, but in a good way. A small smile crept on my lips. I unlocked the door, standing, holding it open while I waited for him to come in.

"Is your nose sore? Your eyes watered so bad." I let out a little giggle.

"Yeah, it is a bit, it was more when they first did it. Can't numb the nose." He shrugged.

"Why both sides?" I asked curious as I flicked the full

kettle on.

"Not sure, always liked it. Once it's healed, I want a stud one side and a small ring the other," he said as he perched himself on the stool by my breakfast bar, his elbows resting on the worktop.

"Well, it looks hot." I winked at him as I grabbed two mugs. "Tea or coffee?"

"Tea, please, baby," he cooed, making me melt on the spot.

"How did you find your first tattoo then? As bad as you thought?" he asked, his fingers interlocking.

"I'm not sure, I didn't know what to expect. I knew it was going to hurt, but it was more an annoying pain instead of an, oh fuck that hurts, pain." I shrugged throwing two tea bags in the mugs, covering them with milk and sugar before pouring the boiling water.

"You were brave." He smirked.

"I know, such a big girl." I giggled as I handed him his tea, grabbing the jar full of cookies and leaving them in the middle of the worktop. I sat next to him, watching him dip his cookie in the hot tea, studying his head and neck tattoos.

He had a flower on his throat, it's never ending leaves entwining round his neck. He then had dot work and small tribal patterns moving into his shaved head, round the sides and the back.

"What you looking at?" He snorted a sigh.

PROMISE ME

"Your neck and head tattoos." I cocked my head, nibbling the inside of my lip. "They must have hurt."

"Yeah, they did, but not enough for them to stand out, if that makes sense." He lifted his shoulders up before dropping them again and reaching for another cookie.

"What do you fancy for dinner tonight? I've got a few bits in, but I haven't done a shop. My routine is all over the place," I admitted as I took a sip of tea.

"Something easy, don't want you slaving over a hot stove for me," he said, washing his cookie down with tea before placing it back on the worktop and twisting himself round so he was facing me, his head tipped back slightly, his hands reaching for my thighs.

"Something quick and easy, so then we can spend our time together." He winked. "You're so beautiful." He sighed before standing up and leaning down, pecking me on my lips.

I felt myself blush from his words. "I'm going to call Carter, see if I can get an interview. Wish me luck," he said as he pulled his phone out his pocket.

"Good luck, but you don't need it." I smiled at him, him smiling back at me as he put the phone to his ear, walking out and into the lounge area.

I collected his cup, putting it in the dishwasher along with mine and putting the cookie jar back. I opened the fridge to see what I could rustle up for dinner. I had some chicken, cheese and pasta. I huffed at the lack of food, but knew I could make a quick, light, chicken pasta. It would do.

I turned on my heel when I heard Conor walk back through the room.

"So, how did it go?" I asked, trying to mask the apprehension in my voice.

"Yeah, good. I've got a meeting Monday morning. Going to travel up with Robyn."

"That's amazing. How exciting, what type of security? Do I need to write you a CV?"

"No, Carter just asked for my previous job roles, I said army. He said that was more than enough. And private security, seems he wants to expand from the two he already has," he muttered as he walked close, wrapping his arms around me, being careful of my tattoo.

"Have you shown your mum a picture of your new ink?" He poked his tongue out at me, winking.

"No, not yet. Thought I would do it tonight. I'm so in love with it." I beamed.

"It's hot." He smirked. "You're hot." His lips pressed into my neck, trailing down to my collar bone. I spun round to face him, his eyes burning into me. I hopped onto the worktop behind me, pulling him in-between my legs as our mouths found each other, before he consumed me completely.

CHAPTER 31

CONOR

Monday morning was soon here. I was anxious. This was a big deal for me. My sleep was wrecked last night, I just couldn't settle, my nightmares plaguing me.

I thought I was getting better, thought I was on the home stretch, but now I felt like I had taken ten steps back. Darcey re-assured me, telling me that I was getting better, that we all have bad days. That's what I'm putting it down to, a bad day.

We went suit shopping on Sunday as I didn't have anything smart enough to go and meet this Carter guy. I was up at the crack of dawn, working out in Darcey's gym before going for an early morning jog along the beach. I got back and showered, slipping my fitted white shirt on, my black charcoal suit trousers that were skinny-legged and a matching blazer. I didn't want a tie, even though Darcey tried to tell me otherwise.

I slipped my feet into black brogues. The last time I wore a suit like this was for my mum's funeral. A pain impaled through my chest at the memories, no one showed up. It was just me. I inhaled sharply before I shook away the bad thoughts.

I rubbed a dollop of hair wax into the palm of my hand, then ran my fingers through my thick, naturally wavy hair, styling it to the side then pushing my long hair on top back, combing the back down so it sat neatly on my shaved sides and back. I sprayed creed aftershave before fiddling with the cuffs of my shirt.

I felt her near me, looking in the mirror at her, grinning like the fool in love that I am.

"Hey, handsome," she said sweetly, gripping onto the bedroom door frame. Her legs looked fantastic in her short, frilly shorts, matching them with a navy baby-doll vest, her breasts spilling out. I bit my lip, sucking in my breath.

She really was a sight for sore eyes. And I was the lucky bastard that got her.

I turned round, walking towards her before wrapping my long, toned arms around her waist and pulling her close to me.

"You smell good," she moaned as she placed her luscious lips on my neck, kissing me softly.

"You always smell good," I mumbled, kissing her hair.

PROMISE ME

"You ready?" she asked, eyes bright.

"Ready as I'll ever be," I said in a low voice.

"You nervous?" She held onto my arms as she pulled her upper body back, eyeing me.

"A little, but I'll be okay." I nodded and smiled at her, pulling her back towards me so I could kiss her. "It's gonna be a hell of a commute if I get this job, I don't know how Robyn does it." I groaned.

"Well, we can cross that bridge when it comes to it, for now, enjoy the train ride and call me as soon as you're out," she said, grabbing my large, tattooed hand and walking with me to the front door where Robyn was eagerly waiting.

"Come on, Royce, you don't want to be late for Mr. Cole," she said sternly with a hint of humour.

"Bye, baby," I said, leaning across and kissing Darcey once more.

"Bye, babe." She smiled as she let my hand go. "Go smash it." Her voice was full of enthusiasm.

"I will."

We were on our last train and making good time, according to Robyn. She was sat opposite me on the packed train carriage.

We got lost in easy conversation, mainly reminiscing about school and the early army days. I knew she missed Chase and would rather have him home than me, but she didn't stop being her caring, friendly self.

"I've got something I want to run past you, well, tell you," I stammered, my heart feeling like it was in my throat, coughing a couple of times.

"Spit it out, Royce, not like you to stammer over your words." Her eyes rolled so far in the back of her head I thought they would get stuck.

"Fuck it." I groaned, pushing my hand through my hair then rubbing them on my thighs before taking a deep breath. "I'm going to ask Darcey to marry me." My eyes went wide as I saw her expression.

"You're what?" A grin so big spread across her pretty face.

"Yup." I let out a sigh of relief.

"Have you got the ring?" she asked, jumping up and down in her seat like an excited child.

"Nah, going to have a look while I'm up here. Shame you've got to work…" my voice trailed off.

"If you can hang about until twelve, I can come on my lunch break," she said desperately, her hands pushed together in a prayer.

"Of course I will. Don't know what the fuck I will do with myself, but I'll wait. Was going to call lieutenant Tyrell tonight to see how Chase was, but I'll do it whilst I'm waiting. Has Zara or Tanner heard anything?" I asked, trying to push down the creeping anxiety that was coming over me.

PROMISE ME

"They had a call on Saturday night, just saying he is making progress, but not much. Keeps asking for you." Her eyes darted up to mine, I could see the hurt in them. "He just wants you," she mumbled.

"Fuck, why hasn't Tyrell called me? The prick." I groaned, throwing my head back in frustration.

"He probably would have at some point this week," she said, trying to calm me down.

"I'll call him, the fucker. Fuck." I banged my fist on the train panel under the window, gaining looks from the other passengers.

"Calm down," Robyn said softly, placing her hands on my knees. "Deep breaths." She smiled at me. I took a deep breath through my nose and out my mouth like I was shown in therapy.

"I am, thank you." My voice sounding grateful, "It's just a shambles. He knows that one little bit of contact with a loved one can change your whole mindset. Fuck calling him, I'll go down there tomorrow. If he won't let me in, I'll bulldoze him out the way," I growled, my temper rising again.

"Breathe, Royce, you have an interview in less than twenty minutes. Don't fuck this up for yourself."

Her smart words pulled me from my anger haze. She was right, I couldn't afford to fuck this up.

"I'm sorry," I mumbled.

"Hey, don't apologise, I'm angry too. But not angry

enough to throw my job away. He will be home, eventually." She sighed, wiping a stray tear. "He will," she said in a whisper as she patted me on the leg.

We pulled up at our station, jumping out and into the hustle and bustle of London. I followed her like a lost dog, I didn't have a clue where I was.

After a short walk from the train station, we stopped outside a tall glass building. I shielded my eyes from the sunshine as I looked up.

"Here we are, Coles Enterprise." She beamed, holding her arms out.

"Fuck," I muttered, instantly feeling anxious again.

"You're gonna smash it."

"I hope so, have a good day. Thanks for this, Robyn, thanks for calming me down. See you at twelve." I smiled at her as she pushed herself through the revolving doors and waved at me. I took a deep breath, then followed behind her.

I took a moment, looking around at this extravagant building, imagining this being mine. To have built this empire. What an achievement.

I walked up towards the front desk, a young dark-haired girl sat there.

"Good morning." I smiled, her eyes looked me up and down. "I'm here to see Carter Cole, it's Conor Royce."

"Let me give his receptionist a call, let them know you are here," she said, her eyes darting down to the phone, her face flushed.

I stepped back, giving her some privacy whilst she made her call. When she put the phone down, I moved back towards her desk. "Go down the hall to the lifts, fifteenth floor, turn left as you exit the lift." She smiled at me, handing a visitor pass to me and a guest book to sign in. I took the pen from her, filling my details in before sliding the book back across to her.

"Not a problem, thank you for your help." I beamed at her as I made my way towards the elevator, pushing the button and waiting. My heart was pounding in my chest. I felt so nervous.

I stepped into the elevator, taking some deep breaths as I started the climb towards the fifteenth floor. Once the elevator pinged, the doors springing open, I took the left like the receptionist told me, my eyes looking at my surroundings.

I saw a young male receptionist standing up to greet me. "Mr Royce, Mr Cole is expecting you. Straight through the glass door in front of you. Can I get you a glass of water? Coffee? he asked.

"No thank you," I muttered, fiddling with the lanyard that was round my neck as I pushed the heavy, glass door open. I saw a young man, must be in his thirties, sitting at a white, high-gloss desk with a glass top, looking up from his black leather chair. He had mousy hair, blinding sage eyes and freckles across his nose. His back drop was the city line of London, it was stunning.

"Mr Royce," he said softly, standing as he walked towards me, extending his left hand to shake mine. I couldn't help but notice his wedding band, I wanted that so bad.

"Mr Cole," I said with some assertiveness to my voice.

"Please, call me Carter." He smiled at me before taking a seat back behind his desk. He held his hand out for me to sit in the chair opposite him. I undid my suit jacket, taking it off and hanging it on the back of my chair. My eyes wandered over his desk when I saw a photo of a beautiful woman and two children. He had a beautiful family.

"I like your tattoo's. Always fancied some myself, but not sure if I am quite brave enough to go through with it." Carter laughed.

"Thank you, taken me five years to get this many." I smiled at him, shuffling in my seat, his eyes focussing on my hand tattoos.

It took me a moment to notice the two guys sitting on the sofa to the right of me. One looked slightly older than Carter, maybe late thirties. Dirty blonde hair, stubble and big built. Solid.

The other had black hair with a black trimmed beard. Both intimidating. My eyes quickly flicked back to Carter.

"You know Robyn?" he asked as he took a pen into

his hands, rolling it in his fingers.

"Yeah, she's my girlfriend's best friend." I nodded, linking my fingers together to save me biting them.

"How long did you serve for? Thank you for your service by the way. Incredible job you did." Carter's voice was compassionate.

"Thank you, sir, just over four years."

"Why did you leave? I didn't think you could?" His eyes bored into mine, he intimidated me, and I wasn't easily intimidated.

"Injury, sir, plus post-traumatic stress disorder," I said quietly, realising this was the first time I had said the words out loud, and I smiled from the inside at this next step I had been able to take.

"I'm sorry to hear that. How are you doing now?" he asked, generally concerned, and I instantly felt better than I did a minute ago.

"I'm getting there. Recovery took some time, was put into an induced coma due to the kind of injury. I was shot. But post-traumatic stress, I'm a lot better than I was. I have an amazing, supportive girlfriend who is helping me. I was kept in a retreat for eight months, lots of therapy." I let out a little laugh.

"Well, I am glad you are okay, and that you have the support. But if you ever need anything, you let me know, okay?" His eyes were sincere.

"Thank you, sir." I bowed my head, looking at my

linked fingers.

"Now, about the post," he said, shifting in his seat slightly. "I need to up my personal security. Taron is due to go on paternity leave in a few months with his third baby, so I need someone to come on and take over from him, then stay on with us when he is back. Is that something you would be interested in?" he asked, his elbows now on the desk as he sat forward, pressing his fingers into his chin.

"Absolutely, yes," I said enthusiastically.

"How is your commute?" he asked.

"We live in Devon, same as Robyn." I nodded.

"Quite a commute then, would that bother you? I would need you here at eight in the morning," he said a little more sternly this time.

"Well, I would probably look to move, be closer to work." I smiled.

"Perfect. So, your hours would vary, depending on when I would need you. Normally, when I am at work, Taron and James," Carter nodded over to both the men who smiled at me, "Go about their business. Weekends can be busy, but more so when it's for events that I have to attend and if my wife, Freya, needs someone..." he trailed off looking at the picture of his family, smiling. "I'll start you on two hundred a day, is that okay?"

I couldn't believe my ears. *Was that okay? It was more than okay.*

PROMISE ME

"Of course, yes, thank you, Carter. Thank you so much," I said, absolutely elated.

"Perfect, start next Monday. Come here for nine o'clock, I will be lenient for the first few weeks, give you a chance to get settled in with us. Then from there, it'll be meeting at my home in Surrey, then you will be assigned your week's tasks. Keep me posted on the move if you can, I do have two properties up for rent, if you would be interested. One is a penthouse, the other is a townhouse. Both vacant but fully furnished. Go home and speak to…" his voice trailed off.

"Darcey."

"Darcey, pretty name. Like the famous ballet dancer." He smiled. "Speak to Darcey then let me know on Monday what you wish to do in regards to the houses. No pressure, just trying to help you out." He smiled, standing from his seat. I stood with him as he walked towards me, taking my hand in a vice like grip and shaking it, Taron and James coming over and shaking my hand, then the dark-haired guy patted me on the back.

"Welcome to the team, I'm Taron." He smiled at me.

Carter opened the office door for me, then leant in. "Thank you, soldier, for everything you have done for this country, take care. Don't forget, you ever need anything, I am here." A small smile was on his face before seeing me out and closing the door behind him.

I let out the breath I didn't know I had been holding, relief washing over me. I had done it. I got myself a job.

I handed my visitor pass back to reception and walked out onto the busy London streets, pulling my phone out my pocket and calling Darcey.

"Hey, baby," I cooed down the phone at her.

"How did it go?" she asked, I could hear the apprehension in her voice.

"So well, I got the job. I start Monday." I laughed as I pulled the phone away from my ear as she squealed.

"Happy?" I joked.

"Elated."

"Me too, my little grunge, me too."

"You coming home now?" she asked.

"Soon, just got to sort something out and I'll be on my way. What time will you be finished at the studio?"

"About one, should be able to stay home for the rest of the week like I planned." She sighed.

"That's good, we can spend the whole week fucking," I muttered, eyeing the people passing by as I darted my tongue out to lick my bottom lip. God, I would fuck her all day, every day, if I could. She was my drug, I was fucking addicted to her.

She was my kryptonite.

"Conor," I heard her shocked toned as I burst out laughing. "I'll be home soon, love you, baby girl."

"Love you, king," she said before cutting the phone

off.

I slipped my phone in the inside pocket of my suit jacket before putting it back on and taking a walk, I didn't know where the fuck I was going, but I was just going to walk and wait for Robyn.

I text Robyn, telling her to meet me at Tiffany's. I had spent a while looking round and deciding what I was going to get her, I was ninety percent sure, but I just wanted Robyn's opinion. It had just gone twelve-twenty when I saw Robyn walking towards me.

"Hey, get the job?" she asked.

"Smashed it, didn't I?" I smirked, holding my hand up for a high-five.

"Yes! Knew you would. Welcome to the team. Carter is lovely, so lovely. And hot." She sighed.

"Alright, Rob, I don't want to fuck him." I laughed out loud, bending slightly, holding my stomach.

"Piss off," she scolded me as she marched towards the rings. I was still chuckling to myself as I followed her.

"I think I've found the one, but I want your opinion. Okay?" I asked, my eyes staring into hers.

"Okay," she said as the sales assistant came over.

"Can you show my friend the ring, please?" I smiled at her.

"Certainly, sir," she muttered as she unlocked the glass casing and pulled out the ring, holding it up under the bright lights to show Robyn the shine on the diamond.

"Mate, that's stunning. It's so Darcey." She sighed as she stared at the stunning heart-shaped diamond I had picked out.

"Thought so." I puffed my chest out, feeling proud. "Next question." I side-eyed her. "Diamonds on the arms or just a plain band?"

"Plain, one hundred percent." She nodded.

"Don't even want to think about it?" I asked her.

'Nope. Go for plain, trust me."

"You sure?"

"So sure." She nodded her head again. "I text you her ring size, you got it, yeah?"

"Yeah, an L?"

"Yup."

"Perfect, have you got a two-carat in the heart stone, in a size L?" I asked the sales assistant.

"I will go check for you, take a seat, I won't be long." She smiled at me before putting the ring back in the cabinet, locking it and disappearing.

"That ring is stunning," Robyn said, staring at the beautiful rings on show. "You a secret rich dude?" she asked, raising her eyebrows.

"Ha. No, I wish. Just have savings, you know. Haven't spent hardly anything for four years, it's just been accumulating." I shrugged. "She deserves this, I am so in love with her."

"I know. You used to be such a dick though. God, she

hated you." Robyn scoffed, shaking her head lightly.

"I know I was, but I wanted her so fucking bad. I loved her from the moment I saw her." I sighed. "Chase warned me off, told me I wasn't allowed her, which was the worst thing he could have done because it only made me want her more. So, by me being horrible, I could still be close to her." I shook my head as I dropped it, looking at my brogues as I sat at the jewellery counter.

"I couldn't stop once I started, I loved riling her up. The fire igniting inside me each time, then the comments I used to make. I knew she was going to be mine though, as cocky as that sounds. I knew we were going to be together, she was always mine. She just didn't know it then, but, after her eighteenth, things shifted between us. She wanted me back." My hair flopping forward onto my head, my eyes raw, watching Robyn.

"Conor, through all of her hate, she wanted you too. Fuck, she crushed on you so bad. Hence why she put up with you, because she couldn't have you as she thought you hated her, so her hating you was better than not having you at all." She smiled at me. "Quite sad really."

"It really is, but each day I am trying to make up for my mistakes, promising her the world and more," I mumbled.

"I know you are, Royce, I know you are."

My head snapped up when I saw the sales assistant walking over with the distinctive Tiffany blue box, a beaming smile on her face.

Of course she would be smiling, she was about to take a small fortune off of you, my thoughts snarled at me.

"Here we go, sir, a two-carat heart diamond on a plain platinum band." She placed the box into a bag and tied it with white ribbon.

"Perfect, thank you so much for your help." I smiled at her, reaching into my suit jacket for my wallet and producing my card.

"Okay, that'll be seven thousand, two hundred and fifty pounds, please." The assistant's smile widened as I inserted my card into the card reader. Robyn's eyes were wide as she watched me part with a small fortune. She took the card reader and pulled the receipt out, wrapping it round my card and handing it back to me.

"Thank you for shopping at Tiffany's," she sang as she handed me the bag and walked away.

"Fuck, you are a sucker in love, aren't you?" Robyn muttered, shocked as she walked with me.

"That I am. A complete sucker." I nodded as we walked towards the door.

A sucker so fucking deeply in love.

CHAPTER 32

CONOR

We were close to the rehabilitation centre. I wanted to go on my own, but Darcey insisted on coming with me. I hated doing it, but I had to tell her that she wouldn't be allowed to come in with me. She said she was okay with it, but I could see she was a little upset. She brushed it off, saying all she wanted to know was that Chase was okay. I promised that I would let her know, and she knew I wouldn't sugar-coat it. Plus, my facial expression would give it away.

We pulled up outside the big, black metal gates as the security guard asked for my name. Darcey undid my window as I leaned out.

"Royce," I snapped. He nodded, opening the gates to let us drive through. Nerves were ripping through me, Darcey's eyes on me as we slowed into a parking space.

"You okay?" she asked, her own voice betraying her.

"Yeah, baby, it's just all still a bit raw." I nodded as I leant over the central console, kissing her before getting out.

I pulled my tee out the back of my jeans, my eyes on my white trainers, taking in a deep breath as I walked towards the door, holding Darcey's hand, Tyrell, the prick, standing in the doorway, waiting for me.

"Why are you here, Royce?" he spat at me.

"For Chase, obviously." I couldn't stop my tone. He went to speak but huffed out in frustration before biting his tongue. His eyes left mine and focused on Darcey.

"Who's this?" His eyes looked Darcey up and down.

"Chase's sister." I grabbed her hand even tighter. "And my partner."

"She can't come in, she will have to sit in the waiting room." He nodded, his tone softer towards her.

"That's fine, just let me in to see him," I growled.

I walked Darcey to the waiting room, kissing her softly. "You going to be okay?" I asked as she took her seat.

"Yeah, I'm okay. Just go see him. Tell him I'm here." She smiled, her eyes glassy.

"I will, baby. I'll be back soon, I won't be long," I said cupping the side of her face and winking at her before turning and walking towards Chase's room.

My memories flooded my mind from when I was here, all the feelings and thoughts filling me with dread. I didn't like being here, but I had to be strong for Chase, to be here for him.

After a short walk down the dimly lit hallway, Tyrell stopped outside his door. "He isn't in a good place, Royce, you need to know that," he said as he opened the door. "You've got fifteen minutes," he huffed, nudging me in with his shoulder and closing the door behind him.

I stood frozen to the spot. Chase was just lying there, staring out the window, not even flinching from the noise of the door. It took me a few minutes to be able to move. My feet felt like concrete as I tried to move towards him.

His long, dirty-blonde hair was knotted where it hadn't been brushed, the curls matted, his skin pale and clammy. He looked awful.

"Chase, bro, it's me," I said quietly as I took a seat next to him, taking his hand in mine. I saw his chest rise up as he took a deep breath, his monitor beeping faster as his heart rate sped up. His head turned slowly as he faced me, his eyes locking on mine. I couldn't stop the lump in my throat, I needed to get him out of here and help him.

"Conor," he mumbled. "Is it really you?" His hand clutched mine tightly.

"It is, mate, I'm here," I choked out, tears falling down my face.

"When will this all be over? The nightmares, the thoughts, the memories. They're killing me. I don't know how much more I can take," he cried, his sobs quiet as if he didn't want to be heard.

"They will stop, buddy. I don't know when, as I'm still plagued, but they are less frequent," I spoke to him softly. I patted his hand, his eyes wide on mine.

"I want to go home." He sobbed as he clung to my hand, tightening his grip.

"I know, and you will. I'll make sure of it." I nodded, then wiped my own tears away.

"How's Darcey, Mum and Dad and Robyn? Fuck, Robyn," he choked.

"They're all fine, mate, they just want you home. We all do. Darcey is outside," I mumbled, looking over my shoulder then back at him, his face lighting up. I could see the hope in his eyes in that moment.

"She is?"

"Yeah." I smiled at him.

"Can you get her?" he begged me, his eyes pleading with me. "Please, Conor."

"I'll try. Tyrell is just outside." Looking over my shoulder, my mind racking with ideas to get her in here. It took a few moments before an idea sprung to me.

"I've got a plan." I smiled at him, dropping his hand.

I walked to the door, and as I suspected, Tyrell was standing outside.

"Sir." I saluted him. "I've just seen one of the nurses out in the garden, that is opposite Sawyer's room. They mouthed for help. I think they've got one of the soldiers out there, she looked panicked," I said breathless, putting on my greatest performance ever.

"Thank you, Royce," he snapped as he ran down the hallway.

I turned to face Chase, giving him the thumbs up before pulling my phone out and dialling her number.

"What's wrong?" Darcey said in a whisper.

"Come down the hallway, quick. I'll be waiting outside the door for you," I muttered before putting the phone down and standing in the hallway. I couldn't still my heart, it was thumping in my chest so fast. The adrenaline was pumping through me, the thought that Tyrell could be back any minute as I sent him on a wild goose chase. I let out a sigh of relief when I saw her running down the hallway towards me, her eyes panicked.

"It's fine," I reassured her, scurrying her through the door, her eyes focussing on Chase as he sat up in his bed.

"Darcey," he whispered, his voice breaking.

"Chase." She gasped as she ran over to him, throwing herself over him, hugging him tightly. I stood close, just watching them. She let him go, her hands round his face, cradling him.

"God, I have missed you." She sobbed as her eyes looked at his face, glassing over at the injuries that he had sustained.

"Not as much as I've missed you," he choked back at her, pulling her to him again.

"When can you come home?" she asked as he

squeezed her tightly.

"Soon, I hope, soon."

My eyes were pulled from their reunion when I saw Tyrell on the grass opposite me, staring right through the window.

Fuck.

"Shit, Darcey, you need to go, now," I said, pulling her off of Chase. "Run back to the waiting room as fast as you can. I'll be there in ten," I said, ushering her out the door as she was blowing kisses at Chase, her eyes red-raw from the tears.

I felt awful, but I didn't know what Tyrell was capable of and the last thing I wanted was Chase being the one that got punished because of my careless and reckless behaviour. I closed the door on her and sat back next to Chase.

"Thank you so much," he said. I could hear how grateful he was. "She is going to save me. I am going to get better. For her. For all of you."

I smiled at him, nodding slightly before lifting my head up to look at him. "It's the least I could do." My brows closed together slightly. "Did they manage to do much with the burns?" I asked, my face a grimace, my lips pressed into a thin line.

I vividly remembered the state he was in after being tortured, the burns were the worst. He was slashed from his ear to his nose and had a hefty gash on his face that was going to leave a nasty scar.

"A bit. I had a couple of skin grafts to try and sort them out, but won't know for a few weeks." He sighed. "You've really cheered me up, Conor," he said, smiling at me, but his smile soon disappears when Tyrell bursts through the door like a bull in a china shop.

"Where is the girl?" he asked, his eyes bulging with rage, his voice hoarse.

"In the waiting room, where you asked me to leave her." I looked at him confused, shrugging at Chase. I may have seemed like I was chill about it, but inside, I was petrified.

"I saw her," he said, certainty lacing his voice. "You couldn't have." I shook my head at him, Chase copying me, flicking his eyes down

to his lap and playing with his fingers.

"I know what I saw," he bellowed at me.

"I don't know what you saw, but it wasn't Darcey," I said, shrugging again.

"I'll just go find her then, shall I? Get it out of her?" A wicked grin spread across his face. I felt my anger bubbling. Nobody threatens the people I love. Especially not Darcey.

Standing up from my chair and walking towards him, a small grin appeared on my face when I saw how much I towered over him. Being six-foot-six had its perks. This inner strength ripped through me, maybe it was protectiveness, but whatever it was I was grateful, because Tyrell backed the fuck down. I didn't have to answer to him. I didn't have to answer to anyone. Because I was Conor fucking Royce, and no one would ever threaten the people I loved.

I grabbed him round the throat, slamming him against the door. "Don't you dare, you won't lay a finger on her, do you understand me?" I said through gritted teeth. He nodded like the pussy that he was. All front and no back-bone. He was fucking spineless, like a snake.

"And before I let you go, sign Chase's discharge papers. He leaves with us. Now," I hissed at him before dropping him to the floor in a heap. He scurried to his feet and ran down the hallway.

I turned to face Chase and nodded at him. It wasn't until I left this shithole of a place that I realised that Tyrell was no more than a prison guard. He calls himself the lieutenant, he isn't. He didn't deserve that title, only men deserve that title. Tyrell wasn't a man. He was a bully, no more than a gutter rat. And I knew what one of those was, because I was once a bully, a gutter rat. But I made a deal with myself that I would keep climbing until I was top rank.

A king.

And that's what I was.

A fucking King.

After an hour had passed, we were on our way home,

with Chase.

I drove home whilst Darcey and Chase sat in the back. He hadn't stopped crying since he knew he was going home. I knew it was a rushed decision, but I couldn't leave him there, not for another second. His soul was slowly dying each day he was in there, he was slipping away.

Darcey had called her mum, telling her that we were on our way home with him. She burst into tears, happy of course, but I think it was hard to believe. Every so often, my eyes flicked to him in the rear-view mirror, his stare cold and vacant.

I had been there, I knew exactly what he was feeling.

Only, he must be feeling so much worse, the torture he had been through was sickening. It made me want to hurl just thinking about it. I think that what I had been told was only scratching the surface.

I was thinking about calling Carter, to see if he could recommend a good therapist I could put him in touch with. I'm sure he had his fingers in many pies. I hadn't had the chat with Darcey yet about taking him up on his offer of renting one of his houses, I'm sure it would be fine, but that meant her walking away from her dance studio that she had worked so hard to build, and it meant walking away from her family.

I knew she would follow me, but in doing so she was letting go of her dream.

We had a long drive ahead, now wasn't the time for thinking about that.

It was dark by the time we pulled up. I hopped out of Darcey's mini, stretching my arms out to straighten my back. I was not made for a mini.

I leant across, pushing the driver's seat forward as I took her hand, helping her out before we both helped Chase. He stood on shaky legs as we supported him, his face breaking into a smile when he saw the front doors of his parent's home open.

Robyn ran towards him, throwing herself at him, making me and Darcey tighten our grip so she didn't bulldoze him over.

"Baby," she whispered as she looked into his empty, hollow eyes, searching deeply for her man.

"Hey," he muttered back, a smile still plastered to his face as she let go of him, letting us walk him up the steps and towards his mum. She was crying, running out of the front door and swooping him up in her arms, Tanner running behind her and lifting him effortlessly and walking him into the lounge.

Zara's hands were over her mouth as she was sobbing, Darcey followed her dad in as I stood back with Zara, wrapping my arms around her.

"It'll be okay, Zara, we will get him the help. My new boss offered me help. When I told him about my post-traumatic stress, he said if needed anything, to ask him.

PROMISE ME

So, I wanted to ask you first if I could call him in the morning? See if he can put me in touch with a good therapist for him? He really does need it," I said a little more forceful than intended, but I needed her to know the seriousness of this.

"Honestly, if I didn't get him out of there, he would have been dead within a week. He is petrified, scarred and traumatised. Let me try to help you all, please?" My voice was now sounding desperate.

"Okay," she said in a whimper as she began to cry again.

"I'm going to head out, don't want to intrude. You need this evening with just him. Anything else will be too overwhelming. I'll come say goodbye, then I will shoot off. I will give you a call tomorrow regarding the therapist." I smiled a weak smile at her, rubbing her arm with my hand before walking her back into the house.

She was like a scared child, not sure what to do or say. This was all new to her, it was new to them all.

I walked into the lounge, my eyes seeking him out instantly. He was sat on the sofa, a large blanket wrapped round his shoulders and a glass of water in his hands. I walked over to him, crouching down in front of him.

"Mate, I'm going to leave you now, okay? I'll come and see you at some point tomorrow. You're safe now, okay? No need to be scared anymore. You're home." I smiled, putting my hand round the back of his head and pulling him towards me, my forehead on his. "I promise you, you're going to get through this. Promise me that you will fight Chase, you will fight like you have never fought before?"

His head nodded frantically. "I promise, mate. I can do this." His scared voice was loud, booming through the room so everyone could hear.

"That's right, you can do this," I cheered him on, I needed him to pull through this. I stood up, patting him on the back gently as I walked away before turning to face Darcey. "You can stay if you want? I can grab a taxi." I smiled at her, wrapping my arm around her and pulling her close to me.

"No, it's fine. I'll come home with you. I will come back tomorrow." She smiled, walking over to Chase and kissing him on the forehead before kissing the rest of her family goodbye. "If you need me, Robyn, call me, okay?" I heard Darcey say was we walked towards the door.

"I will." Robyn's voice was tight and quiet. "Thank you again, Conor." Her little smile on her blotchy face broke my heart. Her eyes were brimming with unshed tears. I just hoped Chase would do this, would accept the help and try to get through this. Not just for us, but for him.

I settled Darcey into the car, she was quiet and timid but it was understandable given the events of today. I closed the door on her, giving her a weak smile and wink before I ran back indoors. I looked in the lounge where Zara and Robyn were sitting round Chase, talking softly to him, his eyes fixated on the curtains at the large sash windows. Tanner was standing in the door, looking on as a spectator. I walked up beside him, I knew this wasn't the right time to do this, but I didn't think there would be a right time, given the circumstances at the moment.

"Tanner," my voice was smooth. His blue, dull eyes flitted up to me.

"Conor," he replied, exasperated. His youthful face looked tired, wrinkled in places I had never noticed before.

"Excuse my bad timing, but I didn't think there would be another quiet opportunity than now. But, I wish to ask for Darcey's hand in marriage, but I couldn't even think about doing it without your permission, your blessing." I kept my voice low, my eyes watching the women in the living room.

I felt his eyes leave me, a chill running across my skin as he let out his baited breath.

"How could I deny you that, son?" he said, his voice warm and sincere. "Of course you can, of course you have my blessing." He wrapped his arm round my shoulders, pulling me in, giving the top of my arm a squeeze. "I'm so proud of you."

My eyes went wide, my heart slowing in my chest at that moment. I was rendered speechless, the tears springing to my eyes.

It was the first father-like interaction I had ever had in my life, and it was one I would cherish forever.

CHAPTER 33

DARCEY

I sat in the car waiting for Conor, I didn't know what he went back in for. I didn't think to ask, my mind was exploding in my head. It had been such a whirlwind day, from going to see Chase to then bringing him home. I was so glad he was home, but I couldn't believe he was actually here with us.

I smiled when I saw Conor running down the stairs from the front door, opening the car door, sliding in and starting the engine. It was only a short drive home and I had never been more relieved to get there. I needed a shower, I felt sticky and hot. I didn't say much to Conor as we walked the stairs up to my home, it was nothing that he had done, I just wanted the world to be quiet for a bit. I needed a time out by myself.

I didn't have to say anything, he walked up to me, kissed me and told me to have some *me* time. And I did just that. I decided on a bath, my muscles ached. I felt wiped out and exhausted.

After it was ready, I peeled my clothes off and slipped into the hot bath, the bubbles covering me completely. I instantly felt myself relax, I groaned when I realised we hadn't had dinner. That wasn't helping with the mood I was in. I had just washed my hair when I heard a knock on the door.

"Hey, baby, I'm not coming to interrupt," I heard his voice soft, a hint of a smile gracing my face. "Just to let you know that dinner will be done in about twenty minutes. No rush though, just wanted to let you know."

"Thank you," I called out as I heard him walk down the stairs. I let out a sigh, thinking back over the last few weeks and how far he had come from when he first arrived home. He was in such a bad way, not as bad as Chase, but he was bad. The nightmares were getting less and less which I was grateful for, but his moods were still up and down.

I nibbled my bottom lip as I sunk back under the water. I couldn't get Chase out of my mind, I was battling with myself as to whether it was the right thing to do, dragging him away. But I knew, deep down, it was right, it was just the unknown that lay ahead that was making me uneasy.

I shook away the thoughts, climbing out of the huge bath and wrapping my towel around my slim frame as I padded through to my room. I towel-dried my hair before pulling a silk, black nighty and putting it on. I brushed my long, golden hair through before making my way downstairs.

The smell of food filled my nostrils, my belly grumbling. I walked into the kitchen, a stupid smile on my face, when I saw him standing over the oven as he was trying to start plating up the food. Plates were banging around, and he was burning whatever was in the pan. I let out a small giggle as I walked into the room and sat down at the breakfast bar, my head resting on my hand, my elbow on the worktop as I watched him.

"Hey, good looking, what you cooking?" I chimed.

"It's meant to be Carbonara, but I've fucked it." He looked at me before laughing. "Beans on toast okay?"

"Beans on toast is perfect." I nodded my head, dropping my arm from my head and reaching across for the bottle of red sitting on the side, pouring us both a glass.

"Sorry, baby, I wanted to cook you a nice meal." He sighed, banging the pan on the hob. "Fucking useless." He burst into laughter, grabbing the toaster out, and reaching for a tin of baked beans before heating them in the microwave. I sat and let out an amused sigh. I could watch him all day.

After a lot of f-bombs, he served up our dinner, and after everything that had happened today, it was perfect.

Once dinner was finished, we were sitting in the living room, lazing on the sofa. Conor was sitting upright, I was tucked up the other end, my legs stretched out over his lap, his hand rubbing up and down my bare legs, slowly trailing his fingers around in circles, occasionally.

He turned his beautiful face towards me, pulling his bottom lip between his teeth, sucking in a breath before he began talking.

"So, at my interview with Carter on Monday, he bought up my commute…" He flicked his eyes down to his lap before bringing them back up to mine. "He offered us a house, in the city." His voice was small, I could tell he was nervous.

"A house?" I asked a bit surprised, my eyebrows raised.

"Yeah, either a penthouse right in the city of London or a house away from the hustle and bustle of it. I said I would speak to you though, obviously." His eyes narrowed on mine. "I know you have the studio, and your family. My commute is over four hours. Robyn is lucky, she can get in when she wants and can make up the time if needs be. I need to be at his house for eight in the morning, I would have to leave at like, four."

His eyes go wide at the realisation. "I can't do that, but I want this job. So bad. I know I am asking a lot of you, I am asking you to give up on your dream, to leave it all behind. You've worked so hard to get to where you are now, after everything that happened when you were younger. I admire you, so fucking much. And don't think I don't feel awful asking this of you, because I do. I feel like such a bastard." His eyes flitted away from mine as they focussed on his knotted fingers.

"Wow," I said in barely a whisper, not even sure how the words left me. I felt like the air had been sucked from my lungs. I couldn't make a decision now, not such a big one, not now anyway. I needed time.

"Can you just give me the night to think about it? It's been such a long day and I am absolutely exhausted, and I just can't think about this right now," I said a little more abruptly than intended. My eyes were fixated on my wine glass as I swirled the deep red wine around in it.

"Oh God, of course, yes, sleep on it," he said as he stood up and kissed me on the forehead, trailing them down my nose as his lips brushed over the tip before taking the glass out of my hand. "Go and get yourself in bed, let me tidy up. I'll be up soon."

He smiled at me as he put the glasses in the sink. "I love you."

"I love you more," I said back, walking up next to him and kissing him on his cheek.

I took myself up to bed, walking into my room, my eyes automatically looking at my dusty-pink, silk ballet pumps hanging up on my wall, along with the outfit I was going to wear for my exam. A heart-breaking reminder of what never was, a crushing pain sliced through me. I started to sob as I climbed into my large super-king bed, snuggling under the white pinch-pin-tuck duvet, it was so heavy but so cosy.

Maybe a fresh start was what I needed? What we both needed.

Before I could let the thoughts continue to dance around my head, I gave into sleep.

When I woke in the morning, I rolled over, disappointed not to see Conor next to me. I sat up, hitting my hands down on the duvet as I pulled myself out of bed, looking out my bedroom window, my fingers running over the box that I kept all of his letters in. I couldn't help but smile.

I looked out the window, the sun was shining which instantly lifted my mood. I opened the window, letting the fresh sea breeze through before making my way downstairs. I looked in the lounge and kitchen but couldn't see Conor anywhere. I started to panic.

Maybe he was annoyed at me because of how I was acting last night?

I walked quickly over to the snug, where we normally sit for our morning coffee, opening the sliding doors and walking out onto the decked balcony, when I saw him. He was sitting on the sand, by the shore-line, his arms wrapped round his knees, facing the never-ending sea.

I ran back upstairs, grabbing my silk, ivory dressing gown and wrapped it around my slender frame as I made my way out onto the beach. I walked back out the sliding patio door, and down the steps that left the balcony that led straight onto the beach. I felt a bitter pang hit me at the thought of leaving this place behind. I wouldn't sell it. I had enough money in the bank to keep it running, plus, I assumed Robyn would still want to live here. I hadn't even thought about Robyn.

I sighed as I walked towards Conor, the early morning wind still had a nip in the air. Conor was sitting in just a T-shirt and jeans, he must have been cold. I walked up behind him, my feet burying in the soft sand. I tucked my loose hair behind my ears as the wind battled with it.

"Hey." My voice was low as I sat down next to him, my arms crossed against my chest, my legs out straight.

"Hey," he replied, his face turning towards me, his eyes trailing up and down me.

"What's going on? Why are you out here?" I asked. I was anxious. I wasn't sure why, I was worried he was going to choose the job over me, to escape his reality. Maybe I brought everything back for him?

"I'm just thinking." He smiled at me, his eyes glistening. "I like it here, it's so peaceful." He turned to face the calm ocean.

"Mmm, me too." I nodded, now looking out as well.

"I'm not going to take the job," he said after a few moments of silence, his head now bowing down so he was looking in-between his legs.

"What?" I asked, my voice harsh. "Why not?"

"I can't make you leave. I can't ask you to give up everything for me, it's just a job." He sighed.

I leant across, my fingers running through his shaved hair before clasping them round his head, twiddling with his longer bit of hair on top.

"Look at me," I demanded, even though my voice was still soft and calm. He did, his eyes penetrating through me. He looked like he had the weight of the world balancing on his broad, strong shoulders, which I was afraid were about to collapse any minute.

"I'm coming with you. There is no way you are giving up this job. There is not a chance in hell I am going to let you, do you understand me?"

He didn't say anything, just kept his eyes fixed on me. "I was thinking, last night, in bed. Yes, I have the studio and I love my job, but I love you. So, so much more than any job, or any dream I once had. Because you, Conor Royce, are my dream. You are everything and more. We need this fresh start, for us, and most importantly, for you." I smiled at him, letting go of his head before I wiped the tears away from my eyes with the palm of my hands.

I watched as he turned slightly, his arms coming

across to me as he swooped me up, pulling me down on top of him, his fingers running through my hair as he pulled my lips towards his as we kissed.

The rush coursed through me, I felt like we hadn't kissed like this in forever, the emotion and love that we both felt for each other showing in this one, little moment. I wrapped my arms around the back of his neck, pushing myself closer to him as our tongues started dancing with one another, the strokes soft as our lips locked.

His hands dropped from my hair as they slowly slid against the silk material of my dressing gown, his needy fingers untying the knot that was round the front of my stomach, undoing it and pushing my gown open before his hands pushed round my waist and round to my back. The feel of his hands on my skin through the silk material felt amazing. I broke from our kiss, rubbing my lips together, my blue eyes on his.

"I want you," I whispered.

"Good, because you're gonna have me." His eyes hooded and stormy, all of a sudden. He looked over his shoulder to make sure the coast was clear. We were lucky that only a few houses, one being mine, sat on the beach front, and it was a nice rural beach that didn't get too busy as you wouldn't know it was here without looking for it.

He lifted me up for a moment, as he undid his jeans, pushing them down slightly.

"This is going to be fast and hard, baby." His voice

was desperate and low. His large hands pushed my nighty over my hips discreetly as he lowered me down onto him, slowly.

I moaned at the feel of him. It felt so good to be one with him again.

I needed this, he needed this, we needed this.

His hips pushed up into me hard as I moved with him, his thrusts becoming faster as he pushed himself deeper. I clamped around him as I came close to my release, his breathing harsh as he was close to his. I pushed my lips onto his plump ones, bucking my hips forward over him, his fingers gliding in-between us as he rubbed softly over my sensitive bud, pushing me over the edge as I came.

I couldn't stop the moans that escaped into his mouth, biting down on his lip to try and quieten myself. His grip tightened on my hip as he smashed into me harder before he found his own release.

I couldn't help but let out a shy giggle, his face breaking into a beautiful fucking smile as he laughed with me, our foreheads pressing against each other, our breathing slowing after our quick sex session on the beach.

"I can never get enough of you, I don't ever want to." His eyes burned into mine.

"You will never have to know what that will feel like. It's always going to be me and you." I reassured him.

PROMISE ME

"It is." He smiled, his eyes pulling from mine, looking down between us as he started nibbling on his bottom lip. "Ah fuck it, I was waiting for the perfect moment, but nothing can be more perfect than now. Us both being together, in love and after amazing sex," he grumbled, before his lips curled into a smile.

He pushed me back slightly as he reached into his pocket, producing an iconic blue Tiffany ring box.

"Darcey Sawyer, my grunge, my baby girl. Marry me, please? Be my queen?" he asked as he opened the box and produced a stunning heart-diamond ring. My hands pressed against my lips, my eyes brimming with tears, which left the box and looked at him, burning into his deep, green eyes, my hands dropping to reveal the biggest smile I think I have ever smiled.

"Yes! Always yes!" I cried as I held my shaky left hand out as he slipped the stunning ring onto my finger.

"Always mine," he whispered as he pulled me into an embrace.

"Only yours," I whispered back, my grin still on my face.

"Promise me one thing?"

He nodded.

"Promise me you'll always love me, whatever happens. Promise that you will never leave, and whatever life throws at us, we will get through it together?"

"Always. You don't even need to ask, it's always me and you. Forever," he replied before kissing me.

CHAPTER 34

DARCEY

Three Months Later

I was walking back towards Birchwood, which was Mr Cole's Townhouse. We were going to go for the penthouse, but at last minute, we decided we didn't want to be right in the hustle and bustle of London. Coming from our quiet village in Devon and leaving my rural beach house was a culture shock in itself.

I was starting to get my bearings now, I didn't need to keep googling what train I needed to get on to get home, and how to get to certain places. I liked Mayfair where we lived, it was upper class and pretty. Our street had stunning, tall green trees that lined the pavements for what seemed like miles. It was summer, and the trees were full of blossom which made the street even prettier.

I smiled when I saw the familiar white house's approaching, knowing that ours was the sixth one down

PROMISE ME

as you got to the top of the street. I didn't think I would, but I loved it here. Conor was happy, he loved his job and was excelling at it. It kept his mind busy and he loved looking after the Coles, plus he had made friends with James and Taron which was nice as he didn't have any other friends apart from Chase.

I sighed as the thought of him crossed my mind, he was no better. If anything, he was worse, and it was heartbreaking. Carter pays for his therapist, he will not let my mum and dad put their hands in their pockets, even though they can afford it. I know he will get there but I think we all thought he would bounce back like Conor did. Don't get me wrong, Conor was still nowhere near where he wanted to be, the nightmares and flashbacks still happened, but we both just accepted that this was part of the new him now, and if they do go completely then it is an added bonus.

My mum and dad come to visit once a month, and we go back home once a month as well. It's nice to go home to the quiet every now and again, plus, it's nice to see Chase and Robyn. I haven't seen her much since we moved here, she had to take a leave of absence from work due to Chase, but Carter was fine, he is a very strong advocate of 'family comes first.'

I walked through the black iron gate that sat between two white pillars before walking up the three steps towards the front door, unlocking it and placing my hand bag on the side table that sits in the hallway. I loved how bright and airy the entrance hall was, from the outside you would think that the inside is narrow, but it's not. The marble floors in the hallway and kitchen were a high-gloss cream, which only made it feel bigger and lighter.

There was a sweeping stair case to the left of the front door, a solid oak bannister running alongside them. I walked down towards the kitchen, where it ran along the whole back of the house. The worktops were black marble, again high-gloss. A pain to clean but I wasn't complaining.

The kitchen cupboards were white which went well with the worktop. I put my shopping bag on the side, placing the milk in the fridge along with the steaks and salad before putting the two jacket potatoes in the cupboard, ready for dinner tonight. I walked back over to the bag and grabbed the pregnancy test out, letting out a deep sigh.

I was a week late.

I hadn't said anything to Conor as I didn't want to get his hopes up if it was nothing. I had been putting it down to the stress of the move, and me trying to find a job in a dance school.

One night, I decided to apply for a teaching role at The London Ballet school, but I still hadn't heard anything, each day that went by I was losing more hope of hearing from them. I put my carrier bag in the pantry before walking upstairs to the bedroom. I threw the box on the bed, then stared at myself in the mirror. I turned to the side, lifting my loose white T-shirt and placing my hands on my belly, a small smile creeping onto my face.

I would love nothing more than to be pregnant with Conor's baby, but it was such a big deal. But I knew we could conquer anything together.

I undid the button on my denim shorts, walking back over to the bed and picking the box up before heading towards the en-suite. I couldn't calm my shaky hands as I opened the box, pulling one of the tests out and reading the instructions. I was trying to rack my brains on when it could have happened, if I was. I was on the mini-pill, so my periods were all over the place. I wasn't one of those lucky ones that didn't have periods, but I could go months and months without one. Or months and months with one. There was no in-between.

I took a deep breath as I sat on the toilet and peed on the stick, pulling it away before putting the cap back on. I placed it on the toilet cistern whilst I did my jean-shorts up and washed my hands.

My heart was galloping at full speed in my chest.

I wrapped my fingers round the china sink, dropping my head and breathing in through my nose and out through my mouth as I brought my eyes up to the mirror, staring back at myself. My hair was in a messy bun with loose, golden strands hanging down in various places. I looked a mess. I snorted a laugh to myself before turning round and looking at the test sitting there. I agreed with myself that I would give it a couple of minutes before I walked over there.

I stood facing out towards the bathroom, my fingers curled back round the sink as I tapped them against the cold china. I loved the bathroom in here. For an ensuite, it was massive. The tub could easily fit me and Conor in comfortably, and the shower was huge. But again, it was so light that it just made the rooms so much better.

I snapped my head back over to the test. I knew it was time to check, but I was so scared. What if it was positive and Conor was upset or angry and he didn't want me or the baby? I knew deep down he would be ecstatic, but I couldn't help the little voice in my head who was making me doubt everything.

I let go of the sink, my fingers instantly aching. I hadn't realised how hard I had been holding onto it. I walked over slowly, trying not to look at the test until I got there, but my curious eyes were betraying me. I stopped just in front of the toilet, my hand coming to my mouth when I saw the word PREGNANT on the test.

Shit.

A cold sweat came over me, my stomach flipping and churning before I dropped to my knees, lifted the toilet seat and threw the days contents up, straight down the toilet bowl.

PROMISE ME

I sat anxiously at the dining room table. Dinner was cooked and served, and I filled two wine glasses with water, putting a bottle of red in the middle of the table for Conor. I was filled with nerves, my appetite completely gone.

Once I had found out, I had a shower and washed my hair, hoping it would make me feel better, but it didn't. I got changed into a lounge tracksuit, and all of a sudden, everything felt constricting round my belly. I had my foot on the dining chair, my knee bent as I wrapped my arms around it, bringing my nail to my lips, I started nibbling.

Deep down, I was so happy that I was pregnant. I couldn't believe that we would have a little daughter or son in nine months, but I couldn't stop the nerves that were bubbling inside me. I had the pregnancy test in my pocket. I was planning on leaving it in the middle of the table for him to see, but I just couldn't do it.

So, I put it in my pocket and that's where it would stay. I turned my phone over, looking at the time, it had just gone eight o'clock. He should be home any minute. I didn't really hear from him during the day, only when he was on a quiet day would we exchange a few text messages and phone calls. My heart skipped a beat when I heard the door unlock.

"Baby, I'm home," he shouted down the hallway, his voice echoing.

"I'm in the dining room." My voice was high-pitched. I was trying so hard to control my nerves, but my voice betrayed me.

I stood from my chair and walked towards the door as he ran down the hallway, scooping me up into an embrace, his eyes looking down at me before he kissed me.

"God, I've missed you. I am so glad it's Friday. A whole weekend of just me and you." He beamed at me as he put me down softly and walked into the dining room. "Mmm, smells amazing, thank you, baby," he cooed as he sat down, I took my seat opposite him.

He reached for the bottle of red and poured himself a glass then hovered it over mine.

"No, thank you," I said sweetly, shaking my head and holding my hand over the glass. "I've got a terrible headache, thought best to stay off the wine tonight." I smiled at him before he placed the bottle back down, picking his knife and fork up.

"You okay?" he asked as he started cutting into his steak.

"Yeah, just been a weird day." I shrugged, trying to keep my voice steady.

"No news on a job?" He sighed as he looked at me.

"Nope, I think I might as well kiss goodbye to London Ballet." My voice was trembling now.

"Don't say that, they probably get inundated with

applications, babe, you will get the job. I know you will," he said proudly.

I went to explain what I meant when he piped up again. "It's been a day today, honestly. I had to look after Freya today, and the little baby, the girl. Wow, she is a handful. She doesn't stop crying. Freya looks tired all the time, then they've got Parker at home as well and he is just non-stop. He runs around their house like a bull in a china shop," he said laughing before taking a mouthful of his steak. "I mean, they look exhausted all the time. Why would you want to put yourself through that?" He shrugged as he took a mouthful of red.

"Because they love their children and wanted to take the next step in their relationship," I said deadpan.

"Well, I know that, but aren't you happy that's not us yet? Broken sleep, late nights, early mornings. You can kiss goodbye to the sex life. Taron checked in with us today, he has just had another baby and it sounds like hell. Don't envy them at all," he said shaking his head.

I was clinging onto my knife and fork so tightly, my throat burning from the growing lump that was there, my eyes brimming with hot tears. His eyes shot up to mine, going wide, his mouth still open, ready to take his next mouthful of food. "Baby, what's wrong?" he asked dropping his knife and fork.

"Good job you don't envy them, eh? Because, guess what *Daddy?*" I said with a snarl. "You'll be joining them in a few months," I snapped as I pulled the pregnancy test out of my pocket and threw it into the middle of the table. My eyes were on him as he looked at the pregnancy test, his face going white.

"Is this a wind up?" he asked.

"What do you think, Conor? Don't be such a prick," my voice was raised, the tears now falling down my cheeks.

"Darcey... Baby... No. No, no, no, no." He shook his head as he held the pregnancy test in his hand, his voice getting faster. "Not yet, we aren't ready for this yet. Fuck. It was meant to be me and you for a while, you working at London Ballet, me with Carter. Us getting married and enjoying life... Just us for a while. Just me and you. I'm not ready to share you yet, you're mine and only mine. I don't want to share you with anyone, not even our child," he said.

My heart fell out of my chest right there and then, falling into the pit of my stomach. He had managed to obliterate my heart in thirty seconds flat.

"You arsehole," I screamed at him as I leant across the table and snatched the pregnancy test out of his hand. "How dare you." I shook my head in disgust, the tears in full flow.

"Do you remember the promise you made me three months ago?" I asked him, my voice quivering from the crying.

"Which one?" he asked, his voice timid, he couldn't even look at me.

"When you promised that we would get through anything, no matter what life threw at us?"

"Yeah..." His voice trailed off.

"Well, you've just broken that promise," I snapped at him, pulling my engagement ring off of my finger and dropping it into the middle of the table. "This was meant to be a good thing, a happy thing, and now you've tarnished it. I want you to leave," I said straight, not even looking at him.

"Darcey, baby... Please," he begged. He knew he had fucked up, but I was so past it.

"GET OUT!" I yelled at him.

I kept my eyes on the floor as I heard the dining room chair squeak on the marble floor as he pushed away from it and walked past me, straight down the hallway, slamming the front door behind him.

As soon as he was gone, I fell to the floor in a sea of tears.

Broken and alone.

CHAPTER 35

CONOR

I walked out of the house, confused, angry and heartbroken.

I was such a prick.

I had hurt the one person who meant the world to me. I didn't mean to react that way, I was shocked and confused. She was on the pill, so how was it possible that she had fallen pregnant?

I had a million questions running around in my head and I couldn't even talk to anyone about it. Well I could have, I could have spoken to Darcey about it, but I turned into a pussy, not say anything.

I pulled my phone out, unlocking it so I could call Darcey and apologise, but I decided against it. I knew she wouldn't answer. I knew I had to let her calm down, and I had a lot of thinking to do, then a lot of grovelling. Fuck, I had a lot of grovelling to do.

PROMISE ME

I looked at my phone and called Carter, I didn't know who else I could call.

After a few rings he answered.

"Cole," he snapped.

"Hey, boss, it's me, Conor." I sighed, stammering slightly. I didn't know if this was the right thing to do. Fuck, of course it wasn't. But it was too late now.

"Hey, all okay? Is something wrong?" he asked. I could hear slight concern in his voice.

"I fucked up." I shook my head.

"Work or personal?"

"Personal. I know this is random, but can you meet me? I need to talk to someone."

"Of course, me and Freya are at the penthouse, a weekend off from the kids. It's been a day as I'm sure you know. Come along, I'll get some beers in the fridge."

"Thanks, mate, I'll see you soon," I mumbled before hanging the phone up and making my way towards the train station.

After a short ride, I was standing outside the building where Carter was. I felt bad gate-crashing his night away with his wife, but not bad enough that I wasn't going to go through with it.

I walked through the main entrance and walked towards the lift, pressing the Penthouse floor. A few minutes passed, and the doors pinged open as I walked towards the lounge area. Freya was sitting on the sofa with a glass of white, her long auburn hair curled and tucked over her shoulder.

"Hey, Conor." She smiled at me.

"Hey," I said with a groan, walking towards her and sitting on the sofa.

"How bad is it?" she asked.

"Oh, it's bad." I couldn't help but let out a little laugh before I knitted my brows together. "I fucked up majorly. I am proper in the dog house." I sighed.

"Conor," I heard Carter's voice boom as he walked towards me with a bottle of beer, handing it to me and giving me a pat on the back before he took his seat next to his wife, kissing her on the cheek before he turned his eyes back to me. "Do you mind if Freya stays?" he asked.

"Of course not, she might be able to help me." I let out a little laugh again, nervous. I started picking the label off the bottle, running my hand through my hair, messing it up slightly.

"Hit us," Carter said as he took a sip of his beer.

"Looks like I'm joining the parenting club..." My voice trailed off. Carter's eyes widened, he looked at Freya, she dropped the glass from her lips.

"Well, congratulations, my man." Carter laughed as he stood up and patted me on the back again before sitting next to Freya, knitting his brows together. "Sorry, how have you fucked up?" he asked confused.

"I lost it. Like, shit myself, lost it. Started rambling

on about how I didn't want to share her, not even with a child. That I just wanted it to be me and her, for us to enjoy it just being us for a while, you know, get married, honeymoon etcetera. It didn't help because I was telling her about how your day went Freya, saying I don't know how you do it and I don't envy it." I winced as I said it, looking down at my half-peeled beer bottle, then flicking my hand over to look at my tattoos, trying to focus.

"Conor," Freya's voice was smooth as she said my name. I darted my eyes up to her grey ones, they were so grey, I had never noticed it before.

"Parenting isn't easy," she started talking, "But it is honestly the best job in the world. Some days are hard, like today for example, but you get through it. Once they're in bed, you forget all the bad and only think of the good and how much you miss them, and that you just can't wait for them to wake up, just so you can see their little faces again." She smiled at me.

"You aren't wrong for feeling like that. I remember when we fell pregnant the first time." Her eyes left mine and were now on her husband as he took her hand in his and brought it to his lips, planting small, soft kisses along the back.

"I was so scared to tell Carter that I was pregnant, we hadn't been together that long. We weren't engaged, but we were so happy that it had happened. It wasn't the right time, but there never is a right time. Once we got our head round it, we had our twelve week scan and we couldn't wait to see our little baby on the screen, but…" Her voice trailed off, her bottom lip trembling.

Carter gave his wife such a sad smile as he clung to her hand.

"We lost our baby, there was no heartbeat. And to be given that news was devastating and truly heart-breaking. But, it made us know that we wanted this so bad. It wasn't easy, we had obstacles, but we finally got our rainbow baby and we were so happy. I wouldn't change it for the world." She smiled at me.

"I'm sorry to hear that, guys, but am so happy you have two, beautiful children now." A small smile graced my face. "I'm just not ready." I shook my head.

"No one is ever ready." Carter laughed softly. "I still don't feel ready." He shrugged before rolling his eyes at Freya, her laughing at him before leaning into him and nudging him.

"How was it left?" Carter asked me.

"She told me to get out, took her engagement ring off and told me I broke my promise." My throat was tight, I felt like I couldn't breathe, like someone had put a steel knife into my windpipe.

"That's not good," Carter muttered.

"Nope," I said bluntly.

"Stop moping about," Freya said abruptly. "You have an amazing woman sitting at home, who is probably beside herself, and you've run away at the first hurdle when the going gets tough." She shook her head.

"You need to man up," she said as she took a mouthful of her wine.

Carter looked at her shocked, before looking at me and raising his eyebrows as he took a big mouthful of his beer.

"I know, I'm such a dick." I shook my head, my hair flopping forward.

"Yup," Freya said, taking another mouthful of her wine.

"What do I do?" My voice came out in a plea. I needed their help, I felt out of my depth here.

"Man the fuck up for one." She smirked at me, Carter just sitting there, his lips curling into a smile as he was trying not to laugh.

"Right." I let out a soft chuckle, shaking my head slightly from side to side.

"Apologise, grovel. And when I say grovel, I mean get on your hands and fucking knees and beg for her forgiveness," she said, twirling her hair round her finger.

"Gotcha." I nodded.

"Good. Okay, I have a serious question for you," she said as she placed her wine down on the coffee table.

"Wow, it must be serious for you to put the wine down," Carter joked which got him an elbow in the ribs as a response, her full lips pressing into a pout.

"Anyway…" She rolled her eyes at her husband, before staring into mine. "Do you want this baby?" she said very deadpan.

"I do. I really do. More than anything. I just freaked out," I admitted, instantly feeling guilty for the way I acted.

"Then I suggest, you go home and tell her just how much you do." Freya nodded at me before grabbing the glass of wine and standing up. "I'm going to take a bath, I'll leave you two to it. Do the right thing, Royce. Don't be a prick," she said as she leant down to kiss her husband on the lips before sashaying her hips towards the big, sweeping staircase in the middle of the floor.

Carter's eyes followed her up the stairs before she disappeared. "Such a lucky bastard," he murmured before his eyes were back on mine.

"Right, enough of the girl shit. My wife is right, you do need to man the fuck up. It takes two to tango. You took sex education at school, right? You know what happens when you have sex, yeah? Or do I need to give you a quick run through of that as well?" he said in a sarcastic manner before breaking out into a chuckle.

"Obviously." I rolled my eyes, sitting back against the sofa and letting out a sigh. "What a fuck-up." I shook my head.

"You're not a fuck-up. Yeah, you did fuck up mate. You reacted, and in an immature way." He shrugged. The

PROMISE ME

anger started to rise, but I pushed it the fuck back down. I wasn't going to tear my boss' head off.

"But you do need to grow up. Yes, babies are hard work, yes, they're sleep thieves, but they're the best thing in the world. And it's not true, you still have sex." He smirked. "It just means that you need to work that little bit harder in your relationship as there is another little person to contend with, but honestly, it is the best thing to ever happen to you. I am the happiest I have ever been. It's because of my beautiful wife and two children. It is a shock to the system, of course it is. When Freya told me the first time, I was shitting myself, but I couldn't let her see that because she was freaking out too. How do you think Darcey felt?" he asked me, now sitting forward, his elbows on his knees as his fingers rubbed across the stubble on his chin.

"Scared," I mumbled.

"Scared, nervous, excited, happy..." He trailed off. "And she came to tell you, and you went off at her, losing your shit because a baby doesn't fit into your plan. But I promise you, they fit into your heart and you wonder why the hell you were ever so worried and scared," he said, standing up and downing his beer out of the bottle.

"Now, if you'll excuse me, I have a wife to take care of," he said before winking at me and squeezing me on the shoulder. "There is a spare room down the hall if you wish to stay, but not sure you want to hear your boss having hot sex with his sexy as fuck wife, so maybe head home."

He laughed as he started walking towards the stairs. "And go and fucking apologise," he shouted before disappearing.

I stood up, draining the rest of my bottle and making my way out of the penthouse before I heard things that would scar me for the rest of my life.

I walked along the busy Friday night streets of London, guilt crushing down on me. I couldn't believe I had acted the way I did. I have never, ever seen Darcey that angry with me.

Upset, yes. But that was because I was leaving for the army. My behaviour was appalling, and I was actually disgusted with myself.

I walked past a little shop that was still open, that had some random flowers out the front. I grabbed a sorry bunch of roses that looked like they would die by the time I got them home, and a bar of her favourite Galaxy chocolate. I paid the guy then took my sorry arse home.

I walked through the metal gate, unlocking the front door and kicking my shoes off. I know how upset she gets when she's cleaned the floor.

I walked through to the kitchen, everything was turned off and cleaned up. Her engagement ring was now sitting on the worktop. I picked it up, putting it in my pocket before I made my way upstairs. I was nervous, so fucking nervous. My heart was jack-hammering in my chest, it felt like it was skipping beats it was going that fast.

I felt like such a heartless bastard. I was a heartless bastard.

After everything she had done and sacrificed for me, and this was how I treated her. My heart split when I saw that she was laying on top of the duvet, scattered tissues round her, her eyes black from the smudged mascara from all the sobbing and her ring-less hand cradling her non-existent bump.

I let out a sigh, walking towards the bed and sitting on the edge.

"Baby girl," I whispered, giving her a little nudge. It took a moment, but her eyes fluttered open, her face instantly turning into a frown. She sat up, her lips parting, ready for her to speak. I placed my finger over her lips and shook my head.

"My turn." I nodded at her. I placed the roses on the bed, along with the chocolate. Her face softened slightly. I dropped my finger from her lips, taking her hands in mine before looking deep into her blue pools.

"I am so sorry, baby." My eyes closed for a moment as I took a deep breath. "I freaked out, my day was overwhelming, and I was looking forward to coming home to see you, then you told me we were having a baby and I reacted. And I am so sorry. I've had time to let it sink in. Okay, the timing isn't great." I watched as a scowl came across her face again. "Hear me out." I smiled slightly.

"But, I can't wait for this adventure, I can't wait to have a baby with you. It's a big step, but a step that we are both so ready for." I leant across and kissed her, her not returning it at first, pulling away.

"You really fucked up, do you know that?" she asked me, her little face still frowning at me.

"I do." I nodded.

"I needed you, I was scared, and you reacted like that, then left me alone. I was so happy when I found out earlier on, and I couldn't even be happy with you. You made me so upset, you broke my heart Conor," she said quietly as she nibbled her lips, but her sad eyes didn't leave mine.

"I know, and, Darcey, I will never, ever do that again. I will never run out on you again, never leave your side. I am here, forever. For you and our little bean." I sat anxiously, waiting for her to answer me, but she didn't. She just sat back on the bed, pulling the duvet over her and shutting me out.

I deserved it, I really did. I leant across, kissing her on her forehead, then moved down to her flat stomach.

"I'm sorry," I whispered to our unborn child before walking out of the bedroom and leaving her to hate me. I knew I had fucked up, but I really thought she was going to forgive me.

I walked into the large dressing room that was in the

house, pulling out the jewellery drawer and placing her ring back into its ring box, letting out a deep sigh as I closed it. I peeled off my suit from work, the evening was stuffy, and I needed to wash the shit-show of today off of me. Well, at least try to.

I left my clothes in a pile on the floor. I'll pick them up later. I walked into the fully tiled bathroom, stepping under the levelled shower, turning it on and letting the hot water burn my skin.

How could I have been so fucking stupid? I should have never reacted in that way. Not to her.

I wanted to go back in there, scoop her up in an embrace and kiss the pain away. But I knew I had to leave her, I said what I needed to say.

Once out the shower, I dried myself off, rough-drying my hair and running my fingers through it, the waves starting to show already. I walked back into the dressing room and grabbed a pair of loose, cotton shorts. I pulled them on, then hung the towel back up on the towel rail before putting my clothes in the laundry basket.

I stopped and looked at myself in the mirror, the sight sickened me. I was embarrassed by my behaviour.

My eyes moved down to the tattoo of her on my stomach. I still remember when I had this done. She still hated me. Fuck, I still hated her when I had it done, but the hate was only lacing the love I felt for her.

I ran my hand over it, my lips pulling into a smile. My smile soon faded when the guilt crashed through me, reminding me of what I had done to her tonight. I padded downstairs, trying to be quiet as I walked into the kitchen, then walked down the stairs that were in the large pantry cupboard and down to the basement where Carter had every alcoholic beverage you could want.

I grabbed a bottle of whiskey before walking back upstairs to the kitchen, placing the bottle on the worktop before reaching up and grabbing a crystal tumbler out of the cupboard. I opened the whiskey, bringing it to my nose and sniffing it, wincing and pulling away. It burned my nostrils, that's how strong it was. I hadn't drunk whiskey since before I left for the army. Part of me didn't want to drink it, knowing I would probably spiral down into a dark place, but the other part of me felt like I needed it, just to numb the hurt that I was feeling.

I poured myself a small amount, bringing it to my lips and taking a sip, the brown poison burning my throat on its way down, the smoothness making it slide down like silk. I winced slightly before taking another sip, this time it was more like a mouthful. I grabbed the neck of the bottle and walked through to the lounge. I sat myself on the sofa, in the dark with complete silence round me.

I didn't want noise.

I wanted my thoughts to haunt me, to make me feel like absolute dog-shit for what I had done.

CHAPTER 36

DARCEY

I laid in bed, still hurt from the events of the night before. I know I should have forgiven him when he came home last night, but I was still reeling and angry from dinner. A hint of a smile graced my face at the yellow roses that were still laying on the bed, and the big bar of galaxy.

I looked beside me and realised that Conor hadn't come to bed last night. I mean, why would he when I ignored his apology? I threw the heavy duvet back before climbing out of bed and walking towards the door. I checked the three spare rooms, my heart dropping a little more each time I didn't see him lying in the beds.

I ran downstairs, my hand sliding down the oak bannister as I did. I walked straight into the kitchen, seeing the pantry door open. I knew he had been into the basement for alcohol which scared me to death as he hasn't drunk properly since before the army.

I ran down to the basement, now frantic to find him, but he wasn't there either.

Fuck.

I ran back up the stairs, tripping up and landing on my belly, the edge of the stair pushing into my stomach. A small cry left me, but I couldn't stop, I needed to make sure he was okay. I pushed off the stairs and climbed up them, walking out the pantry and into the kitchen again. I moved down the marble hallway, stopping in the lounge next. I let out a sigh of relief when I saw him on the sofa, curled up and asleep.

I noticed the crystal tumbler in his hand, his thumb still holding onto it, my eyes then moved to the whiskey bottle, my lips curling when I saw that it had hardly been drunk. I was grateful that he had fallen asleep.

I walked over, bending down to take the glass from his grip, placing it on the coffee table. When I stood up, an almighty pain shot through my stomach, causing me to cry out. Conor jumped in his sleep, his eyes wide as he saw me. My hand was over my stomach, and another cramp shot through me, making my scream.

I don't know why, but I moved my hand in-between my legs to make sure I was okay. I paled, my eyes frantic with worry. Conor hopped up, wrapping his arms around me and ushering me to the front door.

"I'll be two seconds, I need a T-shirt." His face was etched in worry.

PROMISE ME

I saw him run up the stairs, taking three steps in each stride. I could hear the wardrobe doors banging before he was at the top of the stairs and jumping them as quick as he could. He grabbed me one of his hoody's as I was only in a vest and shorts. I pulled it over my head before he ushered me slowly down the steps and out to my car that was parked out front.

He opened the passenger door and helped me in, closing the door behind me. He ran round the other side, starting the car and pushing it into gear as we drove towards the hospital. He took my hand in his, squeezing it before bringing it to his lips and kissing the back of my hand, his lips lingering.

His scared eyes came over to mine, there was so much I wanted to say but I couldn't talk, I was petrified. I knew if I opened my mouth to say something to him, I would burst into tears, and I was afraid I wouldn't be able to stop.

"It's going to be okay, baby, I promise," he said softly, his eyes now back on the road. The radio was playing softly in the back ground, when Lewis Capaldi, "Before You Go," started echoing round the car.

My bottom lip was trembling, my throat constricted and tight from the lump that was growing by the second.

It needed to be okay, it had to be okay.

We made it to the hospital in good time, the traffic was light for a Saturday morning. Conor abandoned the car outside the front of accident and emergency, opening the door and running to my side, helping me out before walking slowly with me into the waiting room.

"Go take a seat, baby," he said before he walked to the check-in desk. I was conscious that people were looking at me. I didn't want to be here, I wanted to home with Conor, wrapped in his arms.

He was next to me within minutes, his arm wrapping around me and pulling me close, his kisses on the top of my head. This is what I wanted, just not in a hospital waiting room. It felt like we were waiting hours before I was finally called in to be assessed.

Conor took my hand and walked with me into the doctor's office, helping me take a seat before he sat next to me.

"Darcey Sawyer, is it?" he asked.

"Yes," I muttered, my voice shaky.

"Can you confirm your date of birth?"

"Sure, sixth of September, nineteen ninety eight."

"Thank you. Okay, so your partner told us that you are having bad cramps, how many weeks pregnant are you? Did something happen?"

"I don't know how many weeks I am," I mumbled, nibbling on the inside of my lip. "I found out yesterday and, erm..." My eyes were on Conor. "I was looking for my partner, and when I was running up the stairs, I fell and

PROMISE ME

landed on the stairs."

I felt Conor's eyes burn into me. I'm sure if they could, I would have third degree burns scalding my skin.

"You fell." His voice was so small, he looked so guilty.

"Yeah..." My voice trailed off. Before anything else could be said, the doctor turned to face me.

"Okay, we will give you a scan. Any bleeding?"

"Not that I have noticed," I whispered, my hands protectively cradling my flat stomach.

"Okay, try not to worry. I will fill in your notes and we will get you hooked up to a ultrasound machine, okay?" His eyes were soft as he started typing on his computer.

Within minutes, he was walking me through the brightly lit corridors, my eyes constantly on Conor, his hand gripping onto mine. The doctor showed me to a bed, I sat on it and swung my legs round as I laid down, Conor sitting beside me as the doctor pulled the curtain round and sat down opposite the ultrasound machine.

I took a deep breath, the tears running down the side of my face that I had no control over. Conor brought my hand to his lips again, brushing them against my soft skin. "I love you so much," he muttered, my heart thumping at his words.

"I love you too, I am sorry," I choked out, my eyes on his. His green eyes were starting to glisten, I knew he was trying to be strong for me.

"You have nothing to be sorry for." He shook his

head. "It's me, I am sorry. So sorry. If it wasn't for me, you wouldn't have fallen up the stairs. Fuck, Darcey. I am, I truly am so sorry. Please forgive me, please?" His pleas were heart-breaking.

Just as I went to tell him I forgive him, the doctor squeezed some gel onto my belly before pushing the probe into my skin as he looked at the screen. A few moments later, he pressed a button, freezing the screen then turning it towards us.

"Here we go, here is your baby." He smiled. "Perfectly fine. I would say you are about eight to nine weeks pregnant."

I burst into tears, happy, sad, a mix of everything came crashing down on me. My eyes locked on Conor's, he stood from his seat, leaning over me and kissing me on my lips. My hand fisted his tee, pulling him close to me.

"I love you," I whispered. My eyes were pulled from him when I heard this noise, my eyes facing the screen, watching our little bean flipping round the screen, with a little white dot flickering fast.

"That's the baby's heartbeat, nice and strong. They're going to be just fine." He smiled at me before printing out the ultrasound photos and giving them to Conor.

"I'll give you a few minutes. I'll pass your details onto the midwife department and they will be in contact. Congratulations, Miss Sawyer," he said before standing, walking out the curtain and pulling it back shut.

PROMISE ME

I let out my held in sobs as I clung to the photos, I couldn't believe everything was okay.

Our little bean was okay.

Conor pressed his forehead against mine as he let out his own sobs. "I am so sorry, baby, I really am. Forgive me, please?" His kisses on my forehead, trailed down my cheeks and onto my lips.

"I do, I do," I whispered before retuning his kiss.

"Let's go home," Conor said, scooping me up in his embrace.

We spent the day lying in bed and watching junk television, Conor not letting me out of his grip. Saturday evening was soon upon us, I needed to call my mum and dad about our proposal, and our baby, but I would do it tomorrow.

Now, I just wanted to lay with Conor, and forget about the last few days, just for a moment.

I woke to find Conor snuggled into me, his hands wrapped protectively round my bump. I smiled before turning to look at him, staring at his beautiful face. His dark eyebrows shaped perfectly, it wasn't fair. He was a man and his eyebrows were amazing, his long, black lashes fanned out on his tanned skin.

My eyes trailed down his bare body, his colourful tattoos merging into each other, smiling when I saw the one of me. I would never tire of looking at him.

I traced my finger up the side of his body, over our

matching tattoos. I couldn't possibly love this man anymore if I tried.

I rolled onto my back, lifting the duvet off me and placing it back down, so it was still over him. I tiptoed out of the bedroom and into the main dressing room, my eyes searching for my ring box. I grabbed it, lifting the lid, taking my ring out before placing it back on my finger.

I made my way back to the bedroom before heading towards the shower. I turned it on, standing under the cascading water. I rinsed my hair off when I heard the bathroom door go, and I instantly smiled.

I looked over my shoulder, my hungry eyes on him as I watched him. His black, cotton shorts clung to his hips. His tattoos covered his toned abs, my eyes ran down to his V-lines, disappearing into his shorts. My mouth watered.

He pushed his shorts down, standing stark-bollock naked in front of me before he walked slowly towards the shower. I turned round to face him, instantly wet for him. His eyes were dark, hooded and stormy. That was my favourite look.

He looked so fucking hot, and he was all mine. He wrapped his hand around my waist, pulling me to him before his wet lips trailed down my neck delicately, moving down, his hands kneading my full, aching breast before sucking my nipple. I moaned, my head rolling back before his hand glided in-between my legs, spreading them before he slipped a finger deep inside me.

I pressed my hand against his chest, pushing him away. His brows furrowed together, his dark chocolate hair flopped onto his forehead before I dropped down to my knees, wanting to show him just how much I wanted him.

I wrapped my hand around him before pushing my lips down onto him, taking every single inch of him. His hands flew into my hair, grabbing two fistfuls as he pushed my head up and down, sweet groans leaving his throat which only drove me on more to satisfy and please him.

He pushed me away gently, pushing his arms round my waist before lifting me up, my legs automatically wrapping around his toned body. He lined himself up with me and thrust into me, fast and hard. I needed to feel him close to me, and this still didn't seem close enough.

His pushes into me were fast and hard, giving me what I needed. I clenched down around him, screaming his name as he continued hitting into me, my head tipped back. His lips were on mine, sucking and nipping at my skin, his hands under my bum, squeezing me hard as he pushed in and out of me.

"I'm going to come, baby," he cried out as he came, finding my own release. He gripped onto me, pushing me against the wall as we stilled our breathing.

"I will never tire of you," he muttered.

"Good, I don't want you to ever tire of me." I smirked as I kissed his lips.

"You're all mine, you know that? Every piece of you is mine. I love that I am the only one that branded you, every inch of you belongs to me." He grinned before kissing me again.

"Well, until this little sleep thief comes along and wants you all to themselves," he said against my lips, letting me go before falling to his knees, his large hands on my belly before he kissed it softly.

"I'm only joking, I love you so much already, little one," he said before standing up and pulling me into an embrace.

CHAPTER 37

DARCEY

I sat in my bedroom, by the window, looking out at the beach where we were due to be married. We managed to get this all booked and set up in six weeks. We decided on a small intimate wedding, Conor wanted to invite Carter, James and Taron with all of their families and James' wife Julia.

Everything was being set up in the little cove where Conor took me when he came back from the army. It holds special memories for us both, and we couldn't think of anywhere else to be married.

Robyn walked into the room, wearing a figure-hugging red dress, her red hair pulled into a messy bun. She looked so beautiful.

I finished my make-up and looked at myself in the mirror, my long, golden blonde hair was pulled off of my face and cascaded down my back in beach waves. I had minimal make-up on, my lips covered in a matte red lipstick.

My mum walked into the room with the help of my dad, carrying my wedding dress. She hung it on the back of the door before unzipping it. My hands flew to my face, it was truly stunning.

Robyn and my mum placed it on the floor, letting it pool before I stepped into it. Robyn held my hand, trying to steady my shaky legs, helping me balance as I stood into it. Robyn and my mum shimmied it up my body. I pulled the thin, lace straps over my shoulders, then smoothed my hands down the dress, smiling at myself in the mirror. I loved this dress so much.

The A-line skirt came out from my waist in a stunning ivory satin. The neck-line plunged down into a V, the lace design covering my chest and my straps with a nude chiffon covering my skin.

Robyn appeared in front of me, holding my battered, old Doc Martens. I saw my mum roll her eyes.

"You have got to be kidding." She sighed. "Darling, why can't you just wear a pretty pair of heels or little pumps? Why the clumpy boots? Please, please tell me that you're doing this as a wind up?" She dropped her hand down onto her thigh as she shook her head, a little smile creeping onto her face.

"Nope." I shook my head, a massive smile gracing my face, my white, straight teeth showing. "I couldn't think of any other shoes more perfect." I giggled.

It was late September, the days were still warm but the evenings were cooler. We went for a four o'clock wedding, so it was still warm but not overly, it was pleasant.

My dad stood there, looking at me, his crystal blue eyes glistening as he walked towards me. "Darcey, my darling. You are breath taking. You're such a beautiful woman, you have grown into such an inspiration. I am so proud of you," he said quietly before he pulled me into an embrace. "I love you so much."

"I love you too, Daddy. Thank you for everything, really, everything," I replied, him still holding my hands as he took a step back.

I heard someone approaching, my heart singing when I saw Chase walking into my bedroom. "You scrub up well." I heard him laugh as he walked through the door.

My eyes darted to him, lighting up when I looked at him. "Thank you." I winked at him.

Today was a good day, which made this day even more perfect. He was struggling, he really was. But he was putting on a brave face, and I couldn't love him anymore.

He walked towards me, cuddling me and kissing me on the cheek. "Conor is a lucky man, yet the bastard still didn't listen to me. I warned him off." He laughed. "Told him he couldn't have you, now look at you. You're both getting married." His smile faded. "And I couldn't be more proud to be your brother, and his best friend. The fact that I get to stand by his side, watching you legally become his wife, honestly, Darcey, I am so happy and so proud. I'm glad the stubborn bastard didn't listen." He winked at me.

"I'm going to go and see him, he is a bag of nerves." He poked his tongue out before disappearing.

"It's time," Robyn said.

"Let's do this, it's time to become Mrs Royce." I smiled, my breath vibrating as the nerves kicked in. But they weren't bad nerves, no, they were nerves of excitement.

I looked at myself one more time before walking down towards the beach.

I stood at the end of the aisle, my dad linking his arm through mine as I held a bouquet of yellow roses, smiling at the memory of when Conor left the ones on my bed. Robyn was holding ivory roses as she walked down first, her eyes fixated on Chase as she walked towards him before sitting to the left.

The music started playing out the large speakers, "Kissing You." I smiled, the images of Romeo & Juliet flashing through my mind.

I lifted my eyes up from my feet, looking at Conor. My heart swelled instantly. He was wearing a white fitted shirt, black braces and a long, skinny black tie. His shirt was tucked into his black suit trousers with his black converse on. I couldn't take my eyes off of him. He was just breath-taking.

I watched as he pulled his lip between his teeth, a stupid grin on his face. My dad kissed me on the cheek, placing my hand into Conor's before taking his seat next to my mum, who was a blubbering mess.

I stood in front of him, smiling.

"You look breath-taking, absolutely stunning. You are so beautiful, baby girl," he cooed.

I let go of one of his hands as I lifted the front of my dress up and twisted my foot into the sand. His eyes focussed on my battered boots before his eyes flicked back up to mine as he broke into a laugh, his head tipping back. "Always my little grunge."

My heart started thumping as the vicar started talking. "Dearly beloved, we are gathered here today…"

We decided against writing our own vows. I'll be honest, I don't think I would have been able to get through them if I had. I was an emotional wreck as it was.

I watched as Conor took the rings from Chase, placing a plain platinum band onto my finger, my heart singing. I took the ring, hovering it over Conor's finger, pushing the solid platinum band onto his finger.

He was legally mine, all mine. Forever.

"By the power invested in me, I now pronounce you Mr and Mrs. Royce. You may kiss your bride." He smiled at Conor.

"About fucking time," he groaned, his large hands cradling my face before pulling me in to kiss him.

If anyone was to have told me four years ago I would have been marrying Conor king Royce, I would have told them to go to hell. Because four years ago, I hated him. Four years ago, he hated me. But that hate was laced with a whole lot of love.

I was pulled from my flashback when I felt him beside me, the hairs on the back of my neck standing, the goose-bumps smothering across my skin. A silly smile appeared on my face at the presence of my husband near me.

Conor pulled me up from the table, wrapping his arms around me, pulling me close as Second Hand Serenade, "Fall For You," started playing for our first dance. My lips curled into a smile, my head tipping back as a small laugh came out, his lips on my neck.

"I fucking love you, Mrs Royce. Always mine."

"Only yours." My silky voice was low.

"Promise me?" He winked.

"I promise you, always." I smiled before pushing my lips onto his again.

I would never tire of him.

He was my forever.

My king.

PROMISE ME

-

CONOR

Seven Months Later

I sat and watched Darcey with Arabella, sitting in the gardens of our new house in Surrey. We still had our house in Devon, but once we were married, we wanted to move a little further out, back into the country and I still needed to be near work. Plus, my new neighbour got me a good deal, he wasn't a bad boss.

He was right, about children just fitting in. She was a little sleep thief, but I wouldn't have it any other way. I was head over heels in love with both the women in my life.

Darcey took to motherhood like a duck to water. Shortly after the wedding, she received a call from the Royal Ballet School of London offering her a part-time job as a ballet teacher. Honestly, if I could have taken a picture of that look on her face when they called her, I would frame it everywhere. She was so adamant she wouldn't get it, but she did.

And I was so fucking proud of her.

She explained that she had just had a baby and they were happy for her to start in a year's time. She was honest about her injury and that some days were better than others, but they agreed to let her change up her schedule if needed. She was hesitant, but she was supportive with me, and I had to be supportive with her.

Carter offered Julia, his house keeper, to look after Arabella if needed, but Zara was looking to move down to be near her daughter.

I was hoping Chase and Robyn were going to follow down, he was doing so well, but recently spiralled into a dark hole. The nightmares came back with a vengeance after the wedding. I don't know if it was the thought that we were leaving him as such, even though nothing was changing. I don't know if he felt he lost a bit of himself when me and Darcey got married.

It broke my heart, but I knew he could do this. He was a warrior, and he was going to push through this dark spell and shine on the other side. Because he was a soldier, he was a fucking fighter.

Darcey walked over to me with our little bundle, sitting on my lap. I took her out of Darcey's arms, cradling her in mine, my other arm snaking round my beautiful wife and kissing her.

"Thank you," I muttered to her.

"For what?" Her stunning smile spread across her face.

"For not giving up on me, for staying by my side, for waiting for me. You made a promise when I was away from you, you promised you would marry me. And you did. You asked me to promise you one thing, do you remember?"

She nodded.

"What was it?" I asked cockily, tilting my head to the side, pushing my tongue into my cheek.

"I asked you to promise me that you would come home." Her voice was hushed, and I pressed my forehead against hers.

"Baby girl, I was always coming home. You are my everything. Now, forever and always." My lips brushed over hers softly before she pulled away.

"I love you." She sighed happily.

"I love you too, my queen."

I was Conor king Royce, and this king needed his queen.

And I finally had her, my Darcey Royce.

EPILOGUE

CHASE

The fake smile I plaster across my face was getting tiring, the pretending that I was okay was too much.

Why me?

Why was I kept behind and tortured day in and day out?

What the fuck did I do wrong?

If anything, it should have been Conor that was tortured. He was always so cocky, a right jack-the-lad. Always pushing the boundaries and going that one step too far.

He was my best friend. Yes, I fucking loved him like a brother. But he left me when I needed him most, fucking scurrying away to return home to *my* family.

They were mine.

It was bad enough that he was married to my little sister, worming his way back into my family again.

PROMISE ME

I wanted him to leave me alone, but at the same time, I didn't. I needed him. I needed him to get me through this. But I didn't want him with her, no. I wanted him to be my friend and only mine.

I was tortured with these thoughts, day in, day out.

This is what my head is like constantly, doubting, hating, but I can't stop it. I love my family and my friend, but at the same time, I loathed them.

I scream, lashing out and throwing my room about. But it doesn't help.

But Robyn, my ray of light in my stormy days, she does help.

But I am haunted.

I need her to help me, I need the help from them all. I was beaten, stabbed, burned, and treated like a human punching bag. I thought I was going to die, I was left to die by my country and by my best friend.

I screamed for him to help me, every fucking day. I screamed so loud until my throat burned, no voice left, and my tears were dry.

But no one cared.

No one came.

I needed saving but no one wanted to come to my aid. No, they left me to rot in the dark, damp cell to be tortured by monsters.

I was here to tell my story, to tell you what really happened when I was left behind.

I am scarred, I am broken, I am bruised.

But I won't give up. No. I am a warrior, and I am going to push through this dark spell and shine on the other side.

I am a soldier, I am a mother fucking fighter, and now it's my time to be heard.

I am coming for you, I am coming to torture you like you tortured me. And I will not go down without a fight, because I am better than that, I deserve more than that. I deserve my happily ever after, and I am going to fight to my last dying breath to get it with the woman I love.

A small smirk spreads across my face as I watch Robyn walk towards me, her beautiful fucking smile gracing her pretty face. She sits on my lap, handing me a blue water bottle.

"Have a drink, you've not drunk all day," she mutters before kissing me.

This girl, right here, is going to be my saviour.

She is going to save me.

She is going to be the one to rescue me.

THE END

CHASE, ROBYN, CONOR AND DARCEY WILL

PROMISE ME RETURN IN A COMPLETE STANDALONE FOR CHASE'S STORY – SPRING 2021.

ACKNOWLEDGEMENTS

Firstly, to my husband Daniel. Without you, none of this would have been possible. You support me in my dream, and push me when I feel like giving up. I couldn't do this without you by my side. I love you.

My amigos, thank you for being my ear when I have my moments of doubt, thank you for being my BETA readers. I am so glad I met you.

Lindsey, thank you for editing my book. I am so grateful to have met you.

Leanne, thank you for not only being an amazing, supportive friend but for also making my books go from boring word documents to an amazing finished product. I am so lucky I got to meet you two years ago.

My bookstagram community, my last thanks goes to you. I will never be able to thank you enough for the amount of love and support you show me. Thank you.

If you would like to follow me on social media to keep

up with my upcoming releases and teasers the links are below:

Instagram: http://bit.ly/38nen4b
Facebook: http://bit.ly/38qujyi
Reader group: https://bit.ly/3dkaxfa
Goodreads: http://bit.ly/2hmuxpz
Amazon: https://amzn.to/2hojupf
Bookbub: http://bit.ly/2ssvisd

If you loved my book, please leave a review.

Printed in Great Britain
by Amazon